30p

POLARIS A
STO

POLARIS AND OTHER STORIES

Fay Weldon

HODDER AND STOUGHTON
LONDON SYDNEY AUCKLAND TORONTO

Acknowledgments

POLARIS was first published by Methuen in 1978; HORRORS OF THE ROAD in *Cosmopolitan*, July 1984; THE SAD LIFE OF THE RICH in *Company*, July 1984; CHRISTMAS LISTS in A CHRISTMAS FEAST, Macmillan, 1983; AND THEN TURN OUT THE LIGHT in *Cosmopolitan*, 1983; BIRTHDAY! in WINTER'S TALES, Macmillan, 1981; THE SCHOOL RUN in *Woman's Own*, September 1984; THE BOTTOM LINE AND THE SHARP END in *Cosmopolitan*, January 1985; OH MARY DON'T YOU CRY ANY MORE in *Woman's Own*, 1982.

British Library Cataloguing in Publication Data

Weldon, Fay
 Polaris and other stories.
 I. Title
 823'.914[F]   PR6073.E374

ISBN 0 340 33227 1 ✓

Contents

Polaris

The dog was called Thompson, a name without significance, except that Timmy's nephew, aged ten, had named him so. It was an innocent, respectable name. Thompson was a springer spaniel: a strong, handsome, long-haired creature, silky brown and white and full of powerful, unnamed emotions. 'Never seek to tell thy love,' misquoted Meg, from Blake, trying to stare Thompson out, 'love that never can be told –' And Thompson stared back at Meg, and seemed to be weeping. It was Meg who dropped her eyes.

The dog Thompson loved Timmy as a man loves another man, and the man Timmy loved Thompson as a man loves a dog. That, Meg decided, was the cause of Thompson's distress.
'He's perfectly happy,' protested Timmy, in the face of all evidence to the contrary. 'That is just the way dogs look at their masters. There is nothing unhealthy in it.'

They were plastering and painting their first house, their first marital home, on the hills above the naval base where Timmy was stationed, there where the cold North Sea meets the sandy Western Scottish shore, there where Polaris dwells. They were using white paint; no frills, just a bleak beauty, a background. That was what they both wanted. Security insisted they put in a telephone, otherwise they'd have gone without that too. They needed only each other. The telephone was in and working before anything else, before even the electricity cable arrived to link them to the mainstream of the world.
Now they mended and smoothed and renovated, making good what had gone before. The shaggy Scottish sheep came

to stare at them through gaps in the old stone walls, where once windows had been, and soon would be again. The sheep made Thompson jump.

'Silly beast,' said Timmy fondly. 'He's afraid of them. He only understands southern sheep.' Yet he expected Meg, also transplanted from south to north, to be brave.

Meg and Timmy prayed that it would not rain until the roof was watertight, and God answered their prayers and sent a long hot dry summer, heather-scented. And Meg and Timmy sawed and hammered and twisted pipes and made love when the spirit moved them, which was often. Down at the Base the other wives trotted in and out of each other's nice new bungalows, with papered walls in pretty pinks and greens, and said that Meg was mad; but no doubt time would cure her, as it had cured each of them in turn. Time, and experience and winter. A cold lonely winter or two, with Timmy away, and she'd move down to the Base, for the company and the coffee and the moral support.

'I'll never be like them,' Meg told Timmy, of course she did. 'I'm different. I married you, I didn't marry the Navy.' 'You'll have Thompson for company,' was all he said, 'when I'm away.'

'Oh, Thompson!' scorned Meg. 'Scratching and bouncing and fussing! All feeling and no brain.'

'He's just alive,' said Timmy. 'He can't help it.'

'I'd rather look after a brain-damaged child than a dog,' said Meg. 'Any day! At least you'd know where you were.'

'You wouldn't rather,' Timmy said, his face not loving and laughing at all but serious and cold, just for an instant, before relaxing again into its pleasant ordinariness.

Her own, her lovely Timmy! How could she be afraid of him? He was handsome in the way heroes are handsome – broad-shouldered, big-framed, blond and blue-eyed – and had made her, who was accustomed to being always slightly delinquent, somehow not quite like other people, into the heroine of her own life. Timmy had given her a vision of perfectibility. He had married her. But she wished he didn't have a beard. If she couldn't see his mouth, how could she properly judge his feelings? Perhaps his flesh was warm but his bones were cold?

Timmy's beard and Thompson! Well, she could live with them.

She had had lovers more temperamental, more experimental, more – if it came to it – exciting than Timmy, but none who had made her happy. He moved her, she tried to explain to him, into some other state. He changed her in his love-making, she said one morning as they puttied glass into window-frames, into something that belonged to somewhere else, somewhere better.
'Perhaps it's the somewhere else you say Thompson comes from,' he said, joking, no doubt because her talking about intimate and emotional matters made him uneasy. But she chose to take it the wrong way, and didn't talk to him for a full six hours, banging and crashing through their still fragile, echoing house until he dropped a hammer on his toe, and made her laugh and she forgave him. Her anger was a luxury: both understood that and thought they could well afford it. Her little spats of bad behaviour were a status symbol of their love.

They made love outside in the yellow glow flung back from the old stone walls as the sun set.
'Never let the sun go down on thy wrath,' said Timmy. Sometimes he said such obvious things she was quite shaken; phrases that merely flitted through her head, and out again, Timmy would give actual voice to. She thought perhaps it was because she'd had more experience of the world than he. He'd spent a long time under the seas, some six months out of every twelve, since he joined the Navy as a cadet.

Besides, he'd been to a public school and a naval college and only ever mixed with the same kind of people; she'd been to art school and had a hard time with herself in one way and another, brought up by a mother she never really got on with: without a father. Timmy took life simply and pleasantly and did as he wanted, without worrying, and was generous. She worried and was mean: she couldn't help it. She couldn't throw away a stale crust unless there was a bird waiting to eat it, whereas Timmy would pour milk down the sink, if the sink was nearer than the fridge and he was tidying up. She had to save, he to spend. But in a sense it didn't matter: between them the opposites balanced out. His prodigality and her frugality, caught steady on the fulcrum of their love.

Thompson slept under the bed, and when they made love at night would be both jealous and fascinated. He'd roam the room and shuffle and lick their toes.
'Dogs shouldn't be in bedrooms,' said Meg.
'Love me, love my dog,' said Timmy, and she found she'd been waiting for him to say it for a long time. Once he had, she settled down to put up with Thompson, third party to their marriage, the fixture under the marital bed. She even bought flea powder down at the PX on the Base, on one of their weekly trips in. And a special comb for Timmy's beard.

In the Autumn Timmy must expect to go on his tour of duty on Polaris. Three months on, three months off, more or less; sometimes longer, sometimes shorter. Security demanded uncertainty. But Meg could not believe it would ever happen. Timmy would say things like:
'You've got to take a driving test before the Autumn, Meg,' or,
'I have to have at least the kitchen finished before I go,' and she would somehow wonder what he was talking about. Her father had died when she was six. The death had been

expected for a year, but how can a child expect a thing like that?

Timmy made her read a book about the care of dogs, and said, 'My brother used to take Thompson when I was away, but now I've got you he's your responsibility.'

But then September did come and the first cold wet day, and they lit the fires in smoky chimneys, and marvelled that the roof was rainproof and the walls windproof. The phone rang at six the following morning and Meg woke from sleep to hear Timmy saying, 'Aye-aye, sir', and she thought it must be a dream, but the space beside her in the bed became cold, and she saw Timmy, lean and naked, dragging out the suitcase from beneath the bed, and he put on a blue shirt and navy socks, and she saw, or thought she saw, Timmy put a pistol into a kind of shoulder harness which he slung over the shirt, and then a navy woollen jersey over that. Could one imagine such a nasty, arid, deathly black metal thing as that pistol? Surely not! And all of a sudden Timmy looked like one of his nephew's Action Men, the one with the beard. She thought his movements had become jerky. She closed her eyes. Timmy bent and kissed her.
'You can't go!' she cried, in panic. 'You can't!'
'Someone has to,' he said.
'What, blow up the world?' she demanded.
'Darling,' he said patiently, 'stop the world from blowing up. If you wanted to have this conversation you've had four months to do it. It isn't fair to start it now. I have to go.'
'But there has to be more notice than this!'
'There can't be,' he said. 'Security.'

His face had its carved look again, but elevated from the simple planes of the child's toy to the more complex and serious kind one might see on a monument to the dead, at the entrance to a War Graves Cemetery, where the rows of simple white crosses stand as such a dreadful rebuke to the frivolous. 'Look after Thompson for me,' he said, and left. closing the door between himself and the dog, and of course himself and her, but she felt that Thompson came first. She watched from the window as Timmy bounced down the stony path on his bicycle into the valley fog, and vanished into the white nothingness of the rest of the world.

Timmy left his bicycle with the security guard down at the docks. It was padlocked next to Rating Daly's new lightweight eight-speed racer, and the security guard undertook to oil it at weekly intervals.

'Hurry up, sir,' said the security man. 'They're waiting to do the fast cruise: said they needed their navigator.'

Polaris submarines, before setting off to sea, which they like to do at unprecedented times and unexpected states of tide, need to test their engines by running them at full speed. But so that the whole coast can't tell by the sudden rumble that a Polaris is on its way out, the engines are fast-cruised just for the sake of it, from time to time. A rumble in the water, the quivering of the sea and sand where children play, may mean something, but equally may not. No one wants to think about it too much.

There are five British Polaris submarines: these compose Britain's independent nuclear deterrent. They have a home base. They have to have that in the same way that people have to have beds. They are very large, like whales. They can't be hidden, so they try to be unexpected. In theory each Polaris slips in to home base every three months or so, under cover of dark, usually in the early morning. First Crew goes home silently, by bicycle or car. Second Crew, warned by a single phone call, eases itself from its bed and is on board with as little fuss as possible. Security would like to keep the crews secluded in barracks for maximum secrecy, if only they could. But you can't push submariners more than a certain way, or who's going to choose to be one? Polaris's crew have to stay sane; and it is common wisdom that the way to stay sane (at least for men) is to have lots of sex and lots of children. So they have to put up with married men, and though they prefer them to live on Base (as second best to barracks) if they insist on living with their wives in crumbling crofters' cottages on the bare hillside they put up with that too. It just makes a little more work.

Instead of hurrying on board Timmy asked if he could use the telephone in the security hut to call his wife.

'Just married, aren't you, sir,' said the security man enquiringly, and dialled the number himself. But he used a coded number from a list he held. He took no chances. Only then did he hand over the instrument.

'Meg,' said Timmy, 'how are you?'

'I'm in bed,' said Meg, 'and Thompson's on it, not even under it, and he's licking my face.'

'Look after yourself,' said Timmy, 'and think of me every morning at eleven-thirty.'

'I'll think of you all the time.'

'Make a special effort at eleven-thirty – it's a quiet time on board – and I'll try and pick up the signals.'

'Is it allowed?' asked Meg, not without bitterness. 'Isn't telepathy a breach of security?'

'It depends,' said Timmy, in all seriousness, 'on what you do with the information received.'

'Where are you calling from?' asked Meg.

'Somewhere,' said Timmy. 'But there's a grey wharf and a shiny wet bright sea. Has the mist cleared up there?'

'It has,' said Meg, and she looked out of the window on to a pristine day resting over autumn hills, and felt her sense of loss and anger subside. All the same, she said, crossly, 'I think all this security business is nonsense.'

'It's only for a few hours every now and then,' said Timmy. 'And we shouldn't be talking about it.'

'I don't care who's tapping this phone,' said Meg. 'The way

to confound the tappers is to overwhelm them with detail! And what's to stop me ringing my cousin whose friend works in the Russian Embassy perhaps, and weeping on her shoulder and saying Timmy's just left me for his tour of duty?'

'My dearest,' said Timmy, cautiously. 'Two things. First, we'll lie about on the bottom of the loch for a while, before actually moving off, and secondly I expect you'll find you can't make outgoing calls on our phone, at least for a little while. It's for all our sakes. You want me home safely, don't you?'

That silenced her.

'Of course,' she said, presently, in a small voice. 'Darling, I love you, and every morning at eleven-thirty I'll think of you and you'll think of me.'

'Two minutes to eleven-thirty, for two minutes. Every day a Remembrance Sunday,' he said. 'I must go now. I'm not supposed to be ringing you, really. It's just that I left – well, you know – all Navy and no man, and I want you to know the man always wins, and darling –'

'Yes?'

'If Thompson does actually ever catch a rabbit, make sure he gets worm pills. Tape as well as round: dogs pick them up if they hunt. Remember? It was in the book.'

'I'll look after Thompson,' she said, and meant it, and he said, 'I love you. I'll see you in three months. Well, roughly three months,' and put the phone down, leaving her to wonder if the reminder about the pills had been the real purpose of the call.

Timmy went on board, into the belly of leviathan, and joined the captain and the first officer on the bridge.

'Now we can get on with the fast cruise,' said the captain, reproachfully. That was as far as reprimand ever got. He was careful of his officers' feelings. They were to be a long time together beneath the sea. He had a beard so full you could hardly tell what his features were, and bright, bright blue eyes; a gentle manner and a reputation, even amongst submariners, for eccentricity.

'Sorry, Alec, sir,' said Timmy. 'I've never been last on board before,' he added in his defence.

'You've never been married before,' said the captain, but whether that compounded or excused Timmy's failing was not made clear. Those who captain Polaris submarines have to keep abreast of the private lives of their crew. They have, after all, to watch for signs of instability. There is a lot at stake.

The countdown for the fast cruise had begun, when Ratings Percival and Daly appeared to say there had been a mishap of which the captain should be at once informed.

'Some of the exotic veg, sir, aren't on board,' said Percival. 'We have no aubergines, no fresh chillies and no fresh ginger.' The captain turned a concerned face towards his crewmen. 'Of course, sir,' said Rating Daly, 'we have powdered chilli and powdered ginger: that's stock issue. But I know how keen you are on the fresh, and it doesn't solve the aubergine question. The pimentos, courgettes, celeriac and so on came on board by crate okay, but the order clearly wasn't made up properly.'

'Chilli powder and fresh chilli have nothing in common at all,' said the captain, seriously discomposed. 'Only fools think they have.'

'Aye-aye, sir,' said Percival.

'Aye-aye, sir,' said Daly.

'The root of the trouble is, sir,' said Jim, the first officer, pouring oil on troubled waters, as was his habit, 'that down in Stores they've only just about caught up with the mushroom as an exotic vegetable. Fresh ginger and so forth is way beyond them.'

But the captain just stared gloomily at Ratings Percival and Daly as if it were all their fault.

'And we hadn't even left port,' Percival complained later to Daly. 'I knew then what kind of tour this was going to be. Never allowed near the galley for the men's food, for hamburgers and beans, because the officers have commandeered it for sweet-and-sour pork with hot chilli sauce, or worse. It will all end in mutiny, not to mention ulcers.' But that conversation came later. Now another thought struck the captain.

'Olive oil?' he asked, over the murmur of warming engines.

'Some left by Crew No. 1, sir. Two litre bottles.'

'Not enough,' said the captain and closed down the engines.

An urgent approach was made to Security and in about an hour Zelda, Jim's wife, drove up to the dock gates with a couple of crates, which Security checked. They prodded ginger and peered into chillies, and nodded and let them through.

'This isn't alcohol?' they enquired, opening up one or two big plastic containers full of green liquid.

'It's olive oil,' said Zelda crossly, in her fluty officer's wife's voice.

She wore a headscarf decorated with ponies' heads and had rather large, brilliant teeth in a long thin face. She seemed to know what she was doing.

'Taste it,' she said, and made them; they put their fingers into the liquid and sucked and shuddered. Olive oil! Their wives still fried in lard, and used Heinz Salad Cream on the salad.

Polaris submarines are dry. No alcohol is allowed on board. To be drunk in charge of a submarine is an offence. Stores did let Captain Alec's crew take cooking wine with them, on condition that it was used in cooked dishes, never uncooked. Heating sends off alcohol in vapour, they explained. Thus sherry could be used in soup, so long as that soup was simmering when the sherry was added; but never in cold trifles. The regulations were strict.

16

Timmy left the boat to collect the crates.

'Where's Jim?' asked Zelda. 'Why did they send you?'

'You know what it's like,' said Timmy, embarrassed.

'I know what *he's* like,' she said. 'And more than one set of goodbyes in one day he just can't face.'

'That's about it,' said Timmy.

'Never mind,' said Zelda. 'I'll just have to say goodbye to you' – and she kissed him long and passionately on the mouth.

'Hey, hey,' said the security man, uneasily. 'That man's got to be celibate for the next three months. You should think of that.'

'It's just for old times' sake,' said Zelda, and Timmy looked flushed and self-conscious.

'Mind you look after Meg for me,' said Timmy. 'And not for old times' sake.'

'I'll look after her,' said Zelda.

'And do be discreet, Zelda,' said Timmy. 'And make sure she looks after Thompson.'

'Bloody Thompson,' said Zelda. 'Always licking one's toes in bed.'

Timmy went back inside, and the hatches were finally battened down, and the rumble of the fast cruise began. Presently Polaris slid away from its dock. Halfway down the estuary it submerged, and was gone.

A knock came on Meg's door as she sat on a clean, smooth patch of floor, doing yoga exercises. She had a small bony body, no-nonsense straight hair and a wide brow and a straight nose and rather thin lips. She had always wanted to live in the country. She'd been a fabric designer who thought she should have trained as a potter but might one day write novels, and had assumed she'd marry some country craftsman. Then she'd bring up her children (when she had them, which she would) without the aid of television or yellow additives in the food, and so forth. And now here

17

she was, married to a man about whom she knew very little, except that she was addicted to him, body and soul, so that his profession and his politics and his social values meant nothing. And all she knew was that her chest ached from lack of him; and she had a pain where her heart was.

Yoga was part of her plan for self-improvement, put into action ten minutes after Timmy's phone-call, when she had stopped crying. Three months to achieve physical perfection, perhaps learn a language – certainly get the house in order. She would dedicate the time to Timmy.

She'd tried the telephone and found, as Timmy had predicted, that the line was now dead. Presumably it would come to life in its own good time. She didn't mind; the sense of being looked after for her own good was reassuring. It was like being a small child again, with parents at the ready to curb one's follies.

The postman rang the doorbell. Meg opened the door, holding Thompson back by his collar. 'It's all right,' she said. 'He's all bark and no bite. He might knock you down by accident but never on purpose.'
'That's always good to know,' said the postman, who was an elderly Scotsman. He rolled up his trouser leg to show a papery grey shin marked with livid patches, which he claimed were the results of dog bites. 'If he adds to these,' he said, 'you'll be getting no more letters up here, and that's certain. You'll have to come down to the Post Office, forbye. Recorded Delivery, sign here.'
He settled himself for a chat, balancing against the doorpost, but occasionally shifting, the better to balance against Thompson.
'You ought to keep the door properly latched,' he said. 'There're prowlers about.'
'Up here? Surely not!'
'Everywhere,' he said. 'It's the unemployment and

Christmas coming, and worse. A young woman like your-
self, your husband off –'
'How do you know he's off?' Meg was startled.
'First Crew's back, that's why. He's Second Crew, so he's
away. It's not difficult.'
'It's supposed to be secret,' complained Meg, but he was
more interested in the letter for which she signed. It was in
a brown envelope.
'That a bill?' he asked, following her into the kitchen.
'I don't know,' said Meg. 'It's for my husband, not me.'
'You'll have to open it,' he said. 'You're married to a sailor
now. I've got to get on. There'll be a big collection down at
the Base. The minute the husbands go the wives start
writing. It calms down after a week or so. I'll come up here
whenever I can. You're too isolated, you know. But you can
always drive down, I suppose, for a cup of tea and a chat.'
'I don't drive and I don't much care for chats,' said Meg
stiffly. She closed and latched the door after him, but then
regretted her rudeness. She would need friends: the buses
that passed on the hill road, below the cottage, came only
once a week.

She put on another jersey because the wind was suddenly
cold, and looked around the cottage. She realised that there
was no real means of heating it through the winter, and
wondered why it was that Timmy was so impractical, and
why she had left all this kind of thing to him, knowing him
to be so.
Thompson started barking. The milkman. She opened the
door to him. She had always presumed that up here milkmen
didn't just put the bottles on the step and leave, as they did
in the city, and she was right.
'You'll be wanting less milk,' he said. He was even older
than the postman, and wheezed. Perhaps Security vetted
all visitors to the house, in the husband's absence, in the
interests of domestic felicity?
'Will I?'

'With your husband off. Before we had the Base at least we knew where we were. Now it's chop and change all the time. Three pints one day, six the next. It's the goodnight cocoa. Navy men get a taste for cocoa, don't they?'

'Do they?' she said, coldly.

'So you'll be all alone up here for three months! Only the sheep for company, forbye. Pity you don't have kiddies.'

'I've been married for less than a year.'

'I'd get on with it, all the same,' he advised. 'All the Navy wives do. The way I look at my work,' he went on, 'is as a Welfare job. Someone for the lonely wives to talk to. Does that dog bite?'

Thompson was sniffing round the old man's knees. 'Only barks,' said Meg.

'Pity. He'll need to do more than that. Prowlers about. Have you got stores in? What are you going to do when the snow starts? I don't come up here in the snow, you know. Couldn't even if I wanted to. No one's going to send a snow-plough just for you.'

Snow? It was almost impossible to imagine the landscape white. She had never seen it so.

'I'll dig myself out,' said Meg. She came from the city, where snow meant an awkward mush, not the implacable enemy country-dwellers know it to be.

She shut the door on the milkman and his aged crabbiness and went upstairs. She sat back on the bed and lost herself in an erotic haze and thought about Timmy, while Thompson grinned at her, as if he knew and sympathised with the tenor of her thoughts. She felt Timmy's presence near her. She looked at her watch. It was thirty-one minutes past eleven. Sea-lag, she thought. The telephone pinged slightly and when she lifted the receiver she could hear the dialling tone again.

'Hi,' she said, to whoever no doubt listened.

Again she had the feeling that she was known, noticed, that they were on her side, and the ping had been a whisper

from the watchers to say, 'He's off, he's safe, all's clear!
Now watch, and wait, and one morning in the New Year,
or even earlier, you will hear him whistling up the frozen
path, and we will have him home to you. We, the listeners!'

It was quite a sensuous feeling: a lying-back on strong,
supporting arms. She replaced the receiver, smiling.

Polaris lay on the bottom of the loch and waited for the
Routine from Base that would tell them where to go and
how to go, and when. On the bridge, Timmy puzzled rather
closely over the charts.
'Anything the matter, Mr Navigator?' enquired the captain.
'We don't want to end up in the Black Sea.'
It was a joke.
'Let alone up the Yangtze River, sir!' remarked Jim, who'd
been reading about Red China in the papers. Security would
have liked the crews not to read the papers, or only Rupert
Murdoch's *Sun*, but the liberty of the individual in the West
had to be respected, or what was everyone struggling for?
'That's for the politicians to decide,' said the captain,
sternly. 'But I'm glad to hear you making a joke, Mr First
Lieutenant, so early in the patrol. We're usually halfway
round the world before you so much as smile. Is it the land
that depresses you, or the sea?'
'The land, I think, sir,' said Jim.
Submariners are like artists, thought the captain, regretting
his question. They'd really rather live alone, outside the
married state, in order to pursue their vision in peace; yet
they find the unmarried state lonely and sad. To have to
feel guilty as they plunge seawards to what they really love,
to see wifely tears flowing and hear their children's sobs is
intolerable. But to have no one to care, to mark the difference
between sea and land, is equally dreadful. Normal sub-
marining, the captain knew, suits best the very young man:
the man with parents who both love the child but look
forward to his absence. Then all get the best of all possible

worlds, with the added spice of a little danger, but not too much. Alas, on Polaris it was different. This was submarining-plus! How could you trust a young unmarried man with the future of Moscow, London, Sydney, Peking and so forth? You couldn't. They were too emotional. Down on Polaris every major city in the world was targeted: the co-ordinates ready and waiting. For the time might come (who knew what the future held?) when one of their own cities might have to be taken out, for good strategic or even peace-making reasons. It took a mature and steady man to recognise such necessities.

Timmy stared at the charts and wondered why they were so misty. He would have liked to have talked more to Jim about the land/sea divide but felt inhibited, as he so often was, with Jim, since having the affair with Zelda. A man, it seemed, could not sleep with his best friend's wife, however secretly and with however good intention, and still look him in the eye. Now that Timmy was himself married he could see more clearly just how great a folly and disloyalty the affair had been. He wished to apologise to Jim; but couldn't, of course. All the same, the fact remained: he was fond of Zelda, and could see that Jim was somewhat cavalier in his attitude towards her. For form's sake, and certainly in Zelda's presence, Jim should at least pretend to prefer life on shore to life at sea.

Under sea. Timmy wanted to be back in bed with Meg, with Thompson under it. Perhaps the mistiness was tears? He took off his glasses and wiped his eyes.

'Oh my God, sir,' he said. 'I've brought my wife's glasses.' There was a short silence.

'Well,' said Jim, 'Yangtze, here we come!'

'It's all right, Alec, sir,' said Timmy. 'It's not too bad. I may get headaches, that's all.'

'Seeing with her eyes,' said the captain, 'while she sees with yours. Love's young dream. Don't let it happen again.' He softened the rebuke by returning to more rewarding subjects.

'How much peanut butter did we bring on board?'
'Two gallons,' said the first lieutenant.
'I hope it's enough,' said the captain. 'Many Indonesian dishes use quite large quantities of peanut butter. It is a country where food is eaten with the hands, and so a thicker consistency is needed.'
Presently the Routine from Base came through. The captain threw a switch or two, and the control board which linked with the nuclear reactor at Polaris's heart glowed warmly, as the mighty engines sucked its power and started up, and minutely vibrated the waves on the far-off shore where the children played, and bounced a grain of sand or so from here to there.

Polaris moved down the Irish Channel and out into the Atlantic. Down in the galley the captain pounded cummin seed and coriander and chilli to make a paste in which to coat a chicken. Jim peeled and diced and blanched baby white turnips preparatory to freezing. They brought fresh vegetables on board and prepared and froze them in the great freezer themselves, not trusting shore-men to do it properly. (There is no shortage of power on a nuclear submarine – lots of light, lots of hot water, lots of cool and elegantly recycled air. The crew swore the air smelt badly of garlic, like a French train on a school trip, but their officers denied it, hotly.)
The captain poured oil from Zelda's plastic can into a jug and thence into a pan. He meant to fry mustard seed in the oil, letting it sizzle for a few moments, then pour it over finely grated carrot, adding lemon juice, salt and pepper, for a simple but interesting salad to serve with the chicken. But the oil spattered in the pan.
'This isn't pure olive oil,' complained the captain.
He investigated and discovered that, beneath a thin top floating layer of olive oil, there was nothing more or less than white wine.
'That was very irresponsible of your wife,' he said sternly

to Jim. 'You, me and Mr Navigator here are an Attack
Team, not a musical comedy act.'

But he didn't pour the wine away; instead he put the canister
up on a top cupboard, out of harm's reach.

While they were eating a Routine came through to say that
Russian submarines were operating in their vicinity.
'When are they ever not?' yawned the captain.
But they took their plates through to the bridge and watched
the lights on the radar screen, and listened to the bleeps as
the leviathans from the other side neared and all but brushed
them, and paused, and passed, in companionable fashion.
'I wonder if they've discovered food,' said the captain.
'I shouldn't think so, sir,' said Jim, who'd once been on a
school trip to Leningrad, and been made sick by soused
herring.
'Then what do they do all day?'
They couldn't remember themselves what they had done,
in the days before they'd discovered the soothing art, and
had dined on hamburgers like anyone else. But now the
weeks were filled with a sense of purpose; and, indeed,
accomplishment.

Two weeks passed. Thompson and Meg settled down to a
state of truce. She tried to keep him out of the bedroom
entirely, while he tried to get into the bed, and they compro-
mised with under the bed. Now that Timmy was away Meg
noticed the landscape. She watched the winter closing in,
suddenly and crossly, like a shopkeeper closing up before a
football match. Slam, slam! Down came the shutters, out
went the sun, up sprang the wind, and life retreated, mutter-
ing, underground, leaving the hills lean and sinewy and
blank. Even the slugs went from the kitchen cupboard. She
missed them. How was it possible to miss such disgusting
slimy things, which clung to damp walls in dark and unexpected places? She was obliged to conclude that it was

because they were, simply, alive and of the animal not the plant kingdom, and had some kind of blind purpose and vague will which carried them into the rockiest and most inhospitable places, where even plants could not survive. They were life, carrying their message into the world of non-life.

Sometimes she was glad Timmy wasn't there. She would have muttered something about missing the slugs and he would have looked quizzical and she would have turned pink and felt silly. Some knowledge simply had to be borne alone: that was one of the penalties of being human. The suggestion was, inasmuch as one had the power of speech, that there was a sharing; but of course there wasn't. It was a pain that the slugs were spared. Thompson, on the other hand, was spared nothing. His suffering was the worse because, observing that humans talked to each other, he believed they would exchange notes on the wonders of the universe. He was wrong in this, but didn't know it. Meg and Timmy's real conversation, real agreement, was wordless and in bed. No wonder Thompson liked to be under it.

The bus was taken off for the winter months. Too few people used it. Meg cycled down to the Base – a half-hour journey going in, two hours back, uphill – to the library, and asked the librarian to find her a book on the life-cycle of slugs. The library had in stock many reference books on crocheting and knitting and jam-making and upholstery and Teach-Yourself-French and First Steps to Philosophy, but there was nothing on slugs.

'You can always try slug pellets,' said the librarian. 'The slugs eat them and simply deliquesce.'

'But that's horrible!' said Meg.

'I expect it is, when you think about it. The thing is, don't think about it. Simply do it.'

Meg met Zelda outside the library. Zelda swooped on her and embraced her and said she must come in for coffee. Wasn't she going mad up there on her own? Meg was looking rather odd, said Zelda. Meg was wearing jeans and an old navy jersey of Timmy's. She felt protected in it. Zelda was wearing pink jeans and a pinker sweater, and a fashionable grey wool scarf tied as a shawl, and many gold bangles and rings.

'In what way odd?'
'You have a funny look in your eye,' said Zelda, 'as if you were pregnant.'
Meg thought.
'When I went to take my pill this morning,' she said, 'I found I had four left and yet I was at the end of the course.'

They went to Zelda's warm, pretty bungalow, with its picture windows and squared-off walls. Thompson had to stay outside. He wailed, but Zelda was ruthless.
'So you've missed four pills,' she said. 'That means you want a baby. It's your unconscious.'
'I don't want a baby,' said Meg. 'I want Timmy.'
'I don't want a baby either,' said Zelda, 'but I'm having one. I only found out this morning. Think of it, Jim won't know for another two months and two weeks. Give or take a day or two, for Security.'
'But you can tell him through the Family Telegram system,' said Meg.
'They only pass on good news, not bad,' said Zelda. 'Bad news waits until the men are back on shore.'
'I suppose your good news and Jim's good news aren't necessarily the same thing,' said Meg.
'Exactly,' said Zelda. 'But that's marriage, isn't it?'
Meg thought in her heart, *not mine and Timmy's, it isn't.*

It was eleven-forty-five and Meg had forgotten to think of Timmy. His thoughts had been flashing all around her but she hadn't noticed. She'd been thinking about the deliquescing of slugs.

At that moment Thompson discovered Zelda's lavatory window ajar and squeezed himself in, bending a hinge or so, and bounced into the living room. He threw himself on Zelda.

'Why does he go to you?' asked Meg, puzzled.

'Because I'm the owner of the house,' said Zelda crossly. 'And he's trying to get into my good books. Couldn't you have left him at home?'

She aimed a kick at Thompson with her little gold boot and he howled. Meg felt protective of him at once and said she must be getting back.

'I don't know much about dogs,' said Meg, as she got on her bicycle, 'but is Thompson extra-specially intelligent?'

'He's extra-specially *mad*,' said Zelda.

The next day Zelda rang Meg and asked her to dinner that very evening to meet Tony.

'You can't say no,' said Zelda, 'because your engagement book is empty.'

'I don't even have one,' said Meg.

'That figures.'

'Who's Tony?'

'He's the spare man, dear. There's always one about. He's a PR man: he deals with the press round here. His wife's away in New Zealand – she always is – and if she isn't she doesn't understand him. He mends fuses and walks dogs and all the husbands trust him. Some sensible woman put the word about that he's queer, which is why his wife's always away, but of course he isn't. He's very nice and funny and he might cheer you up.'

'It's very kind of you, Zelda, but I don't think I'll come.'

'Why not?'

'I don't think Timmy would like it.'

'I don't actually think submariners are very possessive men, or they wouldn't be away so much, would they?' It was an argument hard to refute. Meg tried to think her way round it, but failed.

'I suppose not,' she said. 'Thank you very much, Zelda, I'd love to come.'

Down on the bottom of the Indian Ocean Polaris kept the meal-times of the ships on the surface. Dinner that night was multinational – home-made ravioli done by Jim, who was so good at fiddly dishes; Persian chicken – the kind stuffed with ground mixed nuts and simmered – produced by the captain; and a French *tarte aux poires*, prepared by Timmy, who could produce a more delicate confectioners' cream than anyone aboard. Timmy kept his watch on home time, in order to keep his eleven-thirty appointments with Meg.

When Meg got down to the Base that night she had to push her way through an angry Peace Movement crowd, milling about in the mud with banners and effigies of broken nuclear missiles, like broken phalluses, held aloft. They let Meg through easily enough. She was wearing jeans and an anorak and was riding a bicycle: she seemed near enough one of their own.

'Take the toys from the boys,' they chanted, and Meg thought of the two faces of Timmy, the bouncy, grinning little boy, and the cool, grave features she sometimes glimpsed, that of the man within, and wondered which of them it was she loved, and knew it was the man, who half-frightened her. She had fun with the little boy, and played sexy games with him, but love was reserved for the man, and the man, indeed, was dangerous.

She disliked the women for not understanding this: she thought they weren't adult women at all – just angry little girls in grown-up bodies, which they hated. She was glad that she'd brought a dress and some heeled sandals with her. She'd stuffed them crossly into a carrier bag before she'd left, cursing Zelda's social pretensions, but now she felt pleased with herself. The dress was of fine wool, navy, with white flowers embroidered around the neckline. She'd been married in it.

'What's making you so angry?' asked Zelda, once Meg was inside and changing.

'What do these women want?' demanded Meg.

'Peace,' observed Zelda. 'I always thought you were rather their sort.'

'Then you thought wrong,' said Meg shortly. 'I don't want anything to do with it. Timmy and I just want to be left alone. He's a navigator: all he does is steer ships about by the stars.'

'There are no stars under the sea,' said Zelda. 'It's more complicated than that. Timmy is cleverer than you think.'

'If the Navy chooses to put him on Polaris, that's their responsibility. He's still just a navigator,' Meg persisted. 'A kind of timeless person.' And indeed, she saw Timmy as one of the heroes on Odysseus's boat, underneath a starry Grecian sky, steering between Scylla and Charybdis. She'd met him at a party. 'And what do *you* do?' she'd said. 'I'm a navigator,' he'd replied, and she had hardly heard. Her heart had gone; she had given it away, and that was that. She was like a child: she would not ask more, for fear of finding out more than she cared to know: of having to do what she ought, not what she wanted. A little girl who would not look down at her shoes before school, in case they needed cleaning.

'Darling!' said Zelda, pouring them both rather large gin-and-tonics. Dinner was ham salad and baked potatoes, and already on the table – except for the potatoes, which were keeping warm on the heated Hostess trolley. 'Darling, your husband is one of the Attack Team. There are three of them on Polaris. The captain, the first officer and the navigator. With a little help from the captain, your husband and mine could finish off the world. Didn't he ever tell you?'

'They wouldn't want to finish off the world,' said Meg, presently, taken aback. Timmy had never told her this.

'You know what men are,' said Zelda. 'They just love to obey orders. And if the Routine comes through from Base, "blow up Moscow, or Hanoi, or Peking", that's what they'll do. They'll sit down and push their buttons at the same time and whee! Off go the missiles as programmed. Men have no imagination, you see. One million, two million dead. It's only numbers. And women and children have to be sacrificed to the greater good. Well, we all know that. My father was a doctor; I know better than anyone. He looked after his patients, never us.'

'But the order won't come through,' said Meg.

'It hasn't so far,' said Zelda, glad to see Meg shaken out of what Zelda saw as a virtuous complacency, and pleased to shake a little more. 'But I suppose it must one day. If one owns a pair of nut-crackers one tends to crack nuts. But you knew all this when you married him; you can't complain now. When I meet those Peace Women I just push my way through them, shouting, "The Ruskies are coming, the Ruskies are coming." That makes them crosser still. Well, you have to laugh, don't you?'

'Not really,' said Meg.

'I do,' said Zelda. 'And at least when we're all nuked out of existence by the Ruskies – this whole country is just an unsinkable aircraft carrier for the USA: their forward line – our husbands will be safe enough. They can stay below for ever. We must take comfort from that.'

'Zelda,' said Meg, 'why don't you go and join them outside?'

'I don't have the right shoes,' said Zelda. The doorbell rang: it was Tony, the PR man.

'Tony will make you feel better,' said Zelda. 'He'll explain that we're all perfectly safe and our men are doing a grand job saving the world from itself, and protecting British women and children, and that those women out there are well-intentioned but misguided dupes of the Russians.'

Tony was as lean as Timmy was broad, and his nose hooked and aquiline and his charm very great. He looked into Meg's eyes as if he were looking into her soul, and valued it deeply. He looked past her body and into her mind, and liked it, and made her feel comfortable. She realised that she had never felt quite comfortable with Timmy, and wondered why.

'I can see Zelda's in a naughty mood,' said Tony. 'I hope she hasn't been upsetting you. One has every sympathy with the women outside: and yes, they are misguided, because nuclear weapons are a deterrent – they prevent wars, they don't cause them – but I wouldn't go so far as to say the women are dupes of the Russians. I am no "Reds under the Beds" man. Those women out there are brave and intelligent and have their point of view. We have a different point of view because we know more. We have more facts at our disposal.'

'You are employed by the Admiralty,' said Zelda, 'to say exactly that kind of thing. To pour any sort of oil on any sort of troubled water you happen to come across. Have some ham salad. Don't you think Meg is pretty?'

'Yes I do,' said Tony, 'and Zelda, couldn't I go into the kitchen and whip us up some spaghetti bolognaise? You know I hate salads.'

'I was hoping you'd say that,' said Zelda. 'You know where everything is.'

Thompson growled when Tony rose: that was unusual, thought Meg. Thompson's sins were usually those of over-enthusiasm rather than ill-temper.

After supper Tony insisted on driving Meg home, with her bicycle on his roof-rack.

'I'll be perfectly safe,' she said.

'Good heavens, no,' he said. 'You might get raped by a Peace Woman. I'd never forgive myself. I'm perfectly respectable, aren't I, Zelda? Tell her I'm perfectly respectable.'

Zelda duly told her. Meg gave in, glad to be spared the long ride uphill, glad of the comfort of his smooth white car; uneasily conscious of the benefits money could buy.

They passed through the encampment of makeshift tents where the women had settled for the night.

'Everyone has to make a living,' said Meg sadly. 'And almost no one's occupation is guiltless, I suppose. Just think, Timmy might be an Arms Salesman. Now they're *really* wicked.'

'These women live off the State,' said Tony. 'The wretched tax-payer supports them.'

Tony had another face, too, thought Meg, just as Timmy did. When Tony was off-guard, the all-embracing, all-forgiving urbanity deserted him: she could see the impatient dislike shimmering beneath; a dislike of long-haired lefties, strident feminists, anti-blood-sport nuts, and so forth. She disliked them too, but somehow in a different way. She wanted to change their minds, not root them out. Were all men like this? Pretending to be civilised, but wanting in their hearts nice clean sudden final solutions? The drama of destruction?

She had a vision of After-Armageddon: the missiles flying through crevices in clouds over crowded seas; the hills black and poisoned; the stuff of nightmares. She'd had such nightmares before she'd met Timmy. She'd assumed they were some kind of symbolic reflection of her own inner state, her own fear of sudden, awful events. Her father dying. Sudden, awful, the end of the world. But if everyone had a vision of the end of the world, wasn't that dangerous? Mightn't it then come true? Wasn't it better to keep the mind on what was kind and pure and hopeful? If one acknowledged the devil one gave birth to the devil. She believed that. She thought that was why she so resented the Peace Women. They were bringing Armageddon nearer, not keeping it away. Perhaps she was pregnant? How could she bring a baby into this world? But then again, how could she not? One had to affirm one's faith in the future, and affirm it, and affirm it, and affirm it.

Tony had his hand on her knee. How long had it been there? It was a pleasant hand, warm, sensible, and full of expectation.

She moved it gently away.
'No, thank you, Tony,' she said. 'I love Timmy.'
'Of course you do,' he said, cheerfully. 'And so you should, a nice girl like you.'
She wasn't sure she wanted to be a nice girl. He suggested she admire the landscape. It occurred to her that Timmy never suggested she admire anyone or anything other than himself, or his handiwork.

Tony asked to come in, but she said no, and he acquiesced, again pleasantly.
He offered his services in any way she liked.
'Anything un-innocent,' he said. 'Just say the word. But if I have to put up with the innocent for the pleasure of your company then I will. Mend fuses, fix shelves, lay lino: I'm the original Mr Fix-it. I'll even take the foul hound for walks.'

They lingered on the doorstep. He said he was a woman's man. He said he couldn't get on with Navy men, because they had no conversation. They could exchange information and tell jokes and swap prejudices, but they didn't deal in ideas. And now he had met Meg he wouldn't easily let her go. He had to talk to someone.
'There's Zelda,' said Meg.

She called Thompson and went in and shut the door, and looked at the bare rough decent walls and the plain deal table and was glad to be alone.

'I hope Zelda and Meg get together,' said Jim, the first officer. 'They ought to be friends. I'm afraid your Meg's going to be rather lonely up there on the hills.'
They themselves were under the polar ice-cap: it was a fairly edgy place to be. The radar man never liked it, and Rating Hoskins lay awake in his bunk at night (local night) worrying about what would happen if they set off a missile when they happened to be under some ice mountain. Would the initial thrust be enough to force it through, or would it turn, as in some children's cartoon, and destroy the destroyers? 'She has Thompson to keep her company,' said Timmy.

He felt the touch of Meg's thoughts. She was laughing. He looked at his watch. It was eleven-thirty, Greenwich Mean Time. That night he dreamt that Meg was taking Thompson for a walk in the woods of his childhood.

Meg, indeed, was taking Thompson for a walk, but out on the hills. Thompson had recovered from his fear of sheep since Timmy had gone, and now showed a desire to chase them – only strong words and a stern face prevented him. If she tried to put him on the lead he pulled her along over the rough ground, so she would stumble and fear for her ankles. She had to contain him by force of will alone. She thought that Tony was a good deal more controllable than Thompson.

Even as the notion occurred to her Thompson was off over the brow of the hill and though she yelled for a good five minutes he did not return. A cold wind had got up: the hills were hostile. She did not belong here. She thought she would leave Thompson to find his own way home. He was more part of the elements than she was: leaping and bounding into the chilly blast, exhilarated. The thought that he was Timmy's dog, and she was responsible for him, oppressed her. She could see down to the harbour below, and the docks and the grey sea, and the slow movement of the toy cranes, and on the next fold of hills the Base itself, with its squared-off roads and pretty bungalows and the thin tracery of the high wire fence, and outside it a kind of muddy unevenness, presumably where the Peace tents were pitched, or slung, or whatever they were. She was too far off to make out detail.

It's nothing to do with me, she thought, let them get on with their games, and leave me out of it. Leave me to love my husband, and walk my dog, and get on with my life.

And she ran bounding down the hill.

By five that evening Thompson had not returned and the postman, delivering an envelope marked with many red bands, said, 'A farmer will have got that dog with a gun, forbye. Out there worriting sheep again.'

'He doesn't worry sheep,' Meg said.

The red bands induced her to open the letter and she found inside notification that Timmy's Visa Card had been withdrawn for non-payment of dues. She discovered that they owed the Company £843.72 and at 12½% accumulative interest, too. Timmy had told her to use the card to buy wallpaper, paint, carpets and so forth. She had used it the day before, down on the Base, to buy groceries, finding funds in the joint account she shared with Timmy running low. Timmy's monthly salary had not for some reason shown up on the balance.

Meg shivered. Cold had somehow got into her bones. She put on more jerseys and piled wood on the fire – though stocks were surprisingly low – but kept opening the door to see if she could see Thompson bounding home, which of course she didn't.

Night fell. No Thompson. Meg telephoned Tony and wept over the receiver.
'I'll come right up,' he said.

Thompson arrived home at the same time as Tony. He stood at the door laughing and panting and dropping and picking up a dead rat, for the death of which he expected to be congratulated.
'I hope he hasn't been worrying sheep,' said Tony. 'They shoot dogs for that round here.'

Tony removed the rat from Thompson's mouth, made Meg look for worm pills and thrust one down Thompson's throat. Then he told Meg what to write to Visa and gave her the number of the Families' Officer on the Base who looked after the financial affairs of the wives while their husbands were away. He claimed that submariners were notoriously impractical in money matters and, indeed, in most domestic matters.

'Their minds ebb and flow in tune with the mighty currents of the deep, I expect,' said Meg. 'Their wives have pathetic little sharp foamy wavelet minds. All detail, no grandeur.'
'Not so pathetic,' said Tony.

He put his hand into something he called a soot box in the Rayburn flue and told her the chimney needed sweeping, and he would send a man up to do it, and to fix a cowl to stop the smoke blowing back when the wind was from the north.

He told her he would bring up stores from the Base so she could sit out a snowstorm: otherwise they'd have to send a helicopter to fetch her down and she wouldn't like that, would she? And neither would he. He for one would like to see someone make a go of living independently, outside the

Base. The Navy owned too much of people's souls: it had
no business to.

He said he'd lend her a television set, and she said she
didn't like TV, and he said oh she would, she would. By
the time the New Year was here, and her husband back.

He said he expected nothing from her. He liked to be of use.
He was a solitary kind of person, really. So was she. Let
them both circle each other for a time.

And he went away, leaving Meg warm and comforted and
stirring inside. She tried to remember what Timmy's face
looked like, and was not able to. It was as if the presence of
another man in the croft, his coat hanging on the back of
the chair, seeing to things, doing things, had somehow
driven out the lingering feel of Timmy.

'Did you know,' said the captain – they were back up in the
Pacific now, and coral less of a problem than ice, though
still tricky – 'that we nuclear submariners outnumber the
blue whale? American, Russian, Chinese by the hundred!
We're the rarity – the ones with the GB plates. Every city
in the world with a missile pointed at it. Our five just
provide extra cover for the major capitals: a drop of wine
in the child's glass, to stop him making a fuss, to make him
feel grown up.'
'Ours not to reason why,' said Jim. 'Ours just to do and
die –'
'Only we won't be doing the dying,' said Timmy. 'That's
for those at the end of our doing.'

Men get meditative at the bottom of the sea. On some days
even *haute cuisine* fails. Rating Hoskins played good guitar,
but only knew peace-songs from the sixties; which made
everyone maudlin.

Meg said to Tony, 'The trouble with Thompson is, he acts as if I were his sister, not his mistress. He doesn't respect me.'

'I don't act as if you were my sister,' said Tony. He was in bed with Meg. He had just got in; for warmth, he said. The man who came to sweep the chimney said the whole thing was about to fall down and the fire mustn't be lit until he'd come back, which he would do the following day, with materials to rebuild it.

Cold had struck afresh into Meg's bones. The Families' Officer had explained to her that nearly all Timmy's monthly salary cheque was bespoken on Credit Purchase arrangements, mortgage payments and so forth. There was next-to-nothing left over for daily living; and she, Meg, had been living like a spendthrift, buying cream when top-of-the-milk would do, sending letters first-class, buying wallpaper when whitewash would serve. He would advance her money, of course, against Timmy's next salary. The Navy, he said, believed in looking after wives – and frequently had to. Naval pay was designed to keep single men in beer, not married men in homes. But where was it all to end? If only Meg would agree to sell the croft and come and live on Base, she'd find the living more economical. Meg told the Families' Officer she'd think about it. Tony said he'd pay off the Visa, and they wouldn't tell Timmy. Meg agreed. Meg crept into bed not caring whether Tony followed.

Tony did follow, with a bottle of champagne and two glasses. 'I suppose,' he said, 'you spent most of the last three months in bed with Timmy.'

'Not necessarily in bed,' said Meg. 'It was warmer then – outdoors was always very nice and we grew fond of under the kitchen table, except for Thompson.'

'When it suddenly stops,' he said, 'it must be very hard.'

'Of course it's hard,' said Meg, crossly.

He had all his clothes off. Meg had taken off her jeans, for comfort's sake, but had her other clothes on, the usual vests and body warmers. (And winter not even truly started.) She was in bed for warmth and comfort, nothing else.

'I wish you wouldn't act like some kind of servicing agency,' she said, shaking off his enquiring hand. 'For all I know you're put in by Security to keep me happy.'

'Security don't want people to be happy,' he said. 'Merely silent.'

'It's much the same thing,' she said, 'when it comes to wives.'

And she sat up and accepted the proffered champagne.

'You aren't *really* Security?' she asked, fascinated and a little alarmed.

'Of course not,' he said. 'How paranoid you are. Would they really go to such lengths for the simple wife of a simple navigator?'

'They have to occupy themselves somehow,' said Meg. 'And he *is* one third of an Attack Team: that is, one fifteenth of Britain's Independent Nuclear Deterrent.'

'Is he really Attack Team?' asked Tony. 'How do you know?'

'Zelda told me,' said Meg.

'Ah, Zelda,' said Tony. 'Zelda would never go to bed with a man wearing a body warmer and a thermal vest.'

'Well, you'd know,' said Meg. He did not deny it.

He removed her body warmer and thermal vest.

'I haven't said I will,' she warned him. 'You got into this bed on your own account. I didn't ask you in.'

'You didn't get out of it either,' he said. 'A man takes these little hints to heart. You have lovely nipples. Pinkish. Much nicer than Zelda's.'

'I wish you'd be serious,' she complained. 'How am I going to survive this life? How can Timmy afford to leave the Navy, if he doesn't try and save?'

'Dear heart,' said Tony, 'I am serious, and Timmy doesn't want to leave the Navy.'

'Oh yes he does.' She covered her breasts with the sheet.
'Consciously perhaps, but not deep down in his subconscious, where it really counts.'

Meg believed him and her hand lost its will. The sheet
dropped. There was a noise at the door, a scraping sound,
and the fragile catch gave way. Thompson lumbered in and
lay beneath the bed.
'That's it,' said Meg. 'Please get out of this bed, Tony.'
'Why? He can't talk,' said Tony.
'I wouldn't be too sure of that,' said Meg.
So Tony got out of bed and dressed, forgetting his tie.
Thompson dragged that under the bed and chewed it a
little, having been deprived of his rat, and needing some
small revenge.

Meg felt quite fond of Thompson, for having rescued her.
At the same time the rain had started to fall, and the ground
around the croft, disturbed by months of building work,
had turned to mud. Whenever Thompson went out, which
seemed to be every fifteen minutes, he took shafts of expensive hot air with him; and when he came in, clouts of mud.
He would run upstairs to the bedroom and shake himself
there. If she tried to keep him in, or out, he would holler
and bang like a naughty child until she let him out, or in.
She was plastering and papering the kitchen and it was,
because of Thompson, taking twice as long as she had
estimated.

Meg's mother- and father-in-law came to visit and admire
and sympathise – they were the nicest and remotest of nicest
remote people – and she suggested they take Thompson
away with them. They seemed surprised, even – had they
been a little less nice – a fraction shocked.
'But he's company for you. And protection!'

He is disorder, Meg longed to reply: he is distraction and debacle. He is expensive – 75p a day to feed – he is dirty, and what's more, he is Timmy's. And Timmy, she longed to say, having the uncomfortable feeling that somehow they had shifted the whole responsibility of their son on to her, is yours more than mine. It was you two, after all – and she knew she was being childish – who *thought Timmy up*.

She smiled sweetly and made drop-scones on the stove which, thanks to Tony, roared warmingly and cooked beautifully and was no trouble at all except when Thompson lay too close to it, filling the air with the smell of singeing dog hair. They went away, patting Thompson.

Four more weeks and Timmy would return. Perhaps even in time for Christmas!
'I bet you know when Second Crew's coming back,' she said to Tony, when she met him down at the Base, outside the library. But he only shimmered a smile and said to ask Zelda. She didn't see much of Zelda. She thought Zelda to blame for practically pushing her into Tony's bed (or rather Tony into hers). She was sorry for Zelda's husband, Jim, that nice, simple, beaming man. Wives ought to be virtuous: it was a kind of magic which kept disaster away.

The Peace Women struck camp and moved off, and she felt the magic had worked. When Tony came to help her tile behind the kitchen sink and ran his hand up the back of her jumper she slapped him down very hard, so that tears came to his eyes.
'I didn't expect quite that,' he complained. 'You're so unpredictable.'
'I don't sleep very well.'
'You know the cure for that.'
'It's not that. I think I have cystitis or something. I keep having to get up in the night to spend a penny.'

'You're pregnant,' he said, and took her down to the doctor, who confirmed the diagnosis.
'I wish it was my baby,' said Tony. 'I love babies. But now I'm going south, for a month or so.'

Meg phoned Zelda to tell her the news.
'Should I tell the Families' Officer?' she asked. 'Then he could send a telegram.'
'No point,' said Zelda. 'They'll be back in a few days. And he'll be in a bad temper. They always come back cross. Be warned.'

Timmy stepped out on to firm land, which rocked beneath his feet, and breathed rich cold air which stunned him. It seemed to him that no time at all had passed since he had gone on board. He had two quite different lives. One up here, one down there. It was safer down there, longing for ever for journey's end. He took his bicycle from the security shed. It had been kept well-oiled, he was glad to see. Zelda was waiting for Jim and as Timmy cycled past she said, 'Meg's pregnant,' and he whooped with – what? Pleasure, surprise, shock? – Or just the strength of life in this clean cold unfetid place? He stopped at the Base wine shop to buy champagne. When he got home Meg was in bed and asleep and he got in beside her – as did Thompson, half-mad with ecstasy. Thompson, Timmy observed, had put on weight. Meg couldn't be giving him enough exercise.

'Champagne in bed,' said Meg. 'We're supposed to be saving. It's unbearably extravagant.'
That hurt him.
'Of course I'm glad to see you home.' She shouldn't have said it: it made it sound forced. They had made love furiously and fast and were left uncompanionable and dissatisfied.
'You've put on weight,' she said next, and shouldn't have. 'And you're pale.'
'It's just that the rest of the world is over-coloured,' he said,

retreating, wanting peace, and the gentle lilt of expected life. Just the captain, Jim and himself.

'What do they give you to eat under the sea? Baked beans and corned beef?'

'More or less,' said Timmy.

'I made us a nice cottage pie,' she said. And then: 'Put your head on my tummy. All that life going on down there!'

'It doesn't feel any different,' he said, and shouldn't have.

'I'm glad you forgot your pills,' he added, to make things better.

'How much did the champagne cost?' She returned to the theme of his extravagance. She wished he'd go away again. 'I think you should have trained Thompson to stay out of the bedroom,' said Timmy. 'He's not a poodle or a lapdog; he's a gun dog.'

'I love him being in here,' said Meg. 'I even like the sound of him scratching his fleas.'

'*Fleas?*' said Timmy in alarm.

'All dogs have fleas.'

'Not if they're properly looked after.'

It was intolerable. Meg shrieked and Timmy shouted. She said she was going home to her mother: he said he was going back to sea. She said she'd have a termination and he said good. When both had voiced exhaustion and outrage, and Thompson had stopped pattering and whuffling and fallen asleep with a dribble of saliva drying on his jowls, Timmy laughed.

'Sorry about all that,' he said. They went to bed and to sleep, twined, then woke up and made love again, in a calmer way, and seemed able to resume their life where they had left off. Except not quite. Timmy was alarmed at the consumption of fuel for the Rayburn and said the new chimney was responsible: she shouldn't have had it done. He said she'd have to keep the damper in and she said 'then it smokes' and he said 'nonsense' and she said 'allow me to know my own stove' and he said 'but I installed it' and she said 'badly' and then he laughed and they both stopped, and kissed.

'I'm not supposed to upset you,' confided Meg. 'The Families' Officer said so. Save him from worry: for the sake of the Navy, for the sake of the country, for the sake of the world. He didn't mention for your sake, or mine. But that's what I'm thinking of. See my smile? Set fair for you?' And so it was, until the last day of the leave.

Then, when Timmy had been home for nearly three months, Thompson, cross no doubt because he'd been put on a diet and run off his feet, dragged Tony's tie from under the bed and laid it by Timmy's face as Timmy did his press-ups.

The telephone rang as Timmy stared at the tie. He answered it, listened, said 'yes' and put the receiver down.

She said, 'is that them?' and he said 'yes' again and went on staring at the tie. It was late March. It had been a mild winter, with very little snow. Tony had not been seen, nor mentioned by anyone, except as the person who'd recommended the builder who'd done the damage to the chimney. Timmy had had to rebuild it. They'd spent Christmas with Timmy's nice remote parents, and the New Year with Meg's vaguely reproachful mother. Meg was six months' pregnant.

'How did that tie get there?' asked Timmy.

'I don't know,' she said. 'It's very dusty.'

'How long has it been there? About six months? You were on the pill. How do women get pregnant when they're on the pill? You got pregnant after I left, by a man who wears a green tie with red stars on it. Christ!'

Meg laughed, from shock. She shouldn't have.

'And now you're laughing. No wonder. You have my income, is that it? But you don't have to have me!'

He had on his hard cold face. Meg felt her own grow hard and cold.

'Is your objection to the quality of the tie?' she asked. She did not deign to defend herself.

He did not reply. He was packing his few things. The gun was under his arm. Perhaps he'll shoot me, she thought, and part of her hoped he would.

'Nothing's been right since I've been home,' he said. '*Nothing*. Now I understand why.'

'You must ask the doctor,' she said. 'He'll tell you.'

'How can I ask the doctor? I'm going away for three months, now, with this to think about!'

Meg wept. Thompson howled. Timmy stamped and banged and departed.

'But I'm pregnant!' she called after him, weeping.

'Complain to its father, not to me,' he called back, and was gone. She waited for him to telephone from the dock, but he didn't. She went up to the hills and sat there and watched and presently saw Polaris glide away out of its dock and sink beneath the water halfway down the loch. Thompson laid his bony chin upon her knee and pressed, and the next day she found a bruise there. She bruised easily, now that she was pregnant.

'"Truly the light was sweet,"' misquoted the captain, at the periscope, '"and a pleasant thing it was for the eyes to behold the sun." You see these lumps on my eyelids, Mr Navigator? Cholesterol spots, they say. According to the MD I have to cut down on animal fats. You were first on board this time, Mr Navigator. Have a good leave?'

'No, sir,' said Timmy.

Meg went down to Zelda's, piteously. Zelda was bright and very pregnant. She had new doorbell chimes, 'Pling-plong,' they went, when you rang. 'Pling, pling, plong.'

'Woodland bells!' cried Zelda, in triumph. 'Jim thought I'd like them. Well, that's the way it goes! Work together, live together, think together. What's the matter with you, red eyes? No, don't tell me. You had a row with Timmy and he walked off with a harsh word on his lips.'

'Yes. Several. Whore. Adulteress. That kind.'

'And you won't see him for another three months! Never mind. It always happens. You get used to it. What was it Jim said this time? I can't remember. It doesn't matter. Something perfectly horrid. Ah yes, they want me to help out at the library but Jim said if I took a job I'd grow a worse moustache than I have already. Statistics show career-women grow moustaches. What do they do down on that boat of theirs – study statistics?'

'But Zelda,' Meg wept, 'supposing, supposing – supposing something happens to Timmy and those are the last words he ever said to me.'

'You're very egocentric,' said Zelda. 'You should be thinking of him, not you. Mind you, he'll forget he ever said them. Men do. They have no memory for insults given, only those received. Did you say anything terrible to him?'

'No.'

'Then that will be next leave. Jim and I take it in turns. It's the strain, you know. Bad-tempered when they go, bad-tempered when they get back, and a little bit of peace in the middle. Is it worth it?'

The pling-plong of the woodland chimes sounded and Tony came into the hall.

'Hi,' he said. 'Long time no see.'

'Hi,' said the women, cheering up.

It was late spring. The cold wet weather continued unseasonably into April. A few daffodils came up on the hills, but were paled and shredded by the winds, and if the birds sang no one stood about to hear. Meg stayed in the croft and continued to regard herself as a married woman, and to believe what Zelda had said. She was tempted to storm around Tony, shower him with gusts of blame and torrents

46

of reproaches, but somehow it was all too grave and grown-
up for that. She had to be still, for the baby's sake. It was
an easy pregnancy: she was fortunate.

Thompson grew more excitable, less controllable. He actually caught rabbits now, and came back bloodied, as if he
too had reached man's estate.

It's all the men's fault, thought Meg. All the bombs and
the missiles and the schemes and the theories and the rival
forms of government, and they make believe that the way
to solve things is to see who can blow each other up best:
all male, male and angry and mad.

If the Peace Women had still been there, she thought, she
would have joined them. You couldn't in the full flush of
early sexual love, but you could later on: you could chant
with the rest of them, 'Take the toys from the boys.' Oh
yes, easily.

In the middle of April a strange thing happened. It was on
a morning that had dawned so clear and still and fine that
there was no mistaking winter had ended: and Meg could
see that for weeks now, hidden by the windy, unseasonable
veil, the spring had been preparing for its surprises. The
trees, which only the day before had seemed lean and black,
could today be seen to be plump and hazy with fresh green
leaves. Peonies had sprung up where she'd thought there
was nothing but brown earth: and there were pansies and
polyanthus underfoot. Meg stood on the doorstep, her face
raised to the warmth of the sun, and knew that summer and
good times were coming. Thompson sat on the path and
did the same. She saw now that every branch seemed to
have a bird upon it; and a row of starlings sat on the dry-
stone wall and that they too had their heads turned towards
the warmth. And where the wall had crumbled to the ground
sat a rabbit, perfectly still, and behind that a sheep, quietly
staring in at her. The cat – borrowed from Amanda down
at the library to keep the mice population down – jumped
from the path to the windowsill, and sat there, and one or

two of the assembled company twitched a little, but quickly settled again. It was as if all living creatures united in their pleasure in the day, in their relief that the hard times were over and the knowledge that good times were coming; and that all, in this, were equal and understood one another.

Thompson was the first to break the unnatural peace. He yelped and barked and shot after the rabbit. The sheep trotted off, the birds rose squawking, the cat disappeared into the bushes after them. The normal rules of kill or be killed reasserted themselves. It seemed, at least in the animal kingdom, a kind of game, to which everyone consented.

Meg blamed Thompson. When he came back from his chase, leaping and prancing and slavering, she hit him and shouted at him and chased him through the house, shrieking. Then she was ashamed of herself. Thompson crawled under the sofa and growled when she came near, and when she put her hand beneath it to make friends he snapped at her.

A little later the telephone rang. It was one of the local farmers, asking her to keep her dog under control. He was running the profit off his sheep. If it went on, he'd have to shoot him.

'It's not my dog,' said Meg, feebly. 'It's my husband's, and he's away. He's in the Navy.' She thought that might soften his heart.

'Aye, I know all about that,' said the farmer. 'And I know you're pregnant, and I'm sorry for you, lass. But what are you Navy folk doing up here on our land? You've got your own world, you stick to it. Your dog's your luxury. My sheep are my necessity. That dog's an untrained working dog, and there's nothing worse. He'd be better off dead.'

After that Meg kept Thompson in the house, or took him for walks on a lead, and in her heart Thompson and Timmy became the same thing, the same burden.

Down below the China Seas Jim said to Timmy, 'What's the matter, old man?'

'Nothing's the matter,' said Timmy. He was surprised Jim had noticed anything: he saw himself as a bright clear day, sunny and smiling. The black clouds rolled and swirled about the edges of his unconscious, but with an effort of will he kept them back. Blue skies, smiling at me!

'If it's Zelda,' said Jim, 'don't worry. I know all about that. These things happen. It's all over now. Zelda doesn't like me being in the Navy. It's a half-life for a woman. They have a right to something more. So she has her revenge: then tells me. I don't blame you, old man, and I don't blame her.'

Timmy counted the sentences as Jim spoke them. Nine. He'd never known Jim say more than four in a row before. He was moved by a sense of the importance of the occasion, and presently felt a burden had gone from him he didn't even know he had been carrying.

'I wonder what the time is at home?' he said.

The captain consulted a dial or so.

'Eleven-thirty in the morning,' he said. 'Why?'

'Because that's my time for contacting Meg,' he said.

'Telepathy?' asked the captain. 'The Ruskies do it all the time. I suppose we shouldn't lag behind.'

Timmy listened in, but felt no answering call from Meg, and felt at once lost and vulnerable and said, 'I suppose there are many innocent ways a man's tie could get to be under one's wife's bed,' and the captain said, 'Quite so.'

'I blame myself, sir,' said Timmy.

'That's the secret to it all,' said the captain. 'Let's drink to that!'

'Drink, sir?'

'Life is sweet,' said the captain, 'and a little white wine won't do us any harm.'

He took down from the back of the shelf one of Zelda's two canisters of white wine.

'But, sir,' said Jim, 'it's *bœuf au poivre* for dinner, with green peppers, not black, the way it ought to be. Shouldn't we be drinking red?'

'Desperate times, desperate measures!' said the captain, opening one of the canisters of white wine. Then he pricked his finger with a needle and let a drop or two of blood fall inside. 'Here's to universal brotherhood!' he said. 'And to all our faults!' The blood barely discoloured the wine so he added some drops of cochineal as well. 'We'll leave it a rosé,' he said. 'Compromise, that's the thing.'

The midwife knocked upon Meg's door and found her sitting grimly on a chair, Thompson's lead wound round her wrist, and Thompson sitting at her feet, unwilling, and chafing and wild-eyed. He barked at the midwife, and strained to get to her, not to attack, but to welcome her in.

'I should let the dog go,' said the midwife. Meg did, and Thompson leapt forward and the midwife went towards him instead of cringing back, as most people did when faced with the noisy, welcoming Thompson, and thus managed to keep her balance. Presently Thompson calmed.

'How long had you been sitting like that?' she asked.

'About an hour,' said Meg. 'But I know his moods. If I let him out when his eyes look like that, he goes straight after the sheep, and then he'll get shot.'

'It might be the best thing,' observed the midwife.

'Timmy would never forgive me,' said Meg, who had begun to weep. She was seven months' pregnant. She lay on the bed while the midwife felt round her belly.

'You didn't come down to the clinic,' said the midwife, 'so I thought I'd just pop up here to see if all was well, which it is.'

She took a casual look round the kitchen shelves to see if there was any food, which there was. But she still wasn't easy.

'Hubby away, I suppose,' she said, 'being Crew No. 2. And we mustn't ask when he's due back, must we?'

'No, we mustn't,' said Meg. 'And he couldn't be fetched back, even if I were dying. Not that he'd want to be fetched. He might miss the end of the world, and he wouldn't like that.'

'Can your mother come and stay?' asked the midwife.

'She doesn't like dogs,' said Meg shortly. 'And she doesn't like Timmy, and she doesn't like the Navy, and she told me this would happen and I said let me run my own life, Mother. And I don't think she likes me either, come to think of it.'

'What about your husband's parents? You don't seem to be in a state to be left alone.'

'I hardly know them. What I do know, I don't like. It's mutual, I think.'

'Isn't there somebody who could take the dog?'

'The dog is my responsibility. I'll see it through if it kills me.'

'Your legs are very scratched. Why is that?'

'Because I was taking Thompson for a walk. He pulled me through some bushes.'

'Put him in kennels.'

'Timmy would never forgive me. Perhaps I should go into kennels and Thompson could have the bed all to himself. Until Timmy comes back. Then they'd share it and be perfectly happy. He only married me because he needed a kennel-maid.'

'I think I'd better ring the doctor up,' said the midwife. 'I can't leave you in this state.'

'I'm not in a state,' said Meg, weeping copiously. 'I was only trying to entertain you. Pow! Three schoolboys with their fingers on the trigger. It's all so funny!'

The midwife made Meg take a tranquillising pill, and Meg asked for a few extra for Thompson, but the midwife wouldn't oblige. She said she'd return later with the doctor and Meg was to stay where she was.

But after the midwife had gone for half an hour or so, Meg gave in to Thompson's whinings and snappings and put him on the lead and took him for a walk. Thompson walked sedately for a little but then started pulling and tugging, and finally wrenched the lead right out of her hand – or perhaps she just gave up holding it – and was off after a rabbit. She stood on the brow of the brackeny hill and looked down to a slight valley and a wooded culvert and then the hill rose again and on the opposite slope were sheep. She saw Thompson's small shape pelting downhill: she watched him lose the rabbit in the undergrowth of the valley, and then saw him emerge the other side and stand for a while, watching the sheep.
'But I knew this would happen,' she said aloud. 'It was bound to happen.'

And the sheep scattered as Thompson leapt amongst them, biting and yelping, and she saw a man with a gun coming over the top of the hill. She waved her arms and yelled and started running, but watched the gun being raised and pointed and saw a little puff and then heard a crack, and Thompson had jumped in the air and fallen, in slow motion, and the sheep spread out, away from the centre of the scene, as if interpreting some formal dance routine. And because she was looking at the farmer she didn't watch where she was going, and tripped, with her foot in a rabbit hole, and fell; lost consciousness and, regaining it seconds later, felt a dreadful pain in her side and an even worse one in her head, for which she was totally responsible. She was manufacturing hate, and rage, and pain; all by herself, with enormous energy.

The farmer was putting his coat beneath her head. She felt her eyes cross and wary and her mouth pulled up in a sneer. He said something which ended, as so much did in these parts, 'forbye'; and then his face had gone and so was he, and if she turned her head – her body being pinned by so much pain – she could see where Thompson lay. His skull was partly gone; bits of shredded flesh stuck to something which was white and presumably bone, and also bits of a kind of grey badly wrapped parcel, which was presumably brain; the seat of all Thompson's troubles.

She was glad Thompson was dead. She hoped the baby was dying too, and then herself. She wanted the world to end: if she could have ended it then and there she would have. Pressed the button, finished it all. Ashes and dust and silence. The thought was so strong it seemed like an explosion in her head: not a sharp decent crack, like the one which had shattered Thompson, but a kind of reddish rumble, which presently carried consciousness away with it.

Zelda bent over her; she was in an ambulance. The midwife was there, too. She was knitting a white scarf with red stripes – as best she could, for the road was bumpy. An ambulance attendant studied his nails.
'What *is* Timmy going to say?' reproached Zelda. 'Poor Thompson!'
'Oh, shut up, Zelda,' said Meg, automatically.
'Is she coming round?' asked the midwife.
'She's being very rude,' said Zelda. 'Is that the same thing?'
'What happened?' asked Meg.
'Acute abdominal pain for no apparent reason,' said the midwife. 'It happens sometimes. Don't worry, the foetal heart's strong and steady: so's yours.'
'Did I dream it?' asked Meg. 'Is Thompson dead?'
'Thompson's dead,' said Zelda. 'What *is* Timmy going to say? You should have put him in kennels, Meg.'

'Don't persecute the wee lassie,' said the midwife.
'It's the best thing for her,' said Zelda. 'I know her backwards. Look! It's brought the colour back to her cheeks.'

Meg wept for Thompson.
'I thought I'd blown up the world,' she said, presently. 'I'm glad it's still here.'
'Takes more than you, dear,' said the midwife.
'Three of us like me, and we might,' said Meg, 'all too easily,' but the midwife didn't take the reference. Zelda did. Zelda said, 'Well, I'll have no talk of the end of the world in front of the children. So far as I'm concerned their fathers are guarding our shores and protecting our future, not to mention paying the rent, and to say anything else is negativism. Women for the Bomb, that's me!'
'You've been seeing too much of Tony,' said Meg.
'I just hope,' said Zelda, 'that when my baby's born it manages to look like Jim. So now you know.'

Meg spent the rest of the day in the Base hospital and in the evening they sent her home by ambulance. She kept thinking she saw Thompson, out of the corner of her eye; but when she looked fairly and squarely he wasn't there. But his spirit lingered around the house, on the stairs and under the bed; and every door and window-frame had been scored by his strong claws.

The next morning Meg spoke to him seriously.
'Thompson,' she said, 'you're here and yet you're not here. You'll be off soon, I expect. Did you die for a purpose, to teach me a lesson? I feel there is something to be learned. I wish I knew more clearly what it was. I know I wasn't grateful for what I had, and I should have been. I expected a humble, grateful, easy animal, who would consent to be loved, who could be controlled; and instead I had you. I wanted for a husband the projection of my own fantasies, and instead I had Timmy. No wonder he fought back. I

54

thought it was other people who were angry and violent, not me; but it wasn't so. It was me as well. It's never *them*, is it? It's *us*.'

And she was silent, and seemed to hear Thompson's patient, heavy breathing.

'Thompson,' she said, 'take your spirit out of here, and go to the bottom of the sea, where the big silent ships glide in and out, and tell your master I'm sorry.'

Down on Polaris two Routines came through. One was from the Family News Service. The captain put it in a folder and said nothing.

'I know it's for me, sir. Is it Meg? Is she all right?'

'Perfectly all right.'

'Then what is it, sir? Is it Thompson?'

'Custom is, my boy, to keep bad news to the last day of the tour. Since there's nothing one can do about it –'

But Jim told him.

'Thompson was shot by a farmer. He'd been worrying the sheep.'

Timmy was silent for a while. The smell of chicken *à l'ail* – chicken stuffed with twenty heads of garlic, and simmered in stock – filled the galley and indeed the rest of the boat. It was a comforting smell.

'Poor Meg,' was what Timmy said. 'Poor Meg! All alone up there without even a dog to keep her company. At least I'll be home for the birth.'

'I think I'll just about miss Zelda's,' said Jim, thankfully. 'I'm not much good at childbirth.'

The second Routine was from Operations Base and told them to make for home at all speed. The captain passed the news on to the Engine Room and opened the second canister of Zelda's wine and again he added a little blood, in the interests of universal brotherhood, and a little cochineal: they drank, and Jim carved. The cooked garlic cut and tasted somewhere between fresh young turnip and good potato. They savoured that, and the good red wine. It was half past eleven. (Dinner had drifted earlier and earlier, through the tour. Hunger seemed to gnaw more anxiously as the weeks passed.)

' "Go thy way, saith the preacher," ' quoted the captain. ' "Eat thy bread with joy, and drink thy wine with a merry heart, for God now accepteth thy works." '

Timmy, it being time, thought of Meg and heard a dog barking. It was so firm and real and loud a noise he looked round for its source.

'Sir,' said Timmy, 'do you hear a dog barking?'

'I hear no barking,' said the captain. 'How could I? We are under the sea.'

But whether it was the agreeable sound of the banana and rum fritters frying; or the richness of the red forbidden wine – or perhaps indeed the spirit of poor murdered Thompson touched him – at any rate, presently the captain said –

'You know, if a Routine came through to push those buttons, I wouldn't! What, and lose all this?'

Horrors of the Road

Miss Jacobs, I don't believe in psychotherapy. I really do think it's a lot of nonsense. Now it's taken me considerable nerve to say that – I'm a rather mild person and hate to be thought rude. I just wouldn't want to be here under false pretences: it wouldn't be fair to you, would it?

But Piers wants me to come and see you, so of course I will. He's waiting outside in your pretty drawing room: I said he should go, and come back when the session was up: that I'd be perfectly all right but he likes to be at hand in case anything happens. Just sometimes I do fall forward, out of my chair – so far I haven't hurt myself. Once it was face-first into a feather sofa; the second was trickier – I was with Martin – he's my little grandchild, you know, David's boy, the only one so far – at the sandpit in the park and I just pitched forward into the sand. Someone sent for an ambulance but it wasn't really necessary – I was perfectly all right, instantly. Well, except for this one big permanent fact that my legs don't work.

I'm a great mystery to the doctors. Piers has taken me everywhere – Paris, New York, Tokyo – but the verdict seems to be the same: it's all in my head. It is a hysterical paralysis. I find this humiliating: as if I'd done it on purpose just to be a nuisance. I'm the last person in the world to be a nuisance!

Did you see Piers? Isn't he handsome? He's in his mid-fifties, you know, but so good-looking. Of course he has an amazing brain – well, the whole world knows that – and I think that helps to keep people looking young. I have a degree in

Economics myself – unusual for a housewife of my age – but of course I stayed home to devote myself to Piers and the children. I think, on the whole, women should do that. Don't you? Why don't you answer my questions? Isn't that what you're supposed to do? Explain me to myself? No?

I must explain myself to myself! Oh.

Behind every great man stands a woman. I believe that. Piers is a Nobel Prize winner. Would he have done it without me? I expect so. He just wouldn't have had me, would he, or the four children? They're all doing very well. Piers was away quite a lot when the children were young – he's a particle physicist, as I'm sure you know. He had to be away. They don't keep cyclotrons in suitably domestic places, and the money had to be earned somehow. But we all always had these holidays together, in France. How we loved France. How well we knew it. Piers would drive; I'd navigate; the four children piled in the back! Of course these days we fly. There's just Piers and me. It's glamorous and exciting, and people know who he is so the service is good. Waiters don't mind so much . . . Mind what? . . . I thought you weren't supposed to ask questions. I was talking about holidays, in the past, long ago. Well, not so long ago. We went on till the youngest was fifteen; Brutus that is, and he's only twenty now. Can it be only five years?

I miss those summer dockside scenes: the cars lined up at dusk or dawn waiting for the ferry home: sunburned families, careless and exhausted after weeks in the sun. By careless I don't mean without care – just without caring any more. They'll sleep all night in their cars to be first in the queue for the ferry, and not worry about it; on the journey out they'd have gone berserk. Brown faces and brittle blonde hair and grubby children; and the roof-racks with the tents and the water cans and the boxes of wine and strings of garlic. Volvos and Cortinas and Volkswagen vans.

Of course our cars never looked smart: we even started out once with a new one, but by the time we came back it was dented and bumped and battered. French drivers are so dreadful, aren't they; and their road signs are impossible.

How did the paralysis start? It was completely unexpected. There were no warning signs – no numbness, no dizziness, nothing like that. It was our thirtieth wedding anniversary. To celebrate we were going to do a tour of France in Piers' new MG. It can do 110 mph, you know, but Piers doesn't often go at more than fifty-five – that's the speed limit in the States, you know, and he says they know what they're doing – it's the best speed for maximum safety – but he likes to have cars that can go fast. To get out of trouble in an emergency, Piers says. We were going on the Weymouth/ Cherbourg route – I'm usually happier with Dover/Calais – the sea journey's shorter for one thing, and somehow the longer the journey through England the more likely Piers is to forget to drive on the right once we're in France. I've noticed it. But I don't argue about things like that. Piers knows what he's doing – I never backseat drive. I'm his wife, he's my husband. We love each other.

So we were setting out for Weymouth, the bags were packed, the individual route maps from the AA in the glove compartment – they'd arrived on time, for once. (I'd taken a Valium in good time – my heart tends to beat rather fast, almost to the point of palpitations, when I'm navigating.) I was wearing a practical non-crease dress – you know what long journeys are like – you always end up a little stained. Piers loves melons and likes me to feed him wedges as we drive along – and you know how ripe a ripe French melon can be. Piers will spend hours choosing one from a market stall. He'll test every single one on display – you know, sniffing and pressing the ends for just the right degree of tenderness – until he's found one that's absolutely perfect. Sometimes, before he's satisfied, he'll go through the fruit boxes at the back of the stall as well. The French like you to be particular, Piers says. They'll despise you if you accept just anything. And then, of course, if the melon's not to go over the top, they have to be eaten quite quickly – in the car as often as not . . .

Anyway, as I was saying, I was about to step into the car when my legs just kind of folded and I sank down on to the pavement, and that was six months ago, and I haven't walked since. No, no palpitations since either. I can't remember if I had palpitations before I was married – I've been married for ever!

And there was no holiday. Just me paralysed. No tour of France. Beautiful France. I adore the Loire and the châteaux, don't you? The children loved the West Coast: those stretches of piny woods and the long, long beaches and the great Atlantic rollers – but after the middle of August the winds change and everything gets dusty and somehow grizzly. When the children were small we camped, but every year the sites got more formal and more crowded and more full of *frites* and Piers didn't like that. He enjoyed what he called 'wilderness camping'. In the camping guides which describe the sites there's always an area section – that is, the area allowed for each tent. Point five of a hectare is crowded: two hectares perfectly possible. Piers liked ten hectares, which meant a hillside somewhere and no television room for the children or *frites* stall – and that meant more work for me, not that I grudged it: a change of venue for cooking – such lovely portable calor gas stoves we had: you could do a three-course meal on just two burners if you were clever, if the wind wasn't too high – is as good as a rest from cooking. It was just that the children preferred the crowded sites, and I did sometimes think they were better for the children's French. An English sparrow and a French sparrow sing pretty much the same song. But there you are, Piers loved the wilderness. He'd always measure the actual hectarage available for our tent, and if it didn't coincide with what was in the book would take it up with the relevant authorities. I remember it once ending up with people having to move their tents at ten in the evening to make proper room for ours – we'd driven three hundred miles that day and Brutus was only two. That wasn't Piers' fault: it was the camp proprietor's. Piers merely knocked him up to point out that our site wasn't the dimension it ought to be, and he over-reacted quite dreadfully. I was glad to get away from that site in the morning, I can tell you. It really wasn't Piers' fault; just one of those things. I'm glad it was only a stop-over. The other campers just watched us go, in complete silence. It was weird. And Fanny cried all the way to Poitiers.

Such a tearful little thing, Fanny. Piers liked to have a picnic lunch at about three o'clock – the French roads clear at mid-day while everyone goes off to gorge themselves on lunch, so you can make really good time wherever you're going. Sometimes I did wonder where it was we *were* going to, or *why* we had to make such time, but on the other hand those wonderful white empty B roads, poplar-lined, at a steady 55 mph . . . anyway, we'd buy our lunch at mid-day – wine and pâté and long French bread and orangina for the children, and then at three start looking for a nice place to picnic. Nothing's harder! If the place is right, the traffic's wrong. Someone's on your tail hooting – how those French drivers do hoot – they can see the GB plates – they know it means the driver's bound to forget and go round round-abouts the wrong way – and before you know it the ideal site is passed. The ideal site has a view, no snakes, some sun and some shade, and I like to feel the car's right off the road – especially if it's a Route Nationale – though Piers doesn't worry too much. Once actually some idiot did drive right into it – he didn't brake in time – but as Piers had left our car in gear, and not put on the handbrake or anything silly, it just shot forward and not much damage was done.

How is it that other cars always look so smooth and somehow new? I suppose their owners must just keep them in garages all the time having the bumps knocked out and re-sprays – well, fools and their money are often parted, as Piers keeps saying.

What was I talking about? Stopping for lunch. Sometimes it would be four thirty before we found somewhere really nice, and by four you could always rely on Fanny to start crying. I'd give her water from the Pschitt bottle – how the children giggled – Pschitt – every year a ritual, lovely giggle – and break off bread from the loaf for her, but still she grizzled: and Daddy would stop and start and stare over hedges and go a little way down lanes and find them impossible and back out on to the main road, and the children would fall silent, except for Fanny. Aren't French drivers rude? Had you noticed? I'd look sideways at a passing car and the driver would be staring at us, screwing his thumb into his head, or pretending to slit his throat with his finger – and always these honks and hoots, and once someone pulled in and forced us to stop and tried to drag poor Piers out of the car, goodness knows why. Just general Gallic over-excitement, I suppose. Piers is a wonderfully safe driver. I do think he sometimes inconveniences other cars the way he stops at intersections – you know how muddling their road signs are, especially on city ring roads, and how they seem to be telling you to go right or left when actually they mean straight on. And Piers is a scientist – he likes to be sure he's doing the right thing. I have the maps; I do my best: I memorise whole areas of the country, so I will know when passing through, say, Limoges, on the way from Périgueux to Issoudun, and have to make lightning decisions – Piers seems to speed up in towns. No! Not the Tulle road, not the Clermont road, not the Montluçon but the Châteauroux road. Only the Châteauroux road isn't marked! Help! What's its number? Dear God, it's the N20! We'll die! The N147 to Bellac then, and cut through on the

B roads to Argenton, La Châtre . . . So look for the Poitiers sign. Bellac's on the road to Poitiers –

So he stops, if he's not convinced I'm right, and takes the map himself and studies it before going on. Which meant, in later years, finding his magnifying glass. He hates spectacles! And you know what those overhead traffic lights are like in small country towns, impossible to see, so no one takes any notice of them! Goodness knows how French drivers survive at all. We had one or two nasty misses through no fault of our own every holiday; I did in the end feel happier if I took Valium. But I never liked Piers to know I was taking it – it seemed a kind of statement of lack of faith – which is simply untrue. Look at the way he carried me in, cradled me in his arms, laid me on this sofa! I trust him implicitly. I am his wife. He is my husband.

What was I saying? Fanny grizzling. She took off to New Zealand as soon as she'd finished her college course. A long way away. Almost as far as she could get, I find myself saying, I don't know why. I know she loves us and we certainly love her. She writes frequently. David's a racing car driver. Piers and I are very upset about this. Such a dangerous occupation. Those cars get up to 200 mph – and Piers did so hate speed. Angela's doing psychiatric nursing. They say she has a real gift for it.

I remember once I said to Piers – we were on the ring road round Angers – turn left here, meaning the T-junction we were approaching – but he swung straight left across the other carriageway, spying a little side road there – empty because all the traffic was round the corner, held up by the lights, ready to surge forward. He realised what he'd done, and stopped, leaving us broadside across the main road. 'Reverse!' I shrieked, breaking my rule about no backseat driving, and he did, and we were just out of the way when the expected wall of traffic bore down. 'You should have said second left,' he said, 'that was very nearly a multiple pile-up!' You can't be too careful in France. They're mad drivers, as everyone knows. And with the children in the car too —

But it was all such fun. Piers always knew how to get the best out of waiters and chefs. He'd go right through the menu with the waiter, asking him to explain each dish. If the waiter couldn't do it — and it's amazing how many waiters can't — he would send for the chef and ask him. It did get a little embarrassing sometimes, if the restaurant was very busy, but as Piers said, the French understand food and really appreciate it if you do too. I can make up my mind in a flash what I want to eat: Piers takes ages. As I say, he hates to get things wrong. We'd usually be last to leave any restaurant we ate in, but Piers doesn't believe in hurrying. As he says, a) it's bad for the digestion and b) they don't mind: they're glad to see us appreciating what they have to offer. So many people don't. French waiters are such a rude breed, don't you think? They always seem to have kind of glassy eyes. Goodness knows what they're like if you're *not* appreciating what they have to offer!

And then wine. Piers believes in sending wine back as well as food. Standards have to be maintained. He doesn't believe in serving red wines chilled in the modern fashion, no matter how new they are. And that a bottle of wine under eight francs is as worth discussing as one at thirty francs. He's always very polite: just sends for the wine waiter to discuss the matter, but of course he doesn't speak French, so difficulties sometimes arise. Acrimony almost. And this kind of funny silence while we leave.

And always when we paid the bill before leaving our hotel, Piers would check and re-check every item. He's got rather short-sighted over the years: he has to use a magnifying glass. The children and I would sit waiting in the car for up to an hour while they discussed the cost of hot water and what a reasonable profit was, and why it being a fête holiday should make a difference. I do sometimes think, I admit, that Piers has a love/hate relationship with France. He loves the country; he won't go holidaying in Italy or Spain, only France – and yet, you know, those *Dégustation-Libres* that have sprung up all over the place – 'free disgustings', as the children call them – where you taste the wine before choosing? Piers goes in, tastes everything, and if he likes nothing – which is quite often – buys nothing. That, after all, is what they are offering. *Free* wine-tasting. He likes me to go in with him, to taste with him, so that we can compare notes, and I watch the enthusiasm dying in the proprietor's eyes, as he is asked to fetch first this, then that, then the other down from the top shelf, and Piers sips and raises his eyebrows and shakes his head, and then hostility dawns in the shopkeeper's eye, and then boredom, and then I almost think something which borders on derision – and I must tell you, Miss Jacobs, I don't like it, and in the end, whenever we passed a *Dégustation-Libre* and I saw the glint in his eye, and his foot went on the brake – he never looked in his mirror – there was no point, since it was always adjusted to show the car roof – I'd take another Valium – because I think otherwise I would scream, I couldn't help myself. It wasn't that I didn't love and trust and admire Piers, it was the look in the French eye —

Why don't I scream? What are you after? Abreaction? I know the terms – my daughter Angela's a psychiatric nurse, as I told you, and doing very well. You think I was finally traumatised at the last *Dégustation*? And that's why I can't walk? You'd like to believe that, wouldn't you? I expect you're a feminist – I notice you're wearing a trouser suit – and like to think everything in this world is the man's fault. You want me to scream out tension and rage and terror and horror? I won't! I tell you, France is a joyous place and we all loved those holidays and had some wonderful meals and some knock-out wines, thanks to Piers, and as for his driving, we're all alive, aren't we? Piers, me, David, Angela, Fanny, Brutus. All alive! That must prove something. It's just I don't seem able to walk, and if you would be so kind as to call Piers, he will shift me from your sofa to the chair and wheel me home. Talking will get us nowhere. I do love my husband.

The Sad Life of the Rich

Millie made her confessional to the sea, since there was no priest to receive it. 'All my life,' she said, 'I have cheated and lied to get what I want.' The sad sea scraped against the grey shore, and the wet wind whipped around her Magli shoes. She wondered whether their yellow leather would lose colour where it met the creeping salt damp of the beach, or whether that only happened to cheap shoes? The beach was empty; the other hotel guests stayed in their rooms and waited for the wind to die down and the sun to appear.

Millie assumed there were other guests but it was hard to be sure. Sometimes she caught a flicker of a skirt disappearing down a long pink and gold corridor, or a grey trouser into a carpeted lift, and there was a murmur of chambermaids behind closed doors – so something was going on somewhere. There was a girl who smiled like a robot behind the reception desk, and if Millie left her room for five minutes to buy a paperback in the hotel shop her bed would be straightened and the ashtray emptied by the time she got back. Lights flicked on and off in her room to tell her when the hairstylist was ready. *He* was real: his boyfriend, he said, was a literary agent in Miami. That was a bright spot – he must have liked and trusted Millie to tell her that. But otherwise the staff kept out of her way and the guests kept to their rooms, either because they feared meeting each other or because their arthritic limbs prevented them from reaching the corridor.

'Dear God,' said Millie, 'forgive me!' But she could not raise her eyes to the sky for there was too much rain in the wind. Millie felt her flesh grow goose-pimply. She thought she saw a long greyish bundle rocking in the surf, and looked again and it was gone. Well, this was a beach on Guernsey, and that was imagination, or else a vision. Who cared? A taxi driver had insisted on telling her about World War II on the Channel Isles – the forced labour camps, the starvation, the treacheries, betrayals, slaughter: how the Guernsey beaches, when the high tide receded, would be studded with dead bodies. But that was forty years past, and Millie's was the generation for which the sacrifice had been made – it was for the children; that the children should live in peace and freedom and prosperity. That was what everyone said. 'And so I did,' said Millie, to the bundles which might have been there, and might not have been there. 'Thanks a million.'

The sand spattered up and stung the pink, shiny skin of Millie's calves. Her legs, she feared, had been damaged by the depilatory cream the beautician in the hotel salon had used. Millie had asked for a leg wax but the girl had studied her legs and simply refused. Millie's veins, she said, were too near the surface. It happened to older women. So she had used a cream which had stung far more than the wax would have when it was torn off. There was nothing wrong with Millie's veins: how could there be, when you finally had what you wanted – even though you'd had to lie, cheat, steal and murder to get it – and had started a new life? Didn't your veins somehow start afresh with you?

Well, no. God got you, somehow He got you. Mother always said that He would.

There's nothing wrong with my legs, Millie thought. No one would know they'd been going for fifty years. The wind howled and the clouds parted and Millie managed to look up and saw a beam of sun, like the eye of God, striking down at the sea and now, as the pattern of clouds shifted, it moved on towards Millie and contained her, so that she stood bathed in light.

'It was my fault,' admitted Millie. 'I killed him. The vicar said a special prayer for Stephen on his sick-bed and I didn't join in. I kept my mouth and heart shut because I wanted him to die. Just for a moment, but it was the wrong moment; it was touch and go, and he died. When I got back from church he was dead. I got all his money and now I'm rich. So what are you going to do, send me to hell?'

Oh, thought Millie, I've never in all my life been braver than this; standing on a beach in the very eye of God, defying Him. So bright was the light in which she stood that all around seemed black, and she was alone in the universe. 'So what now, God?' she said. 'What are you going to do about it?'

She waited, and there was silence, just a sense of the grey bundles rocking out at sea. 'I know I was mean to my mother,' said Millie, 'but she was mean to me. I didn't ask to be born!'

Mother was Mary, a trained nurse and a Catholic, and the latter got the better of the former, so Millie had been brought to term. Then Mary pretended Millie was the daughter of her deceased sister. Society was kind enough to unmarried mothers in wartime, but Mary was never one to be kind to herself. So Millie called Mary 'Auntie' and sometimes lived with her and sometimes didn't. Millie's father Bill was the entertainments officer at the US air force camp, and Mary was one of the nice girls bussed in weekly to dance with the brave lads from overseas. But Bill was local and Welsh, and thereafter Mary sometimes lived with him and sometimes didn't, for Bill was not a Catholic and was married to someone in Ireland.

The war disrupted many lives. Mary took a job as a tele-phonist/receptionist in a posh country hotel and her niece came out of the orphanage to live with her. Bill got a job playing the piano in the Nitery at the hotel, and became Uncle. Millie went away to university on a scholarship to do French and German, and one night Bill telephoned and said in his common Welsh/Irish voice that Auntie was very ill, she was to come home, and Millie said she had her finals the next day and couldn't come. Bill wept.

'She's not your auntie,' he said, 'she's your mother.'

'I know that,' said Millie, with a rage such as she had never known before, and put the phone down on the pair of them, and slept soundly and sat her exams, and did very well, and rang home the next day and found that Auntie had died. She went to the funeral, but Uncle wouldn't speak to her, and presently he went home to be father to some other, younger children in Ireland. Millie, going through his papers years back, found photographs of them.

'I'm sorry,' said Millie now, 'Dad and Mum. Or do you only hear me if I say Uncle and Auntie?' It was conditional surrender.

After that, Millie could invent her own parents: an English father who owned a sugar plantation in Barbados; a mother who was an international concert pianist. They travelled a good deal. If you were going to lie, Millie realised, you'd better really lie. Nervous half-truths got found out – proper whoppers seldom did. With her language degree, Millie got a job as a grade one typist in the Foreign Office. Parents who travelled a lot worried Security a little, but not so much that they actually checked up. She'd reckoned on that, and her name and her degree were true enough. Her would-be boss, an under-secretary of trade, liked the look of her legs, which were truly stunning, and indeed the rest of her, and she was obviously not spy-material, this Millie Mason, this well-bred, well-spoken, beautiful, discreet English girl. She worked in Paris, in Bahrain, in Tokyo and all over, keeping company with young men called, vaguely, Teddy Ormly-White, and flat-sharing with young women called, vaguely, Pamela Brown-Cliff-Brown. Money was a problem, but an amazing amount could be extracted from coat pockets in the shadowy cloakrooms of nightclubs and the neat ones of international conferences, but especially the former, and in the right currency, too.

'Forgive me, God,' said Millie, twenty-five years later, trapped in her pool of light, 'but remember that I was being robbed myself, underpaid. I stayed a grade one typist. Men with the same qualifications became administrators.' She thought for a moment that the waves would rock one of the men's bodies right up to her feet, but it drew back again, into the darkness.

Millie fell in love. That was terrible. Millie fell insanely in love with Michael, a young trainee under-secretary with wide blue eyes and the face of a surprised child. She slept with him at once instead of building up to it over three months – as one should, if in love but not wanting marriage – or not at all, at least until after the wedding ring was on the finger, if you wanted a man for good. So of course Michael didn't respect her. She didn't realise it, and blurted out the truth about Auntie and Uncle, and giggled over the plantations and the concerts in the deceptive warmth and safety of that wonderful bed, and he went right off her. 'A tissue of lies,' he said, taking offence, glad of the excuse to get away from the totality of Millie's passion. After that she was careful not to fall in love – if you caught it early, like a cold, there were ways of nipping it in the bud. And when Michael announced his engagement to Susan, she let Susan know about the prostitutes Michael frequented (well, once) and Susan broke it off, and no one ever knew why, except Susan and Millie.

'I'm sorry, God,' said Millie, 'but that was the way the world was in those days. Truth and love just couldn't abide together. As for Susan, I'm sure Michael was gay, at heart, so it was just as well.'

The bodies rocked their reproach: they were all around, she was sure, but she could not see properly beyond the circle of light. 'But how was I supposed to live?' begged Millie. 'Everything changed so fast. There was no one to tell you. So far as you were concerned, God, well, you'd let the war happen so your street credibility, I can tell you, was nix. Nix. A girl had to look after herself.'

Millie got involved with a group of American artists and musicians living in the shadow of Montmartre. Perhaps this was the world she belonged to? She'd leave the formality of the Embassy flat with its shiny issue furniture and the nice girls and the formal, randy men who visited them; and fall into a sea of paint and mess and drink and music and unmade beds with men who laughed and drank and were noisy, and girls who shrieked and raged and swore they'd never marry. Of course in those pre-pill days you had to rely on men to take precautions, and drunken artists are forgetful, or else just plain selfish, and there she was, pregnant, and none of them had any intention of marrying her. And Susan, who'd found she was pregnant by Michael after she'd broken off the engagement, had had an abortion and died from it, and Millie was beginning to understand by now the patterns made by fate, and knew she'd die too if she tried the same thing.

'You'd have done it, too, wouldn't you?' she said, and the sea now lapped her Magli shoes, but she wouldn't move back. Remorse was vanishing: she could never hold on to it long. Resentment kept welling up.

Millie had to marry. There wasn't much time. She chose
Harry Scott-Evans. He had no chin but he loved her and
she'd been using him to take her out when she'd needed a
change. So now she led him on; when he persisted, she
protested – not so much to prevent him but so he was aware
she was more or less unwilling. When it came to it, she cried
out, not in passion, but as if she was a virgin and he
was hurting her. Well, he didn't have much experience.
Afterwards she wept and said, 'What if I become pregnant?'
and he said, 'I'll look after you,' and she saw him every day
after that, as if she truly loved him, and was sweet and
gentle and domestic but shook her head and moved his
hand if he tried to do anything more than kiss her. When
after three weeks she wept again and said she thought she
was pregnant, he said, 'Millie, that's wonderful. I'll marry
you. I've got a leave coming up in two weeks . . .'

'I wasn't stupid, God,' said Millie. 'But you didn't make
me stupid, did you? So what did you expect?'

So there she was, an Embassy wife, and presently had to
admit that her parents were dead – both doctors, killed in
an air raid – and he hadn't been too pleased but had to put
up with it and was really nice to her and she began to feel
better – that is to say bad, because of course baby Julian
wasn't his at all, but he never knew it.

'I don't know why it is, God,' said Millie, 'that getting
better involves feeling worse. What a real bastard you are.'
She took off her bright yellow shoes and kicked them out
into the waves in the hope of dispelling the shadows, but it
didn't work. All that happened was that the shoes were
gone, and the grey bundles still rocked and bumped up
against each other.

Harry got promotion and she had another baby, Sophie,
and gave dinner parties, and yawned behind her hand, and

had an affair with Stephen, who wanted her to run off with him, so she did, leaving Julian and Sophie behind. She'd never be really rich with Harry, who turned out to have very few interesting family connections, and never even went hunting or fishing, but lived off his salary and thought holidays a waste of time. Otherwise, he was thoroughly nice and thoroughly boring, and she had no real complaints. It was just that Stephen was rich and exciting, and a publisher and a patron of the arts, which meant that she'd get the best of all possible worlds. She could be rich and comfortable and secure – and have all that wonderful conversation about whence art and whither literature and what sex who was. And what's more she loved him. Only Stephen didn't want the children. He was right. Julian wasn't bad – and was quite good at drawing – but Sophie was a pain in the neck, and chinless, like her father, and Stephen only ever wanted the best of everything. Better they stayed behind where they were loved and needed. But of course the world never sees it like that.

'You're mad, God,' confided Millie, and waited for death, but death didn't come. The sky just grumbled a little, but still the shaft of light stayed. 'Whatever a girl does, it's wrong. If she has babies, if she doesn't have babies; if she tries to prevent them or she doesn't; if she kills them before they're born, or lets them live and leaves them after. And the penalties are kind of drastic, aren't they? Cancer if you don't, septicaemia if you do; a stroke if you take the pill and a Down's baby if you don't – get yourself sterilised and grow hairs on your chin! Show me a woman who's got it right!'

A kind of breath of assent came from the hotel, where the arthritic limbs of old ladies twinged and stirred in expectation of dinner.

But, of course, marriage with Stephen wasn't what she'd thought it would be. Happy endings kept turning into dire

74

beginnings. After the first affair – which he'd discovered, and forgiven, because though he was still passionately in love with her (he said) he didn't like sex all that much – he'd moved her into the country where there wasn't so much temptation (he was right) and did his entertaining in town. He liked to come home after a hard week's work and relax and enjoy Millie's company and the countryside. Stephen didn't want to go on holidays either. The real trouble was that he was mean: it really hurt him to see money just dribbling away, and the richer he was, the worse he got. So Millie scrubbed her own floors and sewed her own clothes – she had to. She understood him. She'd had a tough upbringing too: when you grew up, the people you were with had to bear the brunt of it. He put up with her, she'd put up with him.

They had an adopted child, Helen. After ten years of having Millie's fertility studied, it was discovered that the fault was Stephen's. That was a whole three years after Millie had agreed to adopt a child Stephen had had – or so Stephen believed – by a girl with whom he was having an affair. 'I'll never see her again, only take in the child, Millie. Then I'll have something of hers; then I can bear it.' So Millie had, and then it turned out that Stephen wasn't the father anyway, couldn't be – what a mess life was! If a man fell insanely in love with you, he could fall insanely in love with someone else, and she supposed she deserved it. If you followed your inclinations into someone else's bed, however temporarily, there was always a penalty to be paid.

And then he'd got Parkinson's disease; he was ten years older than Millie and everyone, it seemed, gets something in the end. There she was, trapped by ties she did not understand – of loyalty, sympathy, compassion, shared experience – to a man trembling in a wheelchair who would not pay out fifty pence for a little gadget to turn pages (so she, Millie, had to hang around and do it), but who had that same week paid over five hundred pounds for a Ben Nicholson sketch. And meanwhile Helen called Millie Mother, for years believing that's what Millie was, when in fact she was some kind of painful honorary auntie.

'I should have let Helen go on believing the lie,' said Millie. 'It did no good to tell her the truth. But she drove me mad; I lost my temper. I'm sorry, God.' She'd been punished enough at the time, she thought. Helen had walked out on the 'pair of them' as she called her surrogate parents, and Stephen had barely spoken to Millie for months. And then he'd just died, while Millie was in church. Murdered, by Millie's act of omission.

'Well, God,' she said now, 'you certainly don't give up! You just sing the same old tune, over and over, until we either go deaf or pay attention.'

She'd sold the house and the art collection and given half to Helen, which was good of her, considering, and here she was, rich as Croesus and missing Stephen – who had done nothing but tremble in a wheelchair for years and drive her mad – on the first proper holiday she had ever had in her life, and of course it had to be on a haunted beach.

Little by little the light faded, as layers of cloud moved over the gap that let through the sun. The grey bundles were just patterns made by surf and sand where the beach was uneven, and the rest of the world faded up, and her yellow shoes came bobbing back on the wavelets to knock into her ankles. She picked them up and went back into the hotel.

She prepared to take a bath before dinner but when she turned on the gold taps the water spurted out of the shower unit above and drenched her head, so she showered instead, and afterwards had just to comb her hair dry. It frizzed out to frame her face and she quite liked the look of that. She put on a silk dress which Stephen had hated because it defined her bosom too much. She stared at herself in the mirror.

'I still look ready for more,' she said. 'Ever-ready Millie!' But somehow the cream and green walls and the pink and green floral curtains and the dappled brown of the armchairs and the ochre of the carpet and barley sugar twists of veneered wood – which were placed here and there for no reason at all – sopped up the words into their dreadful silence.

She went down into the formal, painful elegance of the gold and cream restaurant where penguin waiters busied themselves around the empty tables. She was placed at a central table; one waiter pushed in her chair, another unfolded her napkin and put it with a flourish in her lap, a third lit a candle, a fourth brought the menu, a fifth a wine list, and there were still five more looking on. All these men, thought Millie, but they belonged to a different species. They might as well have been horses and she a cow.

She ate and drank with steady hand, for all they stared. Were they as embarrassed as she? It might be hell, thought Millie, a special hell reserved for the likes of me, for women who murder their mothers and their husbands, defy God, and are vain about their legs.

The pianist took his place at the grand piano, and began to play, especially for Millie. He kept nodding and winking at her. Any minute, thought Millie, I'm going to scream and run. But of course she didn't. She ordered lobster and now wished she hadn't: she had to use a little silver hammer to crack the pincers and made a mess of it; fragments of red shell scattered the floor. Had they done it on purpose? Shouldn't they have done all that themselves, out in the kitchen? Had they guessed, somehow, that she was at heart the kitchen maid?

Now the pianist was playing 'I'll See You Again', and 'The White Cliffs Of Dover'. No, it wasn't hell, it was a madhouse where all the tunes were forty years out of date. And still he nodded and winked. He seemed familiar. He reminded her of her father. Uncle, that is. The same greying sideboards, full puffy face creased from years of false smiles. But of course it was not; Uncle/Father would be ninety now, if he were still alive – this man was fiftyish. As I am, thought Millie, ready for more or not. She smiled back at the pianist, which seemed to please him very much. He struck up 'The Lambeth Walk' with such abandon that Millie's foot began to tap, and only paused, in shock, as the man at the piano began to sing along, in the powerful, guttural half-French, half-Welsh lilt of the Channel Isles, mocking the cavernous gilt pretension.

> *Any evening, any day*
> *As you walk down Lambeth way* . . .

Then Millie sang along as well – tapping her little silver hammer to keep the time.

> *You'll see them all*
> *Doing the Lambeth Walk* . . .

Two of the older waiters joined in the last, vulgar *Oy*, and though the younger ones only managed a laugh and a clap at the end, everyone managed something, and the atmosphere in the room had changed. It wasn't hell at all; merely heaven waiting for the arrival of the angels. And then, of course, with the realisation, they turned up. The first of the old ladies with sticks and diamond rings tottered into the restaurant, and a whole stream behind, and a few men with sandy moustaches and nothing to do, and some younger couples and foursomes who couldn't wait to be old, and soon the restaurant was full. It was just that everyone came down at eight, not seven-thirty. The pianist broke into hit tunes of the fifties, and presently winked at Millie, this time with a rather more relaxed and personal intent. Millie understood it to be an invitation for afterwards, and what's more winked back in acceptance.

Christmas Lists –
A Seasonal Story

Towards the end, as Christmas approached, there had to be
not just a card list but –
    a present list
    a food list
    a drink list
    a party list
    a decoration list
    and a guest list too.

All grew longer with the years. Finally, Louise opened an
actual Christmas file, which would start in the first week of
September, as soon as she had settled down after the summer
holiday. By settling down she meant
— putting piles of post-holiday clothes through the washing
   machine.
— sorting, ironing, folding and finding places for the above.
— drying, shaking, brushing and storing the children's tents
   and backpacks.
— finding space for touring bicycles somewhere other than
   the hall.
— collating, answering and paying accumulated letters and
   bills.
— telephoning, soothing, and generally re-establishing contact with relatives and friends.
— collecting, de-fleaing and worming pets.
— finding, collating and if necessary purchasing assorted
   school, college and sporting wear.
— putting in early orders, before the rush, for coal, wood,
   oil and getting the heating system serviced.
— getting the car serviced.
— getting the garden back under control.

The Christmas file, opened more-or-less as soon as all this was more-or-less done, would be closed in the second week of January, after the last straggling revellers had drifted back to work, and the last thank-you letters or I'm-sorry cards posted.

Then she would look at her hands: she would see broken nails and chapping skin and stand-out veins and know it was as much her fault as the season's. Why didn't she wear rubber gloves or remember to use handcream? Other women did. Perhaps it was her form of protest? But why did she want to protest? It was what she wanted to do, turkeys and tinsel and toys. She loved Christmas. Christmas was a kind of powerful bell, chiming once a year, deep and profound, to mask the passage of life. There was no point staring at her hands and lamenting the passing of the years. They passed anyway. She lived a busy and useful life. She loved her husband, and he loved her. The children were healthy and lively and attractive. She had nothing to complain about, except a kind of extraordinary proliferation, a domestic infiltration, which meant you couldn't keep Christmas in the head any longer, but had to keep lists, and even lists of lists.

'The difficulty is,' Rupert (Louise's husband) said to Louise, when they were both forty-five, 'that we're pinned between the generations. As the family below grows up, the family above grows down. One lot's too young and the other lot too old to be responsible for themselves, so we have to do it.'
She made a list of the people he had to support. She made it on the paper napkin of the restaurant where they were having their twenty-second wedding anniversary dinner. It was 1979. The restaurant had offered linen napkins as late as 1977, before being finally forced, by the increasing costs of laundering, to go over to paper.
'We shouldn't mind,' said Louise, comfortingly, 'it means

the laundry workers are getting a better deal.' But Rupert minded. What was the point of struggle and success, if the traditional rewards melted before your eyes, disintegrated?

The list of the people Rupert supported, according to Louise, in 1979, went like this:
— Louise
— Adam (19)
— Simon (17)
— Polly (15)
— Zoë (12)
— Louise's parents (contributions towards)
— Rupert's parents (contributions towards)
— Rupert's sister-in-law (contributions towards)
— Rupert's nephew and niece (school fees)
— a workforce of 48 people
— secretarial staff of 3
— Louise's cleaning lady
— the unemployed (contributions towards)
— non-ratepayers (contributions towards)
— the sick, the infirm, those too old, too young, or too disturbed in the head to work.

'Not only are we pinned between the generations,' said Rupert, 'but we are squashed by ubiquitous taxes. We, the workers, the wealth-producers of this country, are just a thin, thin filling between thick slabs of non-productive bread. The thirty per cent of the population who work have to carry the burden of the seventy per cent who don't. No wonder we're tired.' He never used to talk like that. Louise supposed it to be just the general drift towards the right that happened as men grew richer and older.

In 1979 Rupert's firm – known as Rupert's Own to the family – was in some slight difficulties, but nothing, no one imagined, that couldn't be lived through. One day the recession would end. It just had to be lived through.

Rupert's Own made dashboard instruments for specialist cars, for both home and export markets. The current difficulties were:
— contracting home markets
— new employment taxes
— inflation
— increasing union pressure
— the high cost and low quality of raw materials
— shortage of skilled labour
— a strong pound, limiting competitiveness abroad
and so forth. If the new light Californian wine they drank with their Osso Bucco – for everyone nowadays was diet conscious and meant to live for ever – tasted slightly sour, and he longed for good old-fashioned rich and gravelly claret, it was hardly surprising.

'Well,' said Louise, 'never mind! I suppose we'll be allowed to grow incompetent with the years in our turn, and then our children will have to look after us, as well as their children and then they'll know what it was like for us.'

But would they? Nothing was what it had been. The children seemed uninterested in careers or earning money, but were content enough to just get by, and there was a distinct lack of grandchildren in their particular patch of the world. Without grandchildren how could there be grandparents? Self-help, it seemed, would have to go on till the grave, and beyond. You'd have to say prayers for yourself, for who else would there be to pray for you?

Louise and Rupert's wedding anniversary was on December 3rd. In their early years together they'd saved the discussion of Christmas plans, such as they were, for that particular day.
— what do you want for Christmas?
— are we going to your parents or mine?
— if we bought Adam and Simon bunk beds would they

accept that as a Christmas present, or would we have to supplement it with, say, a robot for Adam and a teddy bear for Simon, knowing they're each sure to want what the other's got?
— what shall we buy the in-laws?

The first Christmas had been the best – 1957. She and Rupert, students, he of engineering, she of mathematics – defying both sets of parents, neither going home, sharing the Christmas holidays in the days – well, the nights – before people did that kind of thing.
— a fir branch of a Christmas tree
— one silver star upon it
— a chicken and some packet stuffing
— a pound of potatoes for roasting
— some peas, some mushrooms (luxury) for frying
— a Woolworth's Christmas pudding
— top of the milk to pour upon it
— some cigarettes, from her to him
— a new black bra, from him to her
— from both of them unto the other, the gift of themselves, the knowledge that this was the beginning, the great adventure
— a single bottle of wine.

Enough, enough! 'No present,' said her parents, the Parsons, 'not this year, since you're not coming home, but we understand and when you both actually get married we'll put down the deposit on a house for you.'
General, but conditional, as always.

'They really believe,' Rupert and Louise sighed and smiled, unable in their happiness to take offence, 'they really believe we'll end up like them!'

Rupert's parents gave him a dozen pairs of throw-away socks, and her a cookery book, which she still used, year after year, for the Christmas pudding. But at the time she puzzled and brooded. Presents have meanings — if the giver isn't aware of it, the recipient usually is. She wrote alternatives down on the back of the one Christmas card she received that year — it was from a former boyfriend and she despised it.

Throw-away socks to Rupert — significance of
a) I can't be trusted to wash his socks properly: i.e. domestically incompetent.
b) I'm not the kind to wash socks at all: i.e. a slut.
c) I'm eager to wash his socks: i.e. trying to trap him into marriage.
d) I shouldn't waste my time washing his socks: i.e. too good for him.

Well, which did they mean?
'For heaven's sake,' said Rupert, 'they *just gave me some throw-away socks.*'

Recipe book for Louise — significance of
a) Can't cook and should learn: i.e. has at least some kind of future with Rupert.
b) So boring that's all she can do: i.e. has no future at all with Rupert.

The gifts seemed to be throwing up inconsistent signals. She didn't understand them.

'Look,' said Rupert, 'let's not worry about this kind of thing. Stop making lists. It isn't necessary.'
'I have a kind of feeling it is,' she said.
Within a few months she needed more than a suitcase under his bed for her clothes: she needed drawers and cupboards. She had a kind of vision of the way things were going to be. 'Let's just go to bed,' he said. And so they did. Bounce, bounce, on top of the bulging suitcase. They went to the

market and bought a proper chest-of-drawers, and by the following Christmas had a flat, not a room, and a cupboard under the stairs to stack the suitcases, and by the next Christmas were married and on the 1st of December the following year Louise gave birth to Adam. She had to spend Christmas Day in hospital because

a) the baby was slow to suckle

b) her stitches went septic

and Rupert went home to his parents, the elder Branns, and had far too much to drink. Now that would never have happened had it been *her* parents, the Parsons.

— one glass of sherry before dinner

— one bottle of wine with dinner, no matter how many guests

— and more than enough rum in the pudding for anyone, let alone brandy on top of it.

'We'll all be too tipsy to listen to the Queen's speech,' Mrs Parsons would say in alarm, as the wine cork was pulled, and because it was Christmas everyone tut-tutted in sympathetic alarm, instead of saying sadly, 'I wish to God we were!'

For the following ten years the young Branns went alternatively to his parents on Christmas Day, and her parents on Christmas Day. Louise, Rupert, Adam, then Simon, then Polly, then Zoë. The senior Branns lived thirty miles away, the Parsons forty-five, fifteen miles, wonderfully enough, further down the same road. The car would be packed neatly and quickly on Christmas Eve, as would the children's stockings. Into the car, as well as the everyday nappies, wipes, carry-cots and so forth went:

— 1 neat cardboard box, containing four prettily wrapped presents, two for the senior Branns, two for the Parsons.

They'd call in on the Branns for mid-morning sherry and mince pies and to drop off the presents, if they were Christmas lunching at the Parsons, and if lunching at the Branns, would drive on to the Parsons for Christmas high tea, and to drop off their presents. Simple.

86

When the children grew to complaining age – which seemed remarkably early – Adam and Polly complained when they went to the Branns, and Simon and Zoë when they went to the Parsons. The Branns were generous, noisy and slapdash about their Christmases – the Parsons careful, tidy, exact and full of ritual.

'Couldn't we just relax and have our own Christmas, in our own home?' Rupert would lament. 'Do we have to do all this organising?' But neither wanted to hurt anyone. It seemed to them that the parents needed them, to add event to their increasingly quiet and suddenly elderly lives.

In those days, when Christmas still started (just) in December, an allocation of money would be made by Rupert, scrupulously administered by Louise. The sum available went up every year, as Rupert's Own became little by little more prosperous, but every year he had less and less to do with its spending: there was not enough time, not enough energy. 'I suppose it's a sensible division of labour,' said Rupert, sadly, 'but I do miss all the present-wrapping!' And the notion somehow grew up between them, that she was the lucky one, because she had the annual making of Christmas, and he had to do without.

While the young Branns and their children spent Christmas Day away from home, Louise would make do not so much with a list as with a master-plan scribbled on the back of an envelope. If total spending was to be £x, then it would be allocated thus:

$\frac{x}{6}$ Branns & Parsons

$\frac{x}{3}$ Children

$\frac{x}{6}$ Each other

$\frac{x}{6}$ Employees, friends, relatives

$\frac{x}{6}$ Sundries, inc. cards, decorations, wrappings

The initial division in caring, the allocation of love, its spread across the field of acquaintance, was acknowledged on the chart, and then a money value given to that allocation. How else was it to be done?

As the children grew older, the chart had to be adapted; the in-laws received less, the children more, proportionately.

And in the end, after ten years of marriage, on the eleventh Christmas, she abandoned the chart, and started lists.

That was the year they moved to a big Victorian house with a large, long dining room, and Louise picked up a heavy oak refectory table for almost nothing (in the late sixties, when oak was still unfashionable) and they had an excuse for saying, at last – 'Look, come to us for Christmas! Everyone!'

And so they did; though the older Branns were to go on alternate years, for a time, to Rupert's brother Luke, and his wife Veronica, and their two children, Vernon and Lucinda, cousins to Adam, Simon, Polly and Zoë. Louise rather wondered, at the time, at the slight look of relief, not despondency, which crossed the in-laws' faces at the notion that the tradition was to change.

So, every second year, sitting round the Christmas table, would be:
   Louise
   Rupert
   Adam
   Simon
   Polly
   Zoë
   Mr Brann senior
   Mrs Brann senior
   Mr Parsons senior

Mrs Parsons senior
Nye Evans (Rupert's partner)
Wendy Evans (Rupert's partner's wife, with sclerosis)
A child (from the Give-a-Child-a-Christmas-Scheme centre)

And a few friends or visitors from abroad, or business contacts of Rupert's who had nowhere else to go and who wanted to experience a proper Christmas.

Around twenty, usually. Never mind. If there was much to be done, there was much to be celebrated!

One dreadful day, when Louise and Rupert had been married for thirteen years, Luke's wife Veronica woke up to find Luke beside her, dead in bed, and after that she and Vernon and Lucinda came to Christmas dinner too. They never smiled, either, though the years passed and everyone did their best. Veronica would sniff into the stuffing, and Lucinda would mope into the pudding, and Vernon would sulk if he didn't get one of the silver sixpences, and never give it back if he *did* get one, in exchange for an ordinary 50p piece, as her own children were expected to; for silver sixpences, with the years, became in shorter and shorter supply, and modern coins tarnished when in contact with the hot, modern, paraffin-washed and dried fruit of the Christmas pudding.

'The children were like that before Luke died,' said Rupert in exasperation, one Boxing Day, when the noise of quarrelling and wails rose from the children's rooms, as the cousins disturbed the delicate equilibrium of post-Christmas relationships. 'Veronica too. In fact, I daresay that's *why* Luke died. He couldn't stand it a moment longer.'

Everyone tried to like Veronica. They managed to *love* her, and be protective to her, but like, as everyone knew, was a different matter. With some people, hearts simply sank when they entered a room. And the children seemed to have taken after her. And of course it was only fair to take Veronica, Vernon and Lucinda along on summer holidays too.

Never mind. The family spirit, sheer Christmas energy, swept all before it. Roughs and smooths were ironed out. Mrs Parsons still raised her eyebrows as Mrs Brann raised her glass; Louise learned not to intervene, not to worry; not to try to distract her mother's attention as her husband (wilfully?) poured his mother yet another glass of brandy.

She learned not to mind her father watching to make sure Rupert wasn't maltreating her, and his father watching to make sure she wasn't exploiting him. She learned how to manage the delicate transitions, as both sets of parents little by little relinquished the parental role – asked advice, instead of giving it, unasked.

Louise's only sister, Madeleine, had left for Australia years back; she'd opted out. She had a career, not a family. Every few years she'd be there, at the Christmas table, blonde and bold and free, with someone different always in tow, an airline pilot or a screen writer. 'Hard,' Rupert said, softly, gratefully, his arms round soft, sensible, loving Louise. 'She's brittle and hard.'

Madeleine never touched Christmas pudding; pushed the roast potatoes to the side of the plate. In Australia Christmases were salad with cold turkey. Hard to remember this wasn't universal, cosmic: merely some kind of regional obsession!

There were a couple of bad, bad Christmases, well, you only know you're happy if you have something extreme to set it against. One, when Rupert was in love with someone else Louise had never met, and never wanted to meet, but was very like her, she'd heard. Rupert exhibited all the symptoms of a husband illicitly in love:

1) taking extra care dressing in the morning.
2) buying new clothes.
3) looking at himself a lot in the mirror.
4) disturbed sleep patterns.
5) intensive fault-finding alternating with maudlin over-appreciation.
6) Radio 2 on the car radio and Vivaldi on the cassette player.
7) detailed and unnecessary accounts of where he'd been and who he'd seen.
8) making love twice as long and twice as often as usual.

She'd sat that out, grimly, and it had all faded away, and just as well, because otherwise she'd have burned the house down and made the children commit mass suicide, and then done it herself, because the family was *all* of them, and if the *all* was broken, then they were all as good as dead and the sooner it happened the better. She hadn't said this at the time: she'd put no pressure on him. If Rupert didn't know it, what was the point of saying it? But it seemed he did. Rupert had come back, delivered himself again into her safe-keeping. She did not dismay him with reproaches.

And now, of course, later, the children all but grown and gone, the sense of family, as *all*, had diminished. She was amazed, in retrospect, at the savagery, the extremeness, of her reaction to danger. She'd meant it. She'd have done it. The children had been part of her, then. Not so much now.

And then there'd been the Christmas *she'd* been in love, distracted, unable to concentrate: alternately singing and weeping about the house, the children following after her, pattering and puzzled. She'd have sacrificed them at the drop of her lover's hat, run off with him, anywhere, anyhow,

just for the feel of his body against hers, to have his mind caught up in her mind, and hers in his – but he hadn't dropped the hat, in the end. He'd been playing games, teasing his wife.
'You've been using me,' she wept.

'Using you?' He was puzzled. 'I thought you were using me! Being revenged on your Rupert. Weren't you? Did you think it was *real*? Illicit love is never real. That's why it's so powerful.'

She was humiliated in the New Year, unhappy until Easter, guilty until Summer, and better and herself by the following Christmas. Did Rupert know? Perhaps not. It had been a busy year, down at Rupert's Own. Would *he* have killed himself, if she had gone? Probably not! But the thing was, neither *had* gone.

And there had been years when one or other of the children had been difficult, had pushed and heaved against the restraining pressure of the warm Christmas blanket. They had various ways of demonstrating their discontent. They would:
a) stay in bed all day
b) stay out all Christmas Eve
c) get drunk or high
d) vomit at the Christmas table
e) quarrel over Christmas TV programmes
f) forget each other's presents
g) weep all day
h) announce over mince pies: i) loss of virginity, ii) homosexuality, iii) abandonment of education, iv) drug addiction
i) Christmas-out – that is in other people's houses
j) ask grossly unsuitable friends home
k) be rude to parents in public

92

But they seldom all did it at once. They acknowledged a kind of family balance, in which any person at any one time could behave very badly or more than one rather badly, so long as everyone else carried on as usual; that is, with a basic politesse, and sense of continued order. And those who erred had still been contained, loved and understood – which of course drove them wilder still, for a time, until reason reasserted itself.

'Poor things,' Louise would say to Rupert, and Rupert to Louise, with that strange mixture of complicity, love and resentment with which good parents regard their growing children, 'all this understanding must be maddening. We must seem like cotton-wool to them. Butt their heads, as they may, all we do is *give*. They'd be happier, in the short term, with a brick wall to batter at.' 'But not in the long term,' the other would say, and both would nod.

There had been a Christmas or so when she'd been unaccountably irritable and snappy, and had regarded the long rows of expectant faces on either side of the refectory table with less than love. But she had tried, and managed, not to show it. And she had wept and wept one year on discovering that when she handed Rupert his ritual share of the £x (Christmas) in cash, for him to buy her present from him, he had merely put it in the petty cash and sent his secretary out to buy something to its value.

'You have no idea,' he said, 'no idea how busy I am, how worrying everything is. The whole export market is closing down . . . Exchange rates are so firmly and permanently against us!'

'Then let's spend less,' she begged. 'We could halve Christmas, we really could, somehow!'

But she could see how difficult it would be, in a world in which everything grew and grew, to offer suddenly less. The children, who had once expected one present each, now felt aggravated if they received less than three or four. It wasn't that they were greedy, just that the young these days equated giving with love. Give less, and they took it that you loved less, and so construed your explanations and excuses. Not their fault, either, *yours*, for having got caught up in the world, for being what you *were*. How could you say to your ageing parents – 'sorry, cook your own!' – or to Nye Evans, who now had to cut up his wife's dinner on the plate, 'sorry, time's up!' or to poor widowed Veronica, 'Christ! Isn't it time to stand on your own two feet?' when her ankles were so obviously and so permanently weak?

They had to reconcile themselves to it all, and pray it would not just end in bankruptcy. Christmas had become Louise's version of the 'vicious tax spiral' of which Rupert had complained – when you had to pay last year's tax out of this year's earnings, which were taxed higher than last, and that was that. Do it well this year, and you had to do it better the next. Partly Louise's own nature, partly the world's pressure – as in so much else in life, reflected in the way they lived.

1981 was a bad year. The business was in trouble. Not just the export market, but the home market was contracting. There were redundancies, as the business streamlined itself. Rupert was preoccupied, moody, ready to blame anyone for anything, gave up demonstrating his love to her either in bed or anywhere else, fell asleep the minute his head touched the pillow or couldn't sleep at all and thought it was an indignity to use sex as a soporific (which she construed as him saying to her, if I'm not having a good time, I'll be damned if you will either) and Zoë had to re-sit her A-levels, and Polly got pregnant and at first wouldn't have a termination and then suddenly had one much too late, and was ill, and accused Louise of spoiling her life by giving birth to Zoë, so then Zoë was hysterical, and failed more A-levels, and Simon left home too early, and Adam, who had finished college, wouldn't leave home at all, and Veronica had a nervous breakdown and Vernon and Lucinda had to be made room for, so Zoë walked out and went to live with the Branns senior, whereupon Mr Brann had a mild coronary – or so Mrs Brann claimed – and Zoë said what was the point of education anyway, since everything only ended in unemployment and death, and came home. There wasn't any time even to make lists of the troubles, so fast did they occur, that Spring.

By the summer holidays everyone had pulled themselves together, of course, and backpacks were filled and friends organised – and off they *all* went, for once, leaving Louise and Rupert with the wonderful notion that they would have a holiday on their own, for the first time in twenty-one years: except of course then Veronica slipped a disc and so Vernon and Lucinda came along too, to the rented Italian villa. Vernon had a verruca and couldn't or wouldn't walk and Lucinda had sunstroke, of the serve-you-right kind. It didn't really make much difference, Louise thought. To be alone with Rupert suddenly seemed not quite such a good idea. Perhaps he was going mad?

He had the following symptoms:
a) he was careless.
b) he was slovenly in his habits, slopping food and drink and wiping greasy hands on his clothes.
c) he complained of sleeplessness and nightmares.
d) he was rude to guests.
e) he drank too much.
f) he was obsessional – seeing plots where none were.
g) he was for the most part morose, but occasionally noisy and high-spirited.
h) he regarded his wife as his enemy.
i) he went off sex.

A friend, in whom Louise confided her fears – tentatively, for she did not wish to appear disloyal – said 'Mad? That's not madness, that's the male menopause. He'll grow out of it.' Another said, 'Mad? That's not madness, that's business worries. Is he impotent too?' to which Louise could only reply, gloomily, 'How would I know?' 'I expect he is,' said the friend. 'Most men of his age are. It's the women's movement that's done it. All those assertive women going about!'

'I'm not an assertive woman,' protested Louise. 'I'm a traditional woman.'

'Yes, but you're a busy woman,' said the friend. 'God, how busy!'

She wasn't above accepting an invitation to Christmas dinner, all the same. The Branns' Christmas was famous.

In the first week of that September, when Louise brought out her file, Rupert said, 'You can't be thinking about Christmas already, Louise,' and Louise did not reply, so he said, 'Well, I suppose you have to have something to think about.'

In the first week of October Rupert said, 'Let's just keep Christmas simple this year, shall we?' And she did not reply, so he said, 'But I suppose you're just not a simple person any more, are you.'

In the second week of October he gave her the Christmas cheque. It was made out for £1800 which represented a twelve per cent increase over the previous year. He peered at it rather curiously, as if it were nothing to do with him, and at her as if she were an oddity.

'Is that enough?' he asked.

'It just about keeps pace with inflation,' Louise said. Then she said, 'Take it back. I don't want anything. There won't be a Christmas this year.'

'There has to be Christmas,' he said, with a kind of heavy meaningless irony. 'Happy families and all that.'

'I could sell something,' she offered, 'if things are as bad as you say.'

'Sell what?' he enquired, and for a moment she thought he was going to hit her.

She made the Christmas lists as usual, very late, and without pleasure.

At the beginning of November he said, 'If you weren't such an obsessive hausfrau you could have had a career and kept us both.'

He said it in front of her parents, and she thought perhaps she hated him. She knew it was only temporary, but did not know how to endure until it was all over and Rupert was returned to his normal self. She marvelled at the fragility of the male psyche, which dented so under the impact of material misfortune.

The housekeeping money was transferred from his bank account to hers, each month, as usual: index-linked to keep pace with inflation and with a built-in five per cent annual increase on top of that, which they had decided on and kept to, some fifteen years back. The household was accustomed to a small but steady rise in its standard of living. The price of meat went up, but the size of the steak upon the plate remained much the same, and its quality, if anything, was better.

At the end of November, staring at the piece of fillet steak upon his plate, and watching Polly picking at hers, and Zoë pushing hers away and declaring vegetarianism, and Adam devouring his in three mouthfuls — as do many eldest children, he ate as if terrified someone would snatch the food from his fork — Rupert said:

'We do live well, don't we! And all around us are the unemployed and the redundant!'

To which Adam observed, 'The highest good is to consume,

and the second highest good is to employ, which makes you a very good man indeed, Pa,' and Simon remarked, 'Eat now, pay later, that's the only answer to this.' (He was to the far left, politically, the better to annoy his father.) And Rupert got up and left the table, and thereafter appeared at family meals only sporadically. When Louise asked what was the matter, he replied 'nothing'.

But Rupert, she knew, was beginning to take the children seriously, as if their phases were them. She saw a real dislike of him dawning in their eyes, or what was worse, a sort of understanding and forgiveness.

'Mum,' said Simon, returning blithely from college, 'don't take him so seriously. He's going through a hard time.'

Not take Rupert seriously? How could she not? Were they not, each of them, in the other's keeping? Now the children seemed to be suggesting she separate herself out from him. How could she? What did they understand, this new, strange, flaring, kindly, idle generation she and Rupert had created?

On December 3rd, on their wedding anniversary, Rupert said, 'You make such a meal of Christmas. You really shouldn't. It's embarrassing to everyone. A file! Who else keeps a Christmas file? Christmas should come from the heart, spontaneously! What do you put in the file?' She told him, and she went on telling him all night, shaking him awake if he fell asleep; even knowing as she did that he had to be fresh for the next day: that he had a meeting of creditors. She told him about the cards, to begin with.

'Pages 2–8,' she said. 'Cards.'
'What about Page 1?' he demanded. 'You've forgotten page 1. Or do you draw Father Christmas on Page 1?'
'Page 1! Page 1 is the overall spending pattern of the

Christmas. This year x = £1800. Thank God it's neatly divisible by six. I need to know how much to spend on cards. Cards is ⅓ of sundries. Sundries is ⅓ of x. That is if x = £1800 and s = $\frac{x}{6}$ and c = $\frac{s}{3}$ ∴ c = $\frac{£1800}{3 \times 6}$ = £100. Nice and neat, for once! 150 cards or so for £100? You could just about do it. Just.

She continued:

1) She made five initial headings, as an aide-mémoir. Family. Friends. Acquaintances. Business. Duty.

2) She entered recipients under appropriate headings.

3) She checked for extra names from previous files of cards sent and received, and entered those.

4) She struck off those who had received cards but not returned them for two years running, exempting the senior citizens and the mentally deranged.

5) She upgraded and downgraded. Acquaintances could become friends: aunts become duty rather than affection.

6) She checked addresses, with reference to the year's supply of change-of-address cards. Remarkable the number of people whose telephone number one knew but whose address was irrelevant, except at Christmas time.

7) She prepared a section for late cards – unexpected last moment receipts which required immediate response. A small but important section, which would run at 7% of the whole, and had to be prepared for, otherwise the post-Christmas period would be punctuated by telephone calls. Thank-you-for-your-card, I'm-so-sorry – etc.

8) She prepared a section for the children's cards —

'Wait a moment,' he said (he was still at that stage listening), 'the children have their own Christmas money.'

'Yes,' said Louise, 'but on December 23rd they will remember who they have so far forgotten, in the face of constant reminders, tutors, teachers, music-masters, the parents of friends who have loved them and left them and fed them and housed them during the year; those who have helped and are needed to help again and who will expect cards, and certainly should have them.'

'You mean like Polly's abortionist?'

'Quite so,' said Louise. She was beyond taking offence. She hurried on to Section 9.

9) She allocated P, SS or CH ratings to all the names on her various lists, actual and estimated. P = posh, SS = serious, CH = cheap and cheerful, and totalled these. Most P's would be in the business and duty lists, most SS's in the family, most CH's in the acquaintance list – but there were several upgraded CH's every year. The recipients were simply not cheap and cheerful people any more. Now, to find a rough average of what c each P card, each SS card and each CH card could be this year, with c equalling the total of £100, the sums would go like this: no, she would have to refer to the file for the actual workings.

10) E.P.'s warnings would be entered. Early Postings for abroad. Amazing how many people had *left*, over the years.

Cross-references had of course to be made to sundries.

Means had to be found of displaying received cards: the mantelpiece had long ago ceased to be adequate: string strung from wall to wall was unsatisfactory as the cards tended to drift towards the dip in the middle: lately, fortunately, wire card stands had started to appear in the shops, each holding about twenty cards, and these could be stood about here and there in the house. They had a tendency to topple, but it was the best solution she could find. Which cards were to take pride of place where was always tricky: people judged you on that, too. If you put the posh ones too much in evidence, you were boasting: if you put the humble ones forward you were being overly sentimental. Of course, anyone who called liked to see their own card well displayed, and unannounced callers were frequent at Christmas time. You just had to predict them. You needed a lot of sherry too, but that was part of the food and drink section in the file, and she was still only on cards.

She found it best, she told her husband, to make separate expeditions to the shops for her various Christmas purposes, otherwise she ended up forgetting things. She would make one or two journeys for the cards, another for the ingredients for the Christmas pudding, another for decorations and wrappings, another for sundries, three usually for presents, and four carloads of food shopping. Drink, fortunately, was delivered, as were hired glasses. But you had to get in early with an order for those, at Christmas time. More advance planning. If they were giving a party, she would make a separate expedition for the food required for that: two parties over the Christmas season, two expeditions, two separate, and if possible remote, cupboards, to store the food in, once bought. The children and their friends, late home one night and hungry, could eat party tit-bits for fifty and still be looking for more.

But she digressed; Christmas was full of digressions. All she could really say was, one learned seasonal tricks from seasonal experience.

She didn't, she went on, like cutting down on wrappings. Experience proved you always ran out on Christmas Eve, no matter how early you opened the Christmas file, how efficiently you planned. She did try, in the very early hours of Boxing Day, when she was clearing up and the rest of the house slept happily, and boozily, in the knowledge of another good family Christmas spent, to smooth and fold and save at least some of the expensive paper for the following year, but she usually found herself too tired to care: she would just go through the house, abandoning all discrimination, stuffing black plastic sacks with the litter left by generosity and joviality. Twenty-one people to Christmas, each of whom would give a present to everyone else, meant 21 × 20 presents, which meant 420 discarded pieces of paper, not to mention tags, bows, and the debris of crackers. Everyone loved crackers, of course. She had a special page in the file for crackers. Somehow, even so, she always managed to forget the crackers. The children were neurotic about crackers – always had been. Sibling rivalry somehow focused on crackers. Crackers were a winner-takes-all situation. Adam, who had after all suffered three psychic blows, as three times his position in the family had been usurped, had to hold back tears whenever Simon, Polly or Zoë bettered him in cracker-pulling. The only solution was lots and lots of crackers, to make them nothing special. She'd tried no crackers, but Mr Brann had said Christmas isn't Christmas without crackers, did you forget, Louise, good heavens – you're usually so organised about Christmas, Louise, meaning but you have nothing else to do, Louise, but buy crackers . . .

'You're getting upset,' he said. They were in bed. She talked on. He had this meeting in the morning. He wanted to sleep. 'No, I'm not upset,' she said. 'I'm just telling you about Christmas. I'm still on cards: we've just had a minor digression into wrappings and crackers. I haven't started on presents, let alone food, let alone drink.'

She was still talking at four in the morning; he had managed to fall asleep. When he woke, with the dawn, she was describing the unthawing of the turkey and the search for a big enough roasting pan, not too big for the oven, and the hope that the unending roll of foil would not in fact choose that day to end.

Rupert said, as he woke, 'If Luke was alive, he might have been able to help me,' and Louise hit him. He hit her back and they rolled about in the bed, as they had so often in love and laughter, biting, scratching, snarling and hurting. It had never happened before, never.

Rupert went to work without breakfast. His cheek was scored by her nails. She had a sprained wrist.
'A wonderful way to meet my creditors,' he observed as he got into the Jaguar. It was not a new car, but it was splendid. Crimson, with real red leather upholstery.
'*Really*, creditors?'
'You just spend your Christmas money,' he said. 'Open your file, and have a happy Christmas.' She would have slashed his tyres, and possibly his throat, but he left smartly, before she could. He did not deal properly with the creditors – a little more enthusiasm, a little more energy and perhaps he would have carried the day. As it was, he failed.

When he returned that evening she was glad to see him, and he to see her. The habits and affections of years can stand up to a little truth-telling. He could complain, with fairness, that her inability to enjoy the good things he gave her – that is, the family Christmas – undermined the point of his very existence, and she, equally fairly, that he failed to appreciate how much that existence depended on her martyrdom, but each complaint held the other in equilibrium.

Christmas came and went.

In February the factory was closed: in March the Official Receiver was called in. It was amazing how quickly things moved, once they'd begun. The house was put up for sale, and sold, with contents, at a knock-down price. Rupert was morose and drank a great deal: he suffered from nightmares.

He slipped a disc, and had to lie on his back in his parents' home while Louise found somewhere to live, and sorted the children out. Polly moved in with her boyfriend; Zoë, who was still at school, moved in with the Parsons grandparents, and for the first time started working for her exams, as if realising that if she didn't, she'd have to live with them for ever. Veronica, who seemed greatly invigorated by Rupert's and Louise's misfortunes, suddenly got herself a job and a new flat, and said Adam and Simon could stay with her whenever they wanted, and she'd do Christmas that year, for everyone.

By October Rupert and Louise were living in a very small terraced house in an outer suburb, just where the city drifted off into countryside. There was no chance of Rupert finding work for a year or so – until his back was better and his mental state more positive. He was now a declared bankrupt, which meant that he could not sign cheques or engage in business activities. After many visits from social workers and much dealing with bureaucracy, Louise managed to arrange for him to get welfare payments, on which they lived. He did not like going out: he thought people would stare at him. He did not want the children to visit, to witness his failure, his downfall. 'What do you mean, failure?' she would cry out in irritation. 'It isn't failure, it's the way the world is now. There are three million unemployed, apart from anything else, and most of those don't even have bad backs.'
'If you don't know what failure means, you're a fool,' he said. He was not pleasant to her. Much of the time he seemed to actively hate her. He slept as far away from her as he could, at night. She told herself it was because they were so close to each other, he couldn't distinguish which was him and which was her, and since he hated himself must seem to hate her. It was temporary, she told herself. It would pass. She remained as pleasant, and as positive, and as bracing as she could.

The winter closed down. Christmas was coming. She had saved a box of Christmas decorations, from the Fall — as she described it — but she didn't put them up. What was there to celebrate?

'Veronica has asked us for Christmas dinner,' she said, at the beginning of December.
'We can't afford the fares,' he said. She knew he meant that he could not bear the humiliation of sitting at someone else's table, and not the head of his own. She did not press the point. They did not go to Veronica's. Some thirty Christmas cards came through their letterbox that year, most of them with kindly notes inscribed, 'Just a greeting! Don't bother to respond!' Why had she never thought of that? Why, because to accept is so much more difficult than to give. She had never realised that. She began to be sorry for the recipients of her generosity in the past.

It snowed a little. The ground crackled agreeably underfoot. A branch nailed itself, with frost, against the chilly bathroom windowpane. They both stood and admired it.
'It's so simple and so beautiful,' said Louise. 'Chinese!'
'Japanese,' he corrected her. He smiled, she thought for the first time since they had come to live here. He rubbed his hands together.
'Let's light a fire,' he said. 'Get warm. We can gather sticks in the lane.' He built a great mound of dead wood in the back garden, gritting his teeth against the pain in his back. Louise wondered if the wood was not somehow someone else's property, but kept her thoughts to herself.

A very heavy parcel arrived from Madeleine in Australia. When opened, it proved to be a food parcel. It contained Australian tinned and dried fruits and jams, and some kangaroo soup and some dried baby shark.

It was Louise's turn to weep and weep from the shame and desolation of it all, and to rage at him, and her moral collapse seemed to make him better. They were regaining some kind of equilibrium. He dried her tears and was fond of her again.

'Now you know what I feel,' he said. He made love to her that night, and very frequently thereafter.

'We have time to develop the art,' he said. 'At last.'

Welfare provided a ten-pound Christmas bonus that year and she spent it on a chicken, some potatoes, some mushrooms (luxury!) and a Christmas pudding from Woolworth's. The Brann parents sent two bottles of wine, the Parsons parents a kitchen gift-set of washing-up bowl, brushes and so forth, in red plastic. The children appeared with various inappropriate but touching gifts on Christmas Eve, guilty about the proper Family Christmas, now at Veronica's, but unwilling – 'thank God,' Rupert said – to renounce it, and somehow feeling the better and the more united, for their parents' reduced circumstances.

Christmas Day dawned to a clear blue sky and the crackle of frost. They lay in bed for a long time, and presently he got up and put the chicken in the oven. He bent to light it without wincing. His back was much better.

'I suppose,' he said, 'now we're back to the beginning, there's nothing to stop us starting all over again. But let there be no more lists.'

And Then Turn Out the Light

In Newcastle, New South Wales, they have the highest hysterectomy rate in the entire world. There, healthy organs are whipped out by eager surgeons in the nick of pre-cancerous time. There is even a special laboratory, a special building, where removed organs are stored, in a frozen state, so that students can examine them at their leisure. See, a perfect ovarian duct! See the tiny budding eggs: each one the potential half of a human being, that could have loved and been loved, and laughed and wept and planned and hoped. But what use is half a human being: the ageing female organ, everyone knows, no longer attracts the male. So whip it out: cut, nick, clip and sew: implant a source of oestrogen and the organ's owner is good as new: a reliable baby-sitter for its grandchildren, not bleeding, given to moods, hot flushes or the distressing growth-gone-wild of cancer. It's all in the best interests of the community: the operation prolongs life. Statistics prove it.

And here a dozen frozen wombs! Young man, young woman, you, who have no thought of death; of such thawing flesh was your nursery made. Perhaps here, on the slab, is the very one? Did not Mother have her womb out, only last year? And was the surgeon once her lover, when you were ten and she was young? You can thaw and re-freeze the organs only two or three times – after that the texture goes. Never mind: it has served its purpose. Grown a baby or two, and helped in the education of a new race of doctors. Doctors are good people. They do what they can. They have to live, of course, and the more wombs, ovaries and so forth they remove in a year, the richer they are, and the more peacefully the ponies of their little daughters graze in the escarpments that ridge the coast north of Sydney.

Loss and gain, loss and gain! Your loss, my gain.

Tandy was a doctor's daughter herself: born and bred in Newcastle. As a child she had a pony called Toddy. Doctors' daughters experience more sexual assaults at the hands of doctors than do the daughters of men in other professions. Now there's an odd statistic! What can be the look in the doctor's daughter's eye? What can the glint be, that cries out for ravishment at the hands of such normally respectable folk? Oh Daddy, Daddy, pay me some attention! No matter what, no matter how unwelcome: anything will do! Anything! Are we to believe it?

Or perhaps doctors' daughters just go to the doctor more often than other women? Surely that must be it. Doctors don't usually treat members of their own family.

When Tandy was twelve, a paediatrician laid her on her back, divided her legs, put his hand up between them, tweaked and poked and explained that the sudden, terrifying bleeding signified only a ruptured hymen.
'Good thing we live in a civilised country,' he said. 'No blood-stained wedding sheets required for our little Tandy. It's riding that does it!'
'But Toddy's such a well-mannered little horse,' said Mandy, Tandy's mother. She had wide bright eyes and a gentle manner, as did her daughter.
'Even so,' said the paediatrician, 'a sudden bump with the legs parted, and there you are. Virgin no more.'

He came to dinner sometimes. His hair was turning grey. Tandy thought he must have told his wife – a tall woman with hooded eyes – and she no doubt had told her friends. Virgin no more!

When she was fourteen and at school Tandy kept company with a fifteen-year-old boy, John Pierce. Such associations were frowned upon. It was back in the fifties, after all, and Tandy wore a gym slip and a panama hat. They loved each other, filled each other's skies with a kind of pink sunrise glow.

'Something's happened to that girl,' remarked her father, the doctor, over breakfast.
'Oh my God!' said her mother.

John Pierce's mother complained to the school that Tandy Watson was preventing her son passing his exams. Authority had already observed their affection: the way they held hands, leant into each other. The school buzzed with rumours that they'd gone the whole way. Tandy's mother's eyes widened with alarm and fear as the police were mentioned: the possibility of punitive action. Fourteen-year-old girls, in those days, were supposed to be virgins, and anyone who suggested otherwise to them went to prison.

'Good God,' said Tandy's father, 'let's find out. Open your legs, girl.'

Tandy did, up on the patients' couch. Tandy's father frowned, paled, consulted with Tandy's mother.
'But, darling,' said Tandy's mother, 'that business with the horse a couple of years back – had you forgotten?'
He had, of course.
'Goddamned horse,' he said. 'Did you or didn't you, girl?'
'I didn't,' she said. 'I didn't, I didn't and neither did he.'
'Why couldn't you say so before?' he demanded, irate, although nobody had thought to ask her before. 'I believe you, girl. Get your pants back on.'

And she did, and her mother, lying, announced her *virgo intacta* to all the world, but Tandy lost all interest in John

Pierce, and had to think hard before saying anything to her father. Nothing seemed to come naturally any more, between him and her. Perhaps he knew it: he hrummed and hraaed a lot when Tandy was in the room.

Tandy wanted to be a doctor but her father said it wasn't a fit profession for a girl: there were too many terrible sights to be seen, for anyone in that line of business. Tandy went to college to do English literature.

The college gave all its students twice-yearly medical checkups. The rather elderly doctor always had Tandy strip right off so he could palpate her breasts. He gave her internal examinations, too, putting his hand first into a thin rubber glove, then into her to pinch and peek and pry. And then a rectal examination with a light at the end of a metal tube. She'd scream and he'd say crossly, 'just relax.' Doctors always seemed to Tandy to be rather cross. After the fourth of these examinations she checked with her friend Rhoda, who had no breasts to speak of, and discovered that Rhoda was allowed to keep her clothes on and that her inside could do without checking, so after that Tandy ignored the official reminder cards and left her health to luck rather than science.

She raised the question of medical training once more at home. She thought there should be more women in the medical profession.

'Good God, girl,' said her father, 'the thing to do is to marry a doctor, not *be* one. A good doctor's wife is almost as valuable in the community as a good doctor.'

Tandy's mother had good solid-thighed legs, from running up and down stairs to answer the telephone. And indeed there was nothing she didn't know about the early symptoms of mumps, measles and chicken pox, and the management of these diseases. She had a fair, Northern skin, and died rather suddenly from a melanoma, a cancer common in

Australia. A mole on her hand changed shape and size and her husband was too busy to notice it until it was too late to be operable. He had become an excellent golfer, and was playing in an interstate competition, and had a lot on his mind.

'Even if you had noticed,' said his doctor friends, comforting him, for he was very distressed, 'chances are she wouldn't have made it. And how old was she?'

Forty-nine, and coming up to the menopause. Better out of the way, the implication was. After the forties, from a gynaecologist's point of view, it's downhill all the way, tinker as you may with a woman's insides. Bleeding and drying and fibroids and cysts and backache – you name an unhealthy state, the woman has it. She comes to you complaining, fills the surgery with dulled voice and re-proachful eyes. The age of child-bearing is past. All meaning gone, for a woman.

Tandy's father married his receptionist, who was only twenty-nine, and adored him, and raised another family.

'I want to be a doctor,' reiterated Tandy. 'No daughter of mine . . .' reiterated her father. 'I'm not paying for that. Why don't you be a nurse?'

So she did. One year into her nursing course she became pregnant by a medical student who put his faith in coitus interruptus and could not marry her, for various reasons, and Tandy had to have an abortion; at that time a firmly and criminally illegal act. She went to see the local abortionist, a general practitioner known to feel sorry for girls in distress, when she was eight weeks pregnant. He would not accept money, saying he performed these operations from principle, rather than monetary gain: he believed in sex as the great emotional and physical cure-all, and required her to sleep with him before curettage, in order to speed the healing process. She consented, since it seemed to mean more to him than it did to her. He was very short-sighted and kept his pebble lenses on during love-making, saying that seeing was as important as touching. He reproached her for her lack of sexual response and delayed the operation until he had brought her fully to it. He showed her obscene photographs which failed to move her, though they did quite surprise her. Then he was obliged to call his cousin in to have sex with her while he watched, and she feigned the most enthusiastic response, since by now she was ten weeks pregnant and the operation getting daily more dangerous.

When he finally performed it, he did it safely, painlessly and kindly, and she healed with amazing speed. But then she was a healthy girl, and apart from the intimate relationship that doctors seemed to have with her private parts would never have had to visit one at all.

She qualified as a nurse, then as a sister, and could have become matron before she was thirty; but then, as her father remarked, who would have married her? So she stayed a nursing sister, and married an engineer, Roger, and had two children, and apart from the usual peeking and prying, enemas, shaving, cutting and sewing involved in the safe delivery of babies in Newcastle, kept her insides to herself for a considerable time. Roger was an active and pleasant lover, and did not require fellatio, or practise cunnilingus, and they never had the light on, and she managed to separate out the medical aspects of her reproductive organs from the warm, creative, sexual pleasure they now gave her, three or four times a week, during her thirties and forties.

Perhaps Roger was a little boring: perhaps life was rather quiet? She felt untapped, unused: as if she were the kernel of a walnut, and it was withering in the shell, instead of growing plump and interestingly formed and ripe. Roger watched television and played squash: the two boys played football and tennis. No one talked, she sometimes felt: not really talked. They exchanged information, that was all. Life was lived on the surface: sometimes the flesh between her legs tingled in an expectation that infused her whole body, and made her dance and sing and then weep. The boys thought she was mad, but then everyone's mother at a certain age went mad. Everyone knew it. Women did.

Tandy took a part-time job at the local hospital, where they specialised in the care of the handicapped; a place where men lived whose legs grew round their necks, or who had no arms or legs at all, and women with hands grown into claws, and children with brains that still thought better than most, and felt more than most, but could not move limbs, or mouths, or eyes.

How lucky I am to be whole, thought Tandy, even though no longer young, and fell in love with Dr Walker, the medical superintendent, who did not get on with his wife. And he fell in love with her and they managed a weekend or so together, which in a way was a pity because after that she knew what she had missed. She saw that the sunrise glow in the morning of her life, which should have grown stronger and stronger, to suffuse her whole life with a brilliant sexual light, had been deflected, and the day clouded over, and now there were just glimmers, in and out, of a muted radiance.

He went back to his wife and Tandy to her husband, but she told him: which was a mistake. You can trust husbands to love you so far, no more. They, too, have intimations of lost ecstasy. He paced; she brooded.

'Perhaps we would be happier apart,' he said. He was forty-seven; she was forty-four. Either life was going to go on in the suburban house, ordinary and humdrum, eventually to run down into retirement, ill-health and death: or else he would change his job, move out of Newcastle, gain some new access of health and energy, jolt himself into life again. By sleeping with another man she had broken the ties of custom: she had chosen freedom, now he would do the same.

'Go,' she said. 'Very well, go. But we'll stay friends?'
'Of course,' he said. 'And I'll send back the money.'

She had given up the part-time job at the hospital. She found it too painful: not just the sight of so much distressed flesh but the sight of her beloved; the thought of what could have been.

Living apart from Roger was more difficult than she had imagined. She suffered from loneliness, especially in the evenings. Listening to the music she loved, instead of the TV programmes he chose, was not, in the end, sufficient compensation for the simple lack of his presence.

She asked him to come back after six months.
'No,' he said, 'I've found someone else.'

Well, she was still an attractive woman. Other women's husbands sought her out. She decided to become a doctor. She enrolled at the medical school. They hummed and haaed at her age and sex, but accepted her. She loved the work: it came easily to her.

I am happy, she thought. One of her tutors asked her out to coffee, then took her to the pictures. They started sleeping together. He was forty, seven years younger than she, but he said age was irrelevant. They made love with the light on, and she learned to trust him.

One night she had a severe pain in her right side.
'You'd better see someone,' said her tutor, Peter, and she
agreed that indeed she had better. All her contemporaries
had gynaecologists whom they visited, on principle, once
every six months, who would check over their insides and
pronounce them healthy, or unhealthy, and occasionally
would 'just open them up' – for they were licensed surgeons
too – 'to see what's going on in there!'

But Tandy kept forgetting to go: in the end they had even
stopped sending the reminder cards.

The women of Newcastle have wonderfully criss-crossed
stomachs, what with the caesarians, the appendectomies
and a host of openings up. And the ponies are plentiful and
plump on the hillsides, and the little doctors' daughters
laugh and sing, and if the grass is spotted with blood, who
notices?

The gynaecologist was tall and fair, and well-qualified and
new in Newcastle.
'He's wonderful,' her friends said. 'So kind and gentle
and understanding. A conservative surgeon.' That meant
though he opened you up he did not take bits away if he
could possibly help it. The women of Newcastle worried a
little: wondered why they had more abdomen scars per head
of female population than did women anywhere else in the
entire world, so conservative surgeons, these days, did better
than anyone else. There were a few practising women
medicos, but hardly any women surgeons. Women, custom
and practice decreed, do not make good surgeons.

'You look familiar,' said Tandy to the gynaecologist, as she
lay upon the couch, on her side, knees parted.
'Relax, relax! How can I examine you if you stay so stiff?
'Good God,' he said, 'it's Tandy.'

Dr John Pierce, the golden youth from long ago, from sunrise days: thin fair hair and lines of disappointment round his mouth, now that the sun was creeping down the sky.

Well, everyone gets older. He was more shocked than she: he had held an image of her in his mind, a beautiful, laughing girl, with long, thick hair. One day she'd loved him; the next she hadn't. He never knew why. Tossed her head and walked by, and wounded him for ever.

'Good God,' she said, 'it's John Pierce.'
'A long time ago,' he said. 'Do try and relax.'
She tried.
'I think it's just a cyst,' he said, 'causing the trouble. Probably benign, but we'd better open you up and make sure: and of course there are a lot of fibroids here. But then in a woman of your age that's to be expected. How old? Forty-seven? Good God!'
He was forty-seven too. If it's old for a woman it's old for a man but that wasn't the way he wanted to see it. Does anyone? He was married with three children and three ponies, and a receptionist he lusted after, and wouldn't have to lust after if only he had true love, and hadn't lost it long ago to Tandy Watson, who'd tossed her head one day and broken his heart. He blamed her.

He opened Tandy up: and took out everything. Womb, fallopian tubes, ovaries. Snip, snip. Forceps, nurse. (The nurse had glowing eyes above her mask, which reminded him of the past.) He sat by Tandy's bed while she came out of the anaesthetic and told her what he'd done.
'I thought we'd better be on the safe side,' he said.
'But what was wrong with them?'
'Well, nothing,' he said, 'but wombs are a great source of trouble to women your age.'
'You mean you took out three perfectly healthy organs?'
'Well, yes,' he said. 'This cyst was benign but the next one

mightn't be. And I gave you an oestrogen implant so you'll be better off than you were before. Oestrogen slows the ageing process. Well, look,' he said nervously, for her eyes were enormous and witchlike, 'what use are those organs to a woman of fifty? They've served their purpose. They're no use to anyone.'

'Forty-seven,' she said. 'Those organs are *me*. I am nothing, now. You have turned off the light. No one asked you to: no one said you could: you have taken it upon yourself to turn out the light of my life.'

He thought she might sue, but she didn't. She didn't want anyone to know what had happened. She was dull and depressed for a good six months, shocked and zombie-like.

She split up with Peter, who of course had to know, and blamed it on the loss of her organs. He was only forty: what would he want with a half-woman of nearly fifty, without womb, ovaries or fallopian tubes? The few friends she told assured her that in fact no harm had been done: that Peter would have gone anyway; that many women sought out the operation: that she looked, thanks to the oestrogen, slimmer and younger and prettier than before. But Tandy was not convinced. She gave up medical school: it was too much trouble. She became a grandmother and was glad it was a boy.

'They have a better life than girls,' she said, admiring the contained and tidy infant penis.

When she saw John Pierce in the street she would cross the road to avoid him. He seemed to her to walk in a pool of dark. But then she had, after all, turned the light of his life off, carelessly, long ago. She'd slept with him and then denied it to everyone, and failed to love him, and spoiled his life, and he couldn't forgive that. Could anyone, really, man or woman, be expected to forgive?

The Bottom Line and the Sharp End

'I'll get my pennies together,' said Avril the nightclub singer to Helen the hairdresser. 'I'll come in next week and you can work your usual miracles.'

Helen thought the time for miracles was almost past. Both Avril's pennies and Avril's hair were getting thin. But she merely said, 'I'll do my best,' and ran her practised fingers through Avril's wiry curls without flinching.

Avril was scraggy, haggard and pitifully brave. Helen was solid and worthy and could afford to be gracious. Avril had been Helen's very first client, thirty years before, when she, Helen, had finally finished her apprenticeship. In those days Avril had worn expensive, daring green shoes with satin bows, all the better to flirt in: Helen had worn cheap navy shoes with sensible heels, all the better to work in. Helen envied Avril. Today Avril's shoes, with their scuffed high heels, were still green, but somehow vulgar and pitiable, and the legs above them were knotted with veins. And Helen's shoes were still navy, but expensive and comfortable, and had sensible medium heels. And Helen owned the salon, and had a husband, and grown children, and savings, and a dog, a cat and a garden, and Avril had nothing. Nothing. Childless, unmarried, and without property or money in the bank.

Now Helen pitied Avril, instead of envying her, but somehow couldn't get Avril to understand that this switch had occurred.

With the decades the salon had drifted elegantly up-market, and now had a pleasing atmosphere of hushed brocaded luxury. Here now the wives of the educated wealthy came weekly, and the shampooers were well-spoken and careful not to wet the backs of blouses, and decaffeinated coffee was provided free, and low-calorie wholewheat sandwiches for a reasonable charge, and this month's glossy magazines in sufficient quantity – and still Avril would walk in, unabashed, and greet Helen with an embarrassing cry of 'darling!' as if she were her dearest friend, in her impossibly husky and actressy voice. And she'd bring wafting in with her, so that the other clients stirred uneasily in their well-padded seats, what Helen could only think of as the aura of the street: and what is more, of a street in rapid decline – once perhaps Shaftesbury Avenue, and tolerable, with associated West End theatre and champagne cocktails, but now of some Soho alley, complete with live sex shows and heroin-pushers.

Sometimes Avril would vanish for a year or so and Helen would hope she had gone for good, and then there she'd be again, crying 'do something, darling. Work your usual miracles. My life's all to hell!' and Helen would pick up the strands of brown, or red, or yellow or whatever they currently were, and bleach them right down and re-colour them, and soothe and coax them into something presentable and fashionable.

This time Avril had been away all of two years. And now here she was, back again, and the 'do something' had sounded really desperate, as she'd torn at crisp dry henna-and-grey curls with ringed finger-claws, and Helen had been affected, surprisingly, with real sorrow and concern. Perhaps you didn't have to like people to feel for them? Perhaps if they were merely around for long enough you developed a fellow-feeling for them?

She remembered how once – way, way back – when Avril's hair had been long and smooth and shiny, the rings had

had diamonds and rubies on them. Then, at the time of her auburn pony-tail there'd been engagement rings and remembrance rings: and later, once or twice – at the time Avril's hair was back-combed into blonde curls – a wedding ring. Helen could remember. But nowadays the only rings she wore were the kind anyone could buy at a jewellery stall in the market on Saturdays; they came from India or Ethiopia or somewhere ethnic, and the silver was base and the stones were glass. 'Cheap and cheerful,' Avril would cackle, from under the dryer, waving them round happily for all to see, as the other clients looked away, tactfully. They didn't wear much jewellery, and if they did it was either real or Harrods make-believe, and certainly *quiet*.

Avril came in for the latest, desperate miracle on Friday evening. She had the last appointment, and of course wanted a bleach, a perm, a cut and a set. Helen agreed to work late. It was her policy to oblige clients – even clients such as Avril – wherever possible, and however much at her own expense. It was, in the end, good for business. Just as, in the end, steadiness, forbearance, endurance, always succeeded whether at work, in marriage, in the establishment of a home, the bringing up of children. You made the most of what you had. You were not greedy; you played safe; and you won.

Helen rang up her husband Gregory to tell him she would be working late.
'I'll take a chicken pie from the freezer,' he said, 'and there's a nature programme on TV I want to see. And perhaps I'll do a little DIY around the house.'
'Well, don't try mending the electric kettle,' she said, and he agreed not to. Still she did not hang up.
'Is there something the matter?' he said, and waited patiently. He was wonderfully patient.
'Don't you think,' she said presently, 'don't you think some-how life's awfully sad?'

'In what way?' he asked, when he'd given some time to considering the question.

'Just growing older,' she said, vaguely, already fearing she sounded silly. 'And what's it all for?'

There was a further silence at the other end of the line.

'Who's the client?' he asked.

'Avril le Ray.'

'Oh, her. She always upsets you.'

'She's so tragic, Gregory!'

'She brought it on herself,' said Gregory. 'Now I must go and take the pie out of the freezer. It's always better to heat them when they're thawed out a little, isn't that so?'

'Yes,' she said, and they said goodbye, and hung up.

Avril was ten minutes late for her appointment. She'd been crying. Her mouth was slack and sullen. Melted blue eye shadow made runnels down her cheeks. She insisted on sitting in the corner where one of the old-style mirrors still remained from before the last renovation. Avril claimed it threw back a kinder reflection and it probably did, but Avril sitting in front of it meant that Helen was obliged to work with her elbow up against the wall. The neck of Avril's blouse was soiled with a mixture of make-up, sweat and dirt. And she smelt unwashed. But Helen, to her surprise, found the smell not unpleasant. Her Nan had smelt like that, she remembered, long ago and once upon a time, when she'd put little Helen to bed in a big, damp feather bed. Was that where the generations got you? Did they merely progress from chaos to order, dirt to cleanliness? Was that what it was all about?

'Remember when I had long hair?' said Avril. 'So long that I could sit on it! I played Lady Godiva in the town pageant. I was in love with this boy and he said if I wanted to prove I loved him I would sit on the horse naked. So I did. Listen, I was sixteen, he was seventeen, what did we know? My mother wouldn't speak to me for months. We lived in the big house, had servants and everything. What a disgrace! She was right about one thing: I failed my exams.'

'What about the boy?' asked Helen. Whole-head root-bleaches, the kind Avril wanted, were old-fashioned, but were less finickity than the more usual bleached streaks. Helen could get on quite quickly at this stage.

'He was my one true love,' said Avril. 'We'd never done anything but hold hands and talk about running away to get married. Only after I played Godiva he never wanted to run any further than behind the bicycle shed. You know what men are like.'

'But it was his idea!'

Avril shrugged.

'He was only young. He didn't know what he'd feel like later, after I'd gone public, as it were. How could he have? So I went with him behind the bicycle sheds. It was glorious. I'll never forget it. The sun seemed to stop in the sky. You know?'

'Yes,' said Helen, who didn't. She'd only ever been with Gregory and someone else whose name she preferred to forget, at a party, a sorry, drunken episode which had left her with NSU – non-specific urethritis. Well, that's the way it goes. Fate reserves these unlikely punishments for the virtuous who sin only once, and then either get pregnant or catch a social disease. And she'd only ever made love to Gregory at night, so how could she know about the sun stopping? But at least it was love: warm, fond and affectionate, not whatever it was that ravaged and raddled Avril.

'Anyway, then he broke it to me formally that he and me were through. He'd met Miss Original Pure and planned to marry her when he had his degree. I thought I'd die from misery. But I didn't, did I? I lived to tell the tale.'

'I do look a sight, don't I?' Avril said, staring at her plastery hair, but her mind was on the past. 'It was funny. I stood in front of that full-length mirror, at the age of sixteen, and tried to decide whether to do Godiva naked or in a flesh-coloured body-stocking. I knew even then it was what they call a major life decision. Naked, and the future would go one way; body-stocking, another. I chose naked. Afterwards I cried and cried, I don't know why. I've always cried a lot.

'Then of course I couldn't get into college because I'd failed my exams so I went to drama school. I got no help from home – they'd given me up – and I couldn't live on my grant, no one could. So I did a centre-spread in *Mayfair*, perfectly decent, just bra-less, only the photographer took a lot of other shots I knew nothing about and they were published too, and got circulated everywhere, including in my home town. I tried to sue but it was no use. No one takes you seriously once you take your clothes off. I didn't know – well, I guess I was trying to take advantage of him, too, in a way, so I can't complain. And I can tell you this, if the sun stopped behind the bicycle shed, that photographer made the whole galaxy go the other way. Know what I mean?'

'Oh yes,' said Helen, testing a lock of Avril's hair: the bleach was taking a long time to take. She wondered whether to ring Gregory and remind him not to try to mend the kettle, or whether the reminding would merely make him the more determined to do it.

'Do I look as if I've been crying?' asked Avril, peering more closely into the mirror. 'Because I have been. This guy I've been living with: he's a junkie trying to kick the habit. He's really managed well with me. He was getting quite – well, you know, affectionate – that's always a good sign. He used to be a teacher, really clever, until he got the habit. Young guy: bright eyes, wonderful skin – didn't often smile, but when he did . . . Notice the past tense? When I got home from work this morning he'd vanished and so had my rent money. It gets you here in your heart: you can't help it: you tell yourself it was only to be expected, but it hurts, Christ it hurts. I shouldn't have told him I loved him, should I? Should I, Helen?'

'I don't know,' said Helen. She told Gregory she loved him quite often and there seemed no sanction against it. But perhaps the word, as used by her, and by Avril, had a different meaning. She rather hoped so.

'So you only love people who hurt you?' she asked, cautiously.

'That is love, isn't it?' said Avril. 'That's how you know you love them, because they can hurt you. Otherwise, who cares? How am I going to live without him? Just lying in bed beside him: he was so thin, but so hot: he was so alive! It was life burning him up, killing him. Just life. Too strong.' Tears rolled down Avril's cheeks.

She looks eighty, thought Helen, but she can only be my age.

'Anyway,' said Avril, 'I want a new me at the end of this session. Pick yourself up and start all over, that's my motto. Remember when you cut off all my long hair? That was after the *Mayfair* business; I didn't want anyone to recognise me, but of course they did. You can't cut off your breasts, can you? I got picked out of the end-of-the-year show by a director: very classy he was, National and all that, and he and I got friendly, and I got the lead but I wasn't ripe for it, and the rest of the cast made a fuss and that was the end of me; three weeks later, bye-bye National. And he had a wife living in the country somewhere, and it got in the papers because he was so famous, and none of his friends would hire me, they all sided with the wife, so I got a part in a Whitehall Revue and did French maids for five years. Good wages, nice little flat, men all over the place: wonderful dinners, diamonds. You wouldn't believe it, like in a novel, but it wasn't me. I don't know what is me, come to think of it. Perhaps no one ever does. I wanted to get married and have kids and settle down but men just laughed when I

suggested it. I had a blonde, back-combed bob in those days. Remember?'
Helen did. That was in the days when you used so much hair spray on a finished head it felt like a birds' nest to the touch.

'Then I had a real break. I could always sing, you know, and by that time I really did know something about theatre. I got the lead in a Kurt Weill opera. Real classy stuff. You did my hair black and I had a beehive. How we could have gone round like that! And I fell in love with the stage manager. God, he was wonderful. Strong and silent and public school, and he really went for me, and was married, and I've never been happier in my life. But he was ambitious to get into films, and was offered a job in Hollywood and I just walked out of the part and went along. That didn't do me any good in the profession, I can tell you. And I kept getting pregnant but he didn't want us tied down so I'd have terminations, and then he went off with the studio boss's daughter: she was into yoga, and they had three kids straight off. He complained I could never sit still. But I can, can't I? You should know, shouldn't you, Helen?'
'About as still as anyone else,' said Helen, and took Avril over to the basin and washed the bleach off. She hoped she hadn't overdone it: the hair was very fine and in poor condition and the bleach was strong.

'I left them to it; I just came back home; I didn't hang around asking for money. I never do that. Once things are over, they're over – I didn't have any children: why should he pay? We gave each other pleasure, didn't we? Fair exchange, while it lasted. Everything finishes, that's the bottom line. But I never liked beehives, did you?'
'No. Very stiff and artificial.'
'I wept and wept, but it was good-times while it lasted!'
Avril examined a lock of hair.
'Look here,' said Avril, 'that bleach simply hasn't taken.

You'll have to put some more on and mix it stronger.'
'It's risky!' said Helen.
'So's everything!' said Avril. 'I'm just sick of being hennaed frizz: I want to be a smooth blonde again.'

Helen felt weary of the salon and her bank account and her marriage and everything she valued: and of her tidy hair and sensible shoes and the way she never took risks and how her youth had passed and all she'd ever known had been in front of her eyes, and fear had kept her from turning her head' or seeing what she would rather not see. She re-mixed the bleach, and made it strong. Avril would be as brassy a blonde as she wished, and Helen's good wishes would go with her.

'Well, of course,' said Avril, cheerfully, 'after that it was all downhill. Could I get another acting part? No! Too old for ingénue, too young for character and a reputation as a stripper, so Hedda Gabler was out. And frankly I don't suppose I was ever that good. Met this really nice straight guy, an engineer, but he wanted a family and I guess my body had got tired of trying, because I never fell for a baby with him, and he made some nice girl pregnant and they got married and lived happily ever after. I went to the wedding. But how was it, I ask myself, that she could get pregnant and still stay a nice girl, and I was just somehow a slut from the beginning?'

So late, thought Helen, and the perm not even begun. Gregory will have gone to bed without me – will he notice? Will he care?

'So now I sing in nightclubs; I'm a good singer, you know. All I need is the breaks and I'd really be someone . . . I do the whole gamut – from the raunchy to the nostalgic, a touch of Bogart, a touch of Bacall. Those were the days, when love was love. And I tell you, Helen, it still is, and the only thing I regret is that it can't go on for ever – love, sex. The first touch of a man's hand, the feel of his lips, the press of his tongue, the way the mind goes soft and the body goes weak, the opening up, the joining in. I still feel love, and I still say love, though it's not what men want, not from me. Perhaps it comes too easily; always did. Do you think that's what the matter is?'

When Helen took Avril to the washbasin and washed the second lot of bleach away, a good deal of Avril's hair came with it. Helen felt her hands grow cold, and her head fill with black: she all but fainted. Then she wept. Nothing like this had ever happened before, in all her professional career. She trembled so much that Avril had to rinse off what was left of the bleach from what was left of her hair, herself.

'Well,' said Avril, when it was done, and large areas of her reddened scalp all too apparent, 'that's the bottom line and the sharp end. Nothing lasts, not even hair. My fault. I made you do it. Thirty years of hating me, and you finally got your revenge!'
'I never hated you,' said Helen, her face puffy and her eyes swollen. She felt, on the other side of the shock and horror, agreeably purged, sensuous, like her Nan's little girl again. 'Well, you ought to have,' said Avril. 'The way I always stirred things up in here. I just loved the look on your face!'

After a little Avril said, 'I wonder what my future is, as a bald nightclub singer? I suppose I could wear a wig till it grows again, but I don't think I will, it might be rather good. After the Godiva look, the Doris Day look, the Elizabeth Taylor look, then the Twiggy look – the frizz-out, the pile-up and the freak-out – none of which did me any good at all – just plain bald might work wonders for a girl's career.'

A month later Avril le Ray was billed in Mayfair, not Soho, on really quite tasteful posters, and Helen, bravely, took Gregory around to listen to her sing. They went cautiously down into the darkness, where Avril's coarse and melancholy voice filled out the lonely corners nicely, and a pink spotlight made her look not glamorous – for truly she was bald, and how can the bald be glamorous? – but important, as if her sufferings and her experience might be of considerable interest to others, and the customers certainly paid attention, were silent when she sang, and clapped when she'd finished, which was more than usually happened in such places.

'How you doing, Kiddo?' asked Avril of Helen, after the last set, going past on the arm of a glowing-eyed Arab with a hooked nose, waving a truly jewelled ring, properly set in proper gold. 'Remember what I told you about the bottom line and the sharp end? Nothing lasts, so you'd better have as much as you can, while you can. And in the end, there's only you and only them, and not what they think of you, but what you think of them.'

In the Great War

Enid's mother Patty didn't stand a chance. That was in the Great War, in the fifties, when women were at war with women. Victory meant a soft bed and an easy life: defeat meant loneliness and the humiliation of the spinster. These days, of course, women have declared themselves allies, and united in a new war, a cold war, against the common enemy, man. But then, in the Great War, things were very different. And Patty didn't stand a chance against Helene. She was, for one thing, badly equipped for battle. Her legs were thick and practical, her breasts floppy, and her features, though pleasant enough, lacked erotic impact. Her blue eyes were watery and her hair frizzy and cut brusquely for easy washing and combing. 'I can't stand all this dolling up,' she'd say. 'What's the point?'

Patty cooked with margarine because it was cheaper than butter and her white sauces were always lumpy. She wouldn't keep pot plants, or souvenirs, or even a cat. What was the point?
She didn't like sex and, though she never refused her husband Arthur, she washed so carefully before and after, she made him feel he must have been really rather dirty.

Patty, in other words, was what she was, and saw no point in pretending to be anything else. Or in cooking with mushrooms or holidaying abroad or buying a new pair of shoes for Enid, her only child, when she had a perfectly good pair already, or going with her husband to the pub. And, indeed, there very often was no point in these things, except surely life must be more than something just to be practically and sensibly *got through*?

Enid thought so. Enid thought she'd do better than her mother in the Great War. Enid buffed her pre-pubertal nails and arranged wild flowers in jam jars and put them on the kitchen table. Perhaps she could see what was coming!

For all Patty's good qualities – cleanliness, honesty, thrift, reliability, kindness, sobriety, and so on – did her no good whatsoever when Helene came along. Or so Enid observed. Patty was asleep on duty, and there all of a sudden was Helene, the enemy at the gate, with her slim legs and her bedroom eyes, enticing Arthur away. 'But what does she *see* in Arthur?' asked Patty, dumbfounded. What you don't! the ten-year-old Enid thought, but did not say.

In fact, the Second World Male War, from 1939 to 1945, which men had waged among themselves in the name of Democracy, Freedom, Racial Supremacy and so forth, to the great detriment of women and children everywhere, had sharpened the savagery of the Female War. There just weren't enough men to go around. In ordinary times Helene would have gone into battle for some unmarried professional man – accountant or executive – but having lost country, home, family and friends in the ruins of Berlin now laid claim to Arthur, Patty's husband, a railway engineer in the north of England, who painted portraits as a hobby. The battle she fought for him was short and sharp. She shaved her shapely legs and flashed her liquid eyes.
'She's no better than a whore,' said Patty. 'Shaving her legs!' If God put hairs on your legs, thought Patty, then a woman's duty, and her husband's, too, is to put up with them.
Helene thought otherwise. And in her eyes Arthur saw the promise of secret bliss, the complicity of abandon, and all the charm of sin: the pink of her rosy nipples suffused the new world she offered him. And so, without much difficulty Helene persuaded Arthur to leave Patty and Enid, give up

his job, paint pictures for a living and think the world well lost for love.

By some wonderful fluke – wonderful, that is, for Arthur and Helene, if infuriating for Patty – Arthur's paintings were an outstanding commercial success. They became the worst bestselling paintings of the sixties, and Arthur, safely divorced from Patty, lived happily ever after with Helene, painting the occasional painting of wide-eyed deer, and sipping champagne by the side of swimming pools. 'Nasty acidy stuff, champagne,' said Patty.

Enid – Patty and Arthur's daughter – never really forgave her mother for losing the war. As if poor Patty didn't have enough to put up with already, without being blamed by her daughter for something she could hardly help! But that's the way these things go – life is the opposite of fair. It stuns you one moment and trips your feet from under you the next, and then jumps up and down on you, pound, pound, pound for good measure.

You should have seen Enid, when she was twelve, twisting the knife in her mother's wounds, poking about among the lumps of the cauliflower cheese, saying: 'Do we *have* to eat this? No wonder Dad left home!' 'Eat it up, it's good for you,' her mother would reply. 'If you want something fancy go and live with your stepmother.'

And, indeed, Enid had been asked, but Enid never went. Enid would twist a knife but not deliver a mortal wound, not to her mother. Instead she took up the armoury her mother never wore, breathed on it, burnished it, sharpened its cutting edges, prepared for war herself. Long after the war was over, Enid was still fighting. She was like some mad Aussie soldier hiding out in the Malayan jungle, still looking for a foe that had years since thrown away its grenades and taken to TV assembly instead.

At sixteen Enid scanned the fashion pages and read hints on make-up and how to be an interesting person; she went weekly to the theatre and art galleries and classical music concerts and exercised every day, and not until she was eighteen did she feel properly prepared to step into the battlefield. She was intelligent, and thought it sensible enough to go to university, although she chose English literature as the subject least likely to put men off.

'Nothing puts a man off like a clever woman,' said Helene when Enid visited. Now warriors in the Great War thought nothing of swapping secrets. Intelligence services of warring countries, hand in glove, glove in hand! It's always been so. Just as there's always been trade with enemy nations, unofficially if not officially. Helene lisped out quite a few secrets to Enid: her accent tinged with all the poise and decadence of a vanished Europe. 'My foreign wife!' Arthur would say, proudly in his honest, northern, jovial, middle-aged voice. Arthur was the J. B. Priestley of the art world – good in spite of himself.

Oh, Patty had lost a lovely prize, Enid knew it! Her beloved father! What a victory Patty's could have been – and yet she chose defeat. She'd chosen a bra to flatten an already flat chest. 'What's the point?' she asked, when Enid said she was going off to university. Couldn't she even see that?

Little Enid, so bright and knowledgeable and determined! So young, so ruthless – a warrior! And fortune favours the brave, the strong, the ruthless. That was the point. Enid's professor, Walter Walther, looked at Enid in a lingering way, and Enid looked straight back. Take me! Well, not quite take me. Love me now, take me eventually.

Walter Walther was forty-eight. Enid was nineteen. Enid was studying Chaucer. Enid said in an essay that Chaucer's Parfait Gentle Knight was no hero but a crude mercenary, and Chaucer, in his adulation, was being ironic; Walter Walther hadn't thought of that before, and at forty-eight it is delightful to meet someone who says something you haven't thought of before. And she was so young, and dewy, almost downy, so that if she was out in the rain the drops lay like silver balls upon her skin; and she was surprisingly knowledgeable for one so young, and knew all about music and painting, which Walter didn't, much, and she had an interesting, rich father, if a rather dowdy, vague, distant little mother. And Enid was warm.

Oh, Enid was warm! Enid was warm against his body on stolen nights. Walter's wife Rosanne, four years older than he, was over fifty. Rain fell off her like water off a duck's back – her skin being oily, not downy. Enid had met Rosanne once or twice baby-sitting; or rather adolescent-sitting, for Walter and Rosanne's two children, Barbara and Bernadette.

Rosanne didn't stand a chance against Enid. Enid still fought the old, old war, and Rosanne had put away her weapons long ago.

'He's so unhappy with his wife,' said Enid to Margot. 'She's such a cold unfeeling bitch. She's only interested in her career, not in him at all, or the children.' Margot was Enid's friend. Margot had owl eyes and a limpid handshake and not a hope of seducing, let alone winning, a married professor. But Margot understood Enid, and was a good friend to her, and had most of the qualities Enid's mother Patty had, and one more important one besides – self-doubt.

'Men never leave their wives for their mistresses,' warned Margot. It was a myth much put about, no doubt by wives, in the days of the Great War, to frighten the enemy. Enid knew better: she could tell a savage war mask from the frightened face of a foe in retreat. Enid knew Rosanne was frightened by the way she would follow Enid into the kitchen if Walter Walther was there alone, getting ice for drinks or scraping mud from the children's shoes.

Enid was pleased. A frightened foe seldom wins. The attacker is usually victorious, even if the advantage of surprise is gone, especially if the victim is old: Rosanne was old. She'd had the children late. It wasn't as if Walter Walther had really wanted children. He knew what kind of mother she'd make – cold.
Enid was warm. She knew how to silhouette her head against the sunlight so that her hair made a halo round her head, and then turn her face slowly so that the pure line of youth, the one that runs from ear to chin, showed to advantage. Rosanne had trouble with her back. Trouble with her back! Rosanne was a hag with one foot in the grave and with the iron bonds of matrimony would drag Walter Walther down there with her, if Walter didn't somehow break the bonds.

And Enid knew how to behave in bed, too: always keeping something in reserve, never taking the initiative, always the pupil, never the teacher. Enid had seen the *Art of Love* in Rosanne's bookshelves, and guessed her to be sexually experimental and innovatory. And she was later proved right, when Walter managed to voice one of his few actual complaints about his wife: there was, he felt, something indecent about Rosanne's sexual prowess: something disagreeably insatiable in her desires; it made Walter, from time to humiliating time, impotent.

Otherwise, it wasn't so much lack of love for Rosanne that Walter suffered from, as surfeit of love for Enid.

Enid exulted. And Rosanne was using worn-out old weapons: that particular stage in the war had ended long ago. The battle these days went to the innocent, not to the experienced. Modern man, Enid knew by instinct, especially those with a tendency to impotence, requires docility in bed and admiration and exultation – not excitement and exercise.

'He'll never leave the children,' said Margot. 'Men don't.' But Enid had been left. Enid knew very well that men did. And Barbara and Bernadette were not the most lovable of children – how could they be? With such a mother as Rosanne – a working mother who never even remembered her children's birthdays, never baked a cake, never ironed or darned, never cleaned the oven? Rosanne was a translator with the International Cocoa Board – a genius at languages, but not at motherhood. She was cold, stringy and sour – all the things soft, warm, rounded Enid was not. Walter said so, in bed, and increasingly out of it.

'What are you playing at?' asked Helene, crossly. Her own attitude to the world was moderating. She was an old retired warrior, sitting in a castle she'd won by force of arms, shaking her head at the shockingness of war.

Patty now lived alone in a little council flat in Birmingham. As Enid had left home Arthur no longer paid Patty maintenance. Why should he?

'You want Walter because Walter's Rosanne's,' observed Patty to Enid one day in a rare rush of insight to the head. Patty's doctor had started giving her oestrogen for her hot flushes, and side-effects were beginning to show. There was a geranium in a pot on Patty's windowsill, when Enid went to break the news to her mother that Walter was finally leaving Rosanne. A geranium! Patty, who never could see the point in pot plants!

All the same, something, if only oestrogen, was now putting a sparkle in Patty's eye, and she turned up at Walter and

Enid's wedding in a kind of velvet safari jacket which made her look almost sexy, and when Arthur crossed the room to speak to his ex-wife, she did not turn away, but actually saw the point of shaking his hand, and even laying her cheek against his, in affection and forgiveness.

Enid, in her white velvet trouser suit, saw: and a pang of almost physical pain roared through her, and for a second, just a second, looking at Walter, she saw not her great love but an elderly, paunchy, lecherous stranger. Even though he'd slimmed down quite remarkably during the divorce. It wasn't surprising! Rosanne had behaved like a bitch, and it had told on them both. Nevertheless, people remarked at the wedding that they'd never seen Walter looking so well – or Enid so elegant. He'd somehow scaled down to forty, and she up to thirty. Hardly a difference at all!
Barbara and Bernadette were bridesmaids. Rosanne had been against the idea, out of envy and malice mixed. She hadn't even been prepared to make their dresses, which Enid thought particularly spiteful. 'I'd never have made a bridesmaid's dress for you,' said Patty. 'Not to wear at your father's wedding.' 'That's altogether different,' said Enid, hurt and confused by the way Patty was seeing the war, almost as if she, Patty, were Rosanne's ally; more Helene's enemy than Enid's mother.

And then Helene upset her. 'I hope you're not thinking of having children,' she said, during the reception. 'Of course I am,' said Enid. 'Some men can't stand it,' said Helene. 'Your father, for one. Why do you think I never had any?' 'Well, I'm sure he could stand me,' said Enid, with a self-confidence she did not feel. For perhaps he just plain couldn't? Perhaps some of the blame for his departure was Enid's, not Patty's. Perhaps if she'd been nicer her father would never have left? And perhaps, indeed, he wouldn't!

Well, if we can't be nice, we can at least try to be perfect.
Enid set out on her journey through life with perfection in
mind. Doing better! Oh, how neat the corners of the beds
she tucked, how fresh the butter, how crisp the tablecloth!
Her curtains were always fully lined, her armpits smooth
and washed, never merely sprayed. Enid never let her
weapons get rusty. She would do better, thank you, than
Patty, or Helene, or Rosanne.

Walter Walther clearly adored his Enid and let the world
know it. His colleagues half envied, half pitied him. Walter
would ring Enid from the department twice a day and talk
baby-talk at her. Until recently he'd talked to his daughter
Barbara in just such a manner. His colleagues came to the
conclusion, over many a coffee table, that now the daughter
had reached puberty the father, in marrying a girl of roughly
the same age, was acting out incest fantasies too terrible to
acknowledge. No one mentioned the word love: for this was
the new language of the post-war age. If there was to be no
hate, how could there be love?

In the meantime, for Walter and Enid, there was perpetual
trouble with Rosanne. She insisted at first on staying in the
matrimonial home, and it took a lawsuit and some fairly
sharp accountants to drive her out: presently she lived with
the girls in a little council flat. Oddly enough, it was rather
like Patty's. Practical, but somehow depressing. 'You see,'
said Enid. 'No gift for living! Poor Walter! What a terrible
life she gave him.' In the Great War men gave women
money, and women gave men life.

Barbara and Bernadette came to stay at weekends. They
had their old rooms. Enid prettified them, and lined the
curtains. She was a better mother to Barbara and Bernadette
than Rosanne had ever been. Walter said so. Enid remembered their birthdays, and saw to their verrucas and had

their hair styled. They looked at her with sullen gratitude, like slaves saved from slaughter.

Rosanne lost her job. Rosanne said – of course, it was because the responsibility of being a one-parent family and earning a living was too much for her, but Enid and Walter knew the loss of her job was just a simple matter of redundancy combined with lack of charm. Bernadette's asthma got worse. 'Of course the poor child's ill,' said Enid. 'With such a mother!' Enid didn't believe in truces. She ignored white flags and went in for the kill.

Enid had a pond built in the garden and entertained Walter's friends on Campari and readings of Shakespeare's sonnets. They were literary people, after all, or claimed to be. 'Couldn't we do without the sonnets?' said Walter.

But Enid insisted on the sonnets, and the friends drifted away. 'It's Rosanne's doing,' said Enid. 'She's turned them against us.' And she twined her white, soft, serpent's arms round his grizzly, stranger body and he believed her. His students, he noticed, seemed less respectful of him than they had been: not as if he had grown younger but they had grown older. Air came through the lecture-room windows, on a hot summer's day, like a sigh. Well, at least he was married, playing honestly and fair, unlike his colleagues, who were for the most part hit-and-run seducers. As for Rosanne, he knew she knew how to look after herself. She always had. A man, in the Great War, usually preferred a woman who couldn't.

'Let's have a baby of our own soon,' said Enid. A baby! He hadn't thought of that. She was his baby. Or was he hers?

'We're so happy,' said Enid. 'You and I. It doesn't matter what the world thinks or says. We were just both a little out of step, that's all, time-wise. God meant us for each other. Don't you feel that?'

He queried her use of the word God, but otherwise agreed with what she said. Her words came as definite instruction from some powerful, knowledgeable source. They flowed, unsullied by doubt. He, being older, had to grope for meanings. He was too wise, and this could only diffuse his certainty, since wisdom is the acknowledgment of ignorance.

'Of course you should have a baby, Enid,' said Patty. 'Why not?' But she wasn't really thinking. She was having an affair with a mini-cab driver, and had forgotten about Enid. 'Your behaviour is obscene and disgusting,' Enid shouted at her mother. '*He's young.*' 'What's the point in your making all this fuss?' asked Patty. 'I deserve a little happiness in my life, and I'm sure you brought me precious little!'

Enid got pregnant, straight away. Walter went out and got drunk when he heard, with old friends of himself and Rosanne. Enid was so upset by this double disloyalty she went and stayed with her friend Margot for at least three days.

Margot was married and pregnant, too, and by one of Walter Walther's students, who had spots and bad breath. They lived on their grants, and beans and cider. Nevertheless, her husband went with her to the antenatal clinic and they pored over baby books together. Walter Walther took the view, common in the Great War, that the begetting of children was something to do with the one-upmanship of woman against woman, and very little to do with the man.

'Look, Enid,' said Walter, a new Walter, briskly and unkindly, 'you just get on with it by yourself.' Arthur had left Patty to get on with it by herself, too. Her very name, Enid, had been a last-minute choice by Patty with the registrar hovering over her hospital bed, because Arthur just left it to her.

'You can't have everything,' was what Helene said, when Enid murmured a complaint or two. 'You can't have status, money, adoration and what Margot has as well.'
'Why not?' demanded Enid. 'I want *everything!*'

Enid saw herself on a mountain top, a million women bowing down before her, acknowledging her victory. Her foot would be heavy on the necks of those she humbled. That was how it ought to be. She pulled herself together. She knew that, in the Great War, being pregnant could make you or break you. Great prizes were to be won – the best mother, the prettiest child, the whitest white – but much was risked. The enemy could swoop down, slender-waisted and laughing and lively, and deliver any number of mortal wounds. So Enid wore her prettiest clothes, and sighed a little but never grunted when the baby lay on some pelvic nerve or other, and never let Walter suffer a moment because of what he had done to her. (In those pre-pill days men made women pregnant: women didn't just get pregnant.)
His boiled egg and toast soldiers and freshly milled coffee and the single flower in the silver vase were always there on the breakfast table at half past eight sharp and they'd eat together, companionably. Rosanne had slopped Sugar Puffs into bowls for the family breakfast, and they'd eaten among the uncleared children's homework and students' essays. Slut!
Walter was protective. 'We have to take extra special care of you,' he'd say, helping her across roads. But he seemed a little embarrassed. Something grated: she didn't know what. They ate in rather more often than before.

Then Rosanne, who ought by rights to have been lying punch-drunk in some obscure corner of the battlefield, rose up and delivered a nasty body-blow. Barbara and Bernadette were to come to live with Enid and Walter. Rosanne couldn't cope, in such crowded surroundings. She had a new job, and couldn't always be rushing home for Bernadette's asthma. Could she?

'A new boyfriend, more like,' said Walter, bitterly. Enid restrained from pointing out that Rosanne was an old, old woman with a bad back and hardly in the field for admirers.

Now six perfectly cooked boiled eggs on the table each morning – Bernadette and Barbara demanded two each – is twelve times as difficult to achieve as two. By the time the last one's in, the first one's cooked, but which one is it?

Walter looked at his bowl of Sugar Puffs one morning and said, 'Just like old times,' and the girls looked knowingly and giggled. They looked at Enid and her swelling tum with contempt and pity. They borrowed her clothes and her make-up. They refused to be taken to art galleries, or theatres; they refused even to play Monopoly, let alone Happy Families. They referred to their father as the Old Goat.

Sometimes she hated them. But Walter would not let her. 'Look,' said Walter, 'you did come along and disrupt their lives. You owe them something, at least.' As if it was all nothing to do with him. Which in a way it wasn't. It was between Rosanne and Enid.

Enid locked herself out of the house one day and, though she knew the girls were inside, when she knocked they wouldn't let her in. It was raining. Afterwards they just said they hadn't heard. And she'd fallen and hurt her knee trying to climb in the window, and might have lost the baby. Bernadette threw a bad asthma attack and got all the attention.

Walter spent more and more time in the department. She and he hardly made love at all any more. It didn't seem right.

Enid went into labour at eight o'clock one evening. She rang Walter Walther at the English Department where he said he was, but he wasn't. She rang Margot and wept, and Margot said, 'I don't think I've ever known you cry, Enid,' and Margot's spotty husband said, 'You'll probably find him round at Rosanne's. I wouldn't tell you, if it wasn't an emergency.'

'Yes,' said Barbara and Bernadette. 'He goes round to see Mum quite a lot. We didn't like to tell you because we didn't want to upset you.

'Really,' they said, 'the whole thing was a plot to get rid of us. The thing is, neither of them can stand us.' (Barbara and Bernadette went to one of the large new comprehensive schools, where there were pupil-counsellors, who could explain everything and anything, and were never lost for words.)

Enid screamed and wept all through her labour, not just from pain. They'd never known a noisier mother, they said: and she'd been so quiet and elegant and self-controlled throughout her pregnancy.

Enid gave birth to a little girl. Now in the Great War, the birth of a girl was, understandably, and unlike now, cause for commiseration rather than rejoicing. Nevertheless, Enid rejoiced. And in so doing, abandoned a battle which was really none of her making; she laid down her arms: she kissed her mother and Helene when they came to visit her, clasped her baby and admitted weakness and distress to Barbara and Bernadette, who actually then seemed quite to like her.

Walter Walther did not come home. He stayed with Rosanne. Enid, Barbara and Bernadette lived in the same house, shared suspender belts, shampoo and boyfriends, and looked after baby Belinda. Walter and Rosanne visited, sheepishly, from time to time, and sent money. Enid went back to college and took a degree in psychology, and was later to earn a good living as a research scientist.

Later still she was to become something of a propagandist in the new cold war against men; she wore jeans and a donkey jacket and walked round linked arm-in-arm with women. But that was, perhaps, hardly surprising, so treacherous had the old male allies turned out to be. All the same, yesterday's enemy, tomorrow's friend! Who is to say what will happen next?

Birthday!

They met on their birthday, at a party, and discovered that they had been born on the same day twenty-eight years earlier. He in the morning, she in the evening. On 19 June: Gemini – the Twins. Over the cusp and you were into Cancer, which meant you were home-loving, and Molly was if anything a little more home-loving than Mark, which was as it should be.

Molly and Mark. Two Ms. M for mother, morality, meanness, martyrdom, mine. Except for mother, M isn't the warmest of initials, but then mother makes up for a lot. Molly craved warmth, and enclosure and security, and acknowledgment, and Mark craved approval, and love. Well, everyone craves love. To love is almost more important than to be loved. Molly thought that; Mark tended to think the other way round. But then their natal moons were in different Houses – Molly's in the fourth, the House of the Home, Mark's in the tenth, the House of Occupation. Molly's moon was in Capricorn and Mark's in Taurus. Capricorn is a rather sorrowful sign: Taurus just plain sexy.

Molly's mother and Mark's mother were both careful people and had kept an accurate note, in their respective diaries, of their children's hour of birth. That was why both Molly and Mark could be so sure of their natures, as defined at any rate by astrologers, and the old-fashioned kind of astrologer, at that, who works out charts in detail and by tables – not the new-fashioned kind who uses a silicon chip computer, and disregards the moon.

The moon is a strong influence on anyone's character, in particular anyone female, and should not be disregarded.

Molly and Mark were united in dislike of their mothers. It was their unholy bond. They had never admitted it to anyone before. Oh, but it is the worst bond of all. If you are to love your life you must love your mother. Somehow. It is the stuff from which you spring. Deny the good in that and you deny the good of everything.

Mark's mother had grand relatives and a fluty voice and other sons who rose in the ranks of the army and the church and married nice young girls in churches full of flowers. Mark was expelled from school, failed to get to Sandhurst or even university, lived by odd carpentry jobs and married Molly, who was no one, in a Register Office full of plastic roses. Mark's mother was there, but looked rather unhappy. Mark's father was in Uganda, as usual.

Molly's real father lived a Bohemian life with a famous lady artist on whose money he lived. Molly longed to be owned by them, but feared, rightly enough, that they found her boring. Nervousness in their company made her voice hard and her remarks edgy and she knew she was never at her best when she was with them. Her father and stepmother had a row on their way to her wedding, and never got there. Their rows were like that – they would stop the traffic for miles around. Molly was relieved and aggrieved, both at once. Molly longed for Mark, and money. That's another M. Only there wasn't much money.

Did they believe what they were saying, Mark and Molly, in those first few months, as they gazed into each other's eyes? Did they really see themselves written in the stars? Well, why not? They felt it. Love transmuted them: the base metal of reality turned to gold around them.

Perhaps it's better for a man and a woman in love not to be the same age? Perhaps the old tradition, that a woman marries a man a few years older than herself, so that he is not just a little older but a little wiser than she, is after all desirable? So that in every household in the land it can be perceived that the man rules, and the woman acquiesces, and that in this lies natural justice, richness, happiness and fruitfulness? They discussed this too; and then they married. Of course.

Perhaps mothers who keep diaries and don't lose them are not the best mothers in the world? Molly's mother was a complainer. She had been left by her first husband, Molly's father, had had a hard time bringing up Molly by herself, without support, had married again, and still complained – with reason – for her new husband was a mean and rigorous man, and would not give a penny to a starving cat, as Molly's mother put it.

'Ah, but what use would a penny be to a starving cat?' asked Mark, who did not like Molly's mother much, in which he was at one with Molly, and they both giggled, naughtily.

Just money enough to live with a little warmth and peace and fitted carpets and curtains you could close against the world, keeping stress and anger and upset out, and love in. Not money for show – not for minks and gold taps, just money so you didn't have to snatch and save and think about it, or work out how the electricity was to be paid, or even bother to remember when the bills fell due.

Mark liked money to spend; Mark liked money to be there, like magic. Mark believed everyone had money behind them, in securities, and before them, in legacies, and the fact that he had neither, because somehow the family fortune had been lost in Uganda, made no difference to the way he *felt* about money.

Molly had Jupiter in the second House, and Mark had Jupiter in the tenth House, which made money important in their lives. Molly's Jupiter was well aspected to the moon, Mark's badly. Molly was better with money.

They discussed all this in the first weeks of their marriage. 'We've got to start as we mean to go on,' said Molly, looking at the champagne on the bedside table. 'And we can't go on like this.'
Champagne went to her head, deliciously. Part of her loved parties, just as Mark did. Silken shifts and sparkling shoes and lovers' looks across the room. It was just, perhaps, that her natal moon had gazed down from Capricorn, three-quarters full, waxing, and clouds had scudded across it and obscured its brightness.
Molly was a little taller than Mark, who was finely built and wide-eyed, like a naughty faun. Molly's jaw was a little large and her nose a little long: she wished she had been born littler, less competent.

Her natal moon stared sideways and un-squarely at Saturn and made her practical.
'We can't go on like this,' she said.
'We won't,' he said. He loved her, his heavenly twin, his earthly mate. He wished he had been born on a bigger scale, more competent.

His natal moon went hand in hand with Venus; in collusion, as it were. It made him faithless.

'I'll always be true to you,' he said. 'This is all I require for ever and ever, amen.' And he did not even cross his fingers as he spoke. Then.

Well: Mark threw away the champagne bottles, found a job as a junior accounts executive in an advertising agency and took out a mortgage on a little house in the suburbs.

Molly took a part-time job as receptionist to a local dentist. The job was well beneath her capacity but about equivalent to her qualifications. Her schooling had been much disrupted, as her mother changed house and husbands, and no one at home had believed much in education. But the fact that she worked part-time enabled her to paint and polish the little house and cook Mark's dinner when he came home from work.

Molly learned to roof, and plumb, and wire, and carpenter. Someone had to. There seemed to be so very little money. Mark was only a junior executive in his advertising agency, and earned just about enough to keep things going, and came home tired and dispirited. And in a way, having a house and a mortgage and a job and a future had been Molly's idea, not Mark's. Mark, she knew quite well, could have lived from hand to mouth on champagne for ever, not having a moon in Capricorn. So really, thought Molly, it was up to her to make a go of things.

'He should do more,' said Molly's mother, staring at her daughter's lime-chapped hands. Molly had been demolishing a plaster wall, breaking through the division between the two little ground-floor rooms to make one large airy one, and the plaster was old, and lime-filled, and got in her hair and on to her clothes.
It was the kind of thing Molly's mother did say. Mark observed that Molly's mother just didn't like men. (Molly's mother had Mars in Taurus, badly aspected.)

'Mark works hard enough at the office, Mother,' said Molly. Mark's hands were smooth and pale and long-fingered, beautifully manicured. Molly loved them, outside and inside her body.

Molly was, increasingly, somehow workaday herself – she felt it. She read recipe books and lit candles and created an atmosphere of romance, when she could. Mark liked that. It stopped him slumping in front of the television, which was an old man's trick, not a young one's.

'You can't mean to live here for ever,' complained Mark's mother. 'Supposing you had children.'

Through Mark's mother's eyes their street was mean and dingy, strewn with tattered papers and abandoned cars; a street no taxi-driver had ever heard of. (Mark's mother had Jupiter in mid-heaven. She lived grandly.) But Molly loved her house: her little suburban house. Mark came home to it.

Molly was a little vague about what happened at Mark's office. Mark put up with it for her sake; she knew that, and was grateful. And Presentation Day happened about once every three months, and entailed late nights, exhaustion and worry. It was, apparently, when a new campaign was presented to a client and was either accepted, which meant a bottle of champagne – reminiscent of other, carefree days – or rejected, which meant a stiff upper lip and a few sleepless nights, and try again. But Mark was very good.

He didn't bring his work home, either literally or spiritually, if he could possibly help it. That was how Molly liked it. There was the world outside the curtains, which was less and less to do with her, and the world inside, which was her kingdom, with Mark its king.

The new baby had Aquarius rising, the sun in Libra, and the moon in the ninth. A happy, benign, kindly little soul. Her Saturn was in the fourth House, though, the House of the family, and badly aspected. Molly had, for the time, gone off astrology, and didn't give the matter much thought. Nappies and gas-boilers and feeds and pram sheets are such practical things, making the stars in their courses seem irrelevant. A new mother with a new baby gets through her day as best she can. They called the baby Angela. Molly's stepmother, the painter, must have thought it too ordinary a name, for she forgot to send a card, let alone a gift, or money. Molly thought a lot about money, these days – Mark paid a sum into the joint account every month, but he had no idea of the reality of inflation, of course. Men didn't. And he had to look smart for work: he had to have silk ties and shirts with firm collars, and well-cut suits and hand-made shoes. Advertising was like that.

She gathered that Mark didn't like advertising. It seemed to him vaguely immoral. He found his colleagues phoney and tricksy, and prone to stabbing each other in the back. He bought sandwiches for lunch, he told Molly, and walked in the park and thought about nature, and the craft of the woodworker, and whether it wouldn't be possible for his little family, one day, if only they could somehow save enough money, to live in the country, naturally, as God had meant man (and woman) to live.

Well, Mark's moon was strongly aspected in Neptune, which gave him a spiritual side to his nature. Molly's moon made no aspect to Neptune at all.

And how were they to save? Molly managed marvellously – three Ms in a row; add Mark, and that makes four: four square corners to a safe, secure world – but money was so hard to come by. You can buy flaky soap cheap, and Molly did, but a pound of apples is a pound of apples and costs more all the time.

'It's the Common Market,' said Mark, sadly. 'The international conglomerates have done it: it's they who've sent us on this helter-skelter inflationary recession. And to think I'm part of that kind of world! But what can I do?'

What, indeed? It takes money to change jobs, and a man with a house, a wife and a family can't be irresponsible.

Mark sopped up responsibility for Molly, stole light from her moon. It was marvellous. The Ms kept coming.

So did the family. Within three years there were three little girls. Angela, Anthea, and Molly's stepmother shrieked and said, 'No, not another A, not Amelia or Alicia or Annabel,' so they called the third child Bernice instead.

Angela, Anthea and Bernice. Anthea's sun was in Aries and Bernice's was in Taurus and all three were mid-signs, born respectively on the 3rd, 7th and 5th of their months, which kept their characters distinct and unneurotic, and not cuspal. People born as sun-signs change – as were the parents Mark and Molly – can veer uneasily from one nature to another. The transition from Gemini to Cancer is not easy, Gemini being so very undomestic and Cancer so very home-based.

Mark fell in love with a girl called Stella from Market Research. She was a Virgo. 'By name but not nature,' as Mark said to Stella in bed. He told Molly that was what he said to her in bed, because he confessed everything to Molly; everything, after a secretary at the office, a girl called Amantha, a Sagittarian, had telephoned Molly to say Mark was having an affair with Stella. Why did Amantha make such a phone-call? Perhaps, Molly thought, because she *was* a Sagittarian and quick on the telephone and swift to intervene in the cause of natural justice.

Molly wept for days and Mark tried to excuse himself for still more days. Or not so much to excuse, for these things happen, but to explain. Advertising was such a strange world, with strange values, and a strange language of its own, that he always felt ill at ease in it. He could not join in with the others, yet was doomed to live with them from ten to five every day. 'Or six, or seven, or eight, or even midnight,' mourned Molly. 'They work you so hard and pay you so little.'

She had forgiven him days ago. He could not forgive himself.

Their standards were not his: nor their world, as he would explain in the night hours when they lay awake, side by side. He belonged to Molly, and to Angela, Anthea and Bernice. They were *real*, as the world of advertising was not. It was just he had been away for the weekend at a Presentation and Stella had been there, and the hotel so bleak and unfriendly and he had missed his family so much.

'I understand, I understand –' said Molly. 'Let's just get to sleep. I have to get up at six.'

She did, too. She liked to spend her evenings with Mark, just sitting, while he recovered from his day, and that meant leaving the dinner dishes until morning: and as she also liked him to have breakfast in a tidy house with his children, clean and orderly, about him, that meant getting up at six, or even earlier. She was pleased enough to do it.

But Mark's moon was in conjunction with Mercury, and he did not stop explaining easily, once he had started, and in the mornings, long after the Stella episode had finished, she would be bleary-eyed and yawning.

But it had finished. Finally and for ever. Stella had moved to another agency. Sometimes the phone would ring and when Molly picked up the receiver no one answered. But why should that be Stella? These things did happen in a marriage. It had happened all the time to Molly's mother, when living with Molly's father. Molly resolved that her marriage would be strengthened by this assault upon its integrity, and not weakened by it.

She resolved this, not merely for her own sake but for that of Angela, Anthea and Bernice, and took care thereafter to be yet more loving, a still better wife. But the episode with Stella had clouded Molly's happiness, dulled her eyes a little, as the clouds had dulled the moon at the time that she was born. Mark seemed as bright-eyed as ever; well, that was how it went.

Molly had two terminations. There was not really the money for more children, or for the bigger house a larger family would demand. Molly and Mark talked about vasectomy, at the time when it was fashionable, but Molly thought she could not fancy a sterile man, and Mark said he'd be only too happy with a sterile woman, so Molly was sterilised instead. The sun was in opposition to the moon that day; but the operation went well enough.

On their mutual birthday, every year, Mark took Molly out to dinner at a Chinese restaurant and told her how much he loved her. She adored the extravagance, and being waited upon, and impractical food you did not even have to finish. She was shocked, year by year, to see how the cost of restaurant meals soared. So, of course, did the cost of fish fingers and baked beans which, over the years, supplemented by vitamin tablets, seemed to be the staple diet of Angela, Anthea and Bernice. But all three had Capricorn stuffed with rich and benefic plancts, so their lives could be expected to get better as they got older.

Every other year Mark would have to go off on a Presentation, or on a holiday cruise – for he was now account executive for a large travel agency and obliged to travel; journeys from which he would return pale with exhaustion and overwork and fretted by the company of capitalists and idiots. It was a pity that his promotion coincided with the nation's economic recession, and that there was as little money as ever.

Time passed. Molly's parents no longer seemed to loom so large in her life as once they had done, and she was obviously of as little importance as ever. Her mother's complaints reeled faintly into the heavens, and faded into nothingness somewhere out there amongst the stars. Her father no longer even bothered to send her a card at Christmas. Molly, if they remembered her at all, was someone from long ago, a gawky girl full of promise who had long since come to nothing, lost in a suburban street in a world stuffed as full of students as a haystack with straw. Molly no longer minded.

Then all of a sudden she and Mark were forty, and the girls were nine, eight and six, and it was 20 June, the sun was passing from Gemini to Cancer, and three surprising things happened.

Mark gave her a video-cassette recorder for her birthday.
'It must have cost hundreds!' she breathed.
'It's from the office,' he said. 'All the executives have them now: even the junior ones like me. Well, there has to be some recompense for the life we lead. Some danger money for our souls!' And he gave her a bunch of red roses as well, in love and gratitude. The real present. Molly gave Mark, that morning, a book on pond life – for she had built a pond in the garden with her own hands, digging out and cementing and lining, so that Mark could put tadpoles in it and grow frogs and feel nearer to the nature that he loved.

The second surprising thing was that Mark took the three girls to lunch at the office, so that she could have the day off, to do as she wanted. Wonderful! Well, he didn't take them actually *into* the office – not wanting, he said, to subject beings as tender and true as his daughters to the sordid glare of commercial life – but at least out to lunch at a French restaurant nearby.

The third surprising thing, even more surprising to Mark than to Molly (for he tried to eject them when they turned up) was a party from the office, who arrived in drunken hilarity, in three taxis, with champagne, to wish Mark a happy fortieth birthday, just as Mark and Molly were setting off for their Chinese restaurant.

Molly was quite excited. A party! She remembered thoughts of silken shifts and glittery shoes and lovers' glances across rooms, and realised how long it had been since they'd gone to a party, except up and down the street, where the dresses were Crimplene, the shoes came from Marks and Spencer and no one looked lovingly, except perhaps the man from the television rental, who seemed to eye her sometimes with a fleeting nod and wink.

The girls clambered out of bed, the baby-sitter accepted champagne from the tooth-mug, and a good time was had by all. Molly was amazed and gratified by how popular Mark seemed; how he underrates himself, she thought. And how well-heeled they look, she reflected, and imagined that perhaps they regarded her shabby home askance.

Yet how could they? Why should they? She and Mark had what they never could have. If they looked, it was with envy. The malefics fighting in the sky: Mars and Saturn.

They had brought Mark a tribute, they said. A cassette to mark his birthday, made by his colleagues, starring his colleagues. Mark protested, but champagne and bonhomie drowned his protests, and the cassette was slotted into the new video, with its green digital clock and the two dots beating, beating life and time away.

'We made it in the TV Department,' they cried. 'Makes a change from blue films, any day.'

Molly shivered with shock. She could believe it of them, suddenly. Trendy, phoney people, after all, seeking amusement, pushing experience to its ultimate ends, coming slumming down in her nice homely house, intruding where they were not wanted, where they had not been asked. Blue films! And Mark had taken the girls near the place, and she had been glad, selfishly, wanting a day off, just one day.

And there they were on the film, staring at themselves out of the telly. Wouldn't they be spoilt? Surely it was bad for them? Didn't these people care? 'Happy birthday, Daddy!' Yet they seemed so sweet: hand in hand, little mid-cuspians, with their sturdy natures, and their afflicted fourth Houses. The House of the Home.

But what was wrong with their home? Nothing. Astrology *must* be wrong. A false trail.

Then came a tribute from Mark's boss. The senior accounts executive. Red-faced, backed by a massive oil painting of ships at sea. He raised a glass to Mark. Was that the Boardroom? It was *enormous*. Mark's boss was jovial and drunk.
'Are we on camera? Yes? From one king newt to another,' he said, 'here's wishing Mark may the next forty years be as lively as the last! The day he came on the Board was the day I should have handed in my notice, and I didn't, and I haven't looked back, or at any rate, up from under the table, ever since! I daren't, because the Agency's gone from strength to strength and he's after my job. So here's to you, Mark, and may all your tots be doubles!'

The Board? Mark drinking? Mark never drank at work. He said it gave him a headache. He suffered from headaches in the morning, quite badly sometimes. And was somnolent in the evenings. But then many office workers were. Paperwork is a great strain, and dealing with people, and exercising judgments, and in general taking responsibility.

'Here's wishing you many happy returns, Mark,' said a gentle voice, and a simpering, willowy blonde bit her lip and stared out of the camera, 'and this is the best present I can give you. Just a look.' And she edged away a corner of her blouse until a portion of white breast showed, which she rapidly re-covered as the screen went blank and a great cheer went up from the audience.

'Put it away, Wendy! Put it away!'

Now another woman: older and darker and cleverer by far on the screen. Sleek and cross.

'Sod off, Mark,' she said, 'even if you are forty, you can't expect pity from me. I may feel different by August, of course.' And the screen went blank and cries of 'Good for Stella!' went up, and somebody screeched, 'Stella always waits 'til the last minute before she changes her mind.' And somebody else said, 'But just don't tell Amantha!'

Stella? Stella was supposed to have moved to another agency years ago. August? August was when Mark had to go on the bi-annual fact-finding cruise which bored him so. Molly looked over to where Mark leaned against the sideboard – bought eight years ago from the junk shop down the road. She thought he was avoiding her eyes. Well, of course he was.

He was smiling, slightly, a strange, far-away, rueful smile. He is Gemini, she thought, all Gemini. Which twin are you kissing? The one who loves you or the one who doesn't? The one who needs you, or the one who keeps you in reserve? The one who comes home to you, the half-life, to rest while gathering strength for the real life, the true life, the office life: of girls and excitement and power and drink?

Someone else smiled from the screen, now. A restaurateur. French. You could tell from the beret and the menu on the blackboard. Steak au poivre: £14.50. No, that must be a joke. Surely. That was the price of the whole birthday once-a-year celebration Chinese meal.

'Now from the lips of the man whom single-handed Mark has made rich,' sang the commentator, half on screen, half off, for the cameraman seemed to be drunk too, 'Monsieur Victor himself. Sing Happy Birthday, Monsieur Victor.' Monsieur Victor shuffled and grinned and looked embarrassed and could not sing. 'Please,' begged the commentator, 'to the greatest gourmet of them all, to Mark, the man who loves smoked halibut by the pound, and Chablis by the crate! To Mark, on his fortieth birthday!' And the picture crumbled into confusion and laughter and suddenly a few of the guests were looking at Molly as if realising what they had done, and Molly was leaning against the wall, in the Indian kaftan she had ironed and loved and looked forward to, and which now seemed absurd.

The television screen leapt into life again. Now it was a young man with a blond moustache, raising a glass and saying, 'Until I met Mark I never knew that advertising and dirty weekends were synonymous, so happy birthday, Mark, king of the con-men,' and someone abruptly switched off the set and the party evaporated with nervous smiles and cries of, 'Surprise over,' and Mark and Molly were left together, with Angela, Anthea and Bernice, up far beyond their bedtime, flinging their arms around their father, crying, 'Happy birthday, Daddy! Happy birthday, Daddy dear. Oh, and Mummy too, of course!'

The School Run

You know what it's like in the country. Too many roosters strutting round too many farmyards surrounded by adoring hens: too many bellowing bulls mounting too many grateful cows: too much soft-eyed female acquiescence and too much glittery male pride, too many females being chosen and males choosing to allow you to believe, as is possible in the city, that nature can be subdued and men and women made equal. The lesson from nature is too extreme to be ignored, and that, in my opinion, is why the villages hereabouts buzz with destructive scandal, and adultery, suicide, self-mutilation, incest, rape and murder are common occurrences, and cities are, by comparison, sane and peaceful places.

My name is Judith. I come from the city. I am thirty-four. My husband is ill with asthma, which is why we moved down here. We have two children, Colleen and Kieron. We live opposite Ranstrock Farm, in a nice little old sub-Georgian house, rather cheap because it's near the main road. It's a rather new road, carving through the Ranstrock acres. We tend to live in a cloud of pesticide but never mind: the meadows are wonderfully green and lush and fertile. My husband makes architectural models – you know, those miniatures of new hospitals, new schools, new urban centres and so on, which serve to get commissions for architects and go on display to soothe the local inhabitants when it's obvious that change is neither wanted nor needed, but is going to happen.
(Round here I'm described as cynical and am not particularly welcome at the WI, because sometimes their cakes make me laugh. There is a certain Mrs Leaf, who uses at least a teaspoon of green colouring and at least a teaspoon

of orange colouring in her icing, not a drop or two like other people, and when I start laughing, so does everyone else, which is half a relief, half terrifying, because once we start, when will we ever stop? Zen must come to Easter Dundon – our village – too, in the end. Nothing's safe. We all know it, but they'd prefer to put it off for a bit, not welcome it, like me. So I get labelled cynical.)

My husband is what you would describe as a craftsman, and I am what you would describe as a craftsman's wife.

Craftsmen's wives are on the whole good-looking, stable and reasonable. We wear well. Our husbands, after all, are not indifferent to appearance and have an eye for quality, and a weakness for a bit of gloss. They are practical men: they know they will never be rich but will always be *right*, and choose accordingly. They are often overtly gentle men, with anger and envy running in strong torrents beneath. But they love and are loved and are usually faithful. Their wives develop strong and fairly idiosyncratic views of their own, a kind of inner fortress within the outer defences of the craftsman's view of the world. Craftsmen tend to despise the world, because, being genuinely sensitive, they can't quite cope with it.

Artists' wives, if I may digress, have a far harder time. If your daughter must go to Art School, never let her do a Fine Art course. The young male artists are all waiting there to pounce, and pounce one will. Then watch her turn from some slim, bright, energetic girl into Saskia washing-up at Rembrandt's sink, soft, plump-armed, doe-eyed, bare-footed, serving the Artist who serves Art. Art is a convenient mistress for any man. He can drink, beat, steal, fornicate, commit any number of domestic cruelties and excesses in Her name. It's expected. And when your artist has sucked his Saskia dry and turned the corners of her smiling mouth from up to down, he throws her out and, if he can, finds another plumper, less currently weepy one. The process can take years, and a handful of children.

Want to sleep? Your artist wants to wake. Want to work – no – his retrospective's coming up. Want the baby? No – terminate! How can he paint if he can't sleep? *Don't* want a baby? Then you must have one – how can he live with the sterility you impose upon him? Want to eat? No, he wants to drink. And so must you, daughter, you must want what he wants, for you must serve Art too. But Art's a faithless mistress; pity the Artist: he only uses you as he is used. Serve Her as he may, drink, batter, carouse, fornicate at Her bidding, she'll turn her back in the end. Many, many are called, and few are chosen. Many have the symptoms of genius, but very few have the disease itself, and those that do probably look and behave like bank-clerks, and never even realised they were Artists.

(Bank-clerks as husbands are another story. I'll tell it some time.)

Farmers' wives – ah, farmers' wives. Sandra Jephsen lives across the way in Ranstrock Farm. At the Carnival Party last year Geoffrey Jephsen, cock of his dungheap, swaggering young farmer, Sandra's husband, owner of Ranstrock Farm and its three hundred acres, as was his father, his grand-father and his great-grandfather before him, let his eye light on me, and now I love him.

Sandra Jephsen has thin fair hair and a timid eye, fleshy legs and a gentle manner. A proper farmyard female, just right for Geoffrey, who glitters and glistens with male sweat and energy, and has muscles which move beneath the skin as if they had their own separate existence: as if it were they which made love, not he. I know that, I know all that; I don't care.

What does he see in her, when he could have me? I have long slim legs and sharp brown eyes and look and feel a bit like Shirley MacLaine.

He didn't want to marry her, he didn't choose her. He married her because she was a Fenton and the Fenton Farm's two hundred acres verge on to Ranstrock Farm, and that's the way things are done round here: a Jephsen and a Fenton sacrificed, so that two half-acre fields can become one one-acre field and the ploughing made easier. The old order continues alongside the new. They have two pale little children, more Fenton than Jephsen. I'm surprised she managed to impose her genes upon them at all, she has so little will, so little energy. She knows about me: I know she does. We take our cars out at the same time each morning – on the school run. Our children go to the same school, five miles down the road. She looks at me with her sad, pale eyes and looks the other way and I know she knows, and I don't care.

I let her go first, I drive behind her, rather too close. I like her to know I'm there. I know it's cruel, but I don't care about that either. I see her eyes in the mirror, looking back at me if she has to stop and I pull up just behind her. My father was an artist, my mother killed herself (at any rate she died when I was twelve; that's how I interpret it. Suicide or second-hand murder). When *he* died last year there were two hundred canvases in the attic. He'd sold three when he was twenty-six, and nothing since. Nothing. Perhaps I inherit his cruelty? I burnt them all. I and my sister, we presided over the death of his life. It was a wonderful bonfire. Crackle crackle! My husband Roy was shocked. He doesn't like to see anything die that lives. He doesn't like to see Art, Craft's big sister, insulted. I think he changed his view of me a little, then. But how can I tell what's happening between him and me? It's all one-way now, in any case. I love Geoffrey. I've forgotten Roy. I would drive whey-faced Sandra off the road, if I dared, which I so nearly do. Except for the children, in the cars; for this is the school run.

Five miles to school there and back in the morning, and the same again in the afternoon. That's a hundred miles in a school week.

'It's crazy,' says Roy. 'Why don't you and Sandra Jephsen get together and organise something?'

'I like doing it,' I say. She sometimes manages to elude me on the way home, but there I am in the morning, always, falling in just behind her. Well, the children do have to be at school on time. She's not a bad driver.

They closed our village school at the beginning of the year: it was either put the children on the school bus to Polydock Junior, which has a low reputation, or do the hundred weekly miles to Pennyham and back. How was I to know Sandra would choose Pennyham, too? I'm surprised she cares. I'm surprised she can tell a good school from a bad school. I can. I'm a real PTA type. Geoffrey says so.

Geoffrey said so, nuzzling my ear in the back of his Range Rover, my skirt rucked up and tearing, caught on the door handle, with the dogs snuffling and uneasy outside. It's quick, sudden, farmyard and violent with Geoffrey, not slow and gentle and peaceful and reverential as it is with Roy. Roy talks to me while he makes love, admires my body, looks after my feelings, goes on patiently till I'm satisfied: Geoffrey doesn't care about me, only about him. He loves me, in so far as he loves me, and while it lasts, for the sexual pleasure I give him. That's all. Geoffrey says things like, 'what a little slut you are,' or, 'if I were your husband I'd throw you out,' or, if I say I have to go, because of the children, 'what a real little Miss PTA you are!' And then his teeth will nip my ear so I cry out and I don't go until he's finished, and the children wait at the school gate and

I don't care. I love him. Sandra Jephsen collects hers on time, poor thing.

Why does he want her, standing in his kitchen, mashing the potatoes for his supper with her pale suffering eyes? He could have me.

I wonder if Roy knows. I don't care about that, either. He'd never have the courage to leave me. He loves me, he does what I say. He's weak. He's not strong. Geoffrey is strong, and so am I. Roy should have Sandra; I'm sure they'd suit each other.

Roy's asthma is worse down here in the country, not better. I used to feel for his wheezing and gasping – now I despise it. I'm never ill. He's half Geoffrey's size; he is really quite a small man, now I look at him. Is it really a man's job, to sit day after day gluing tiny scraps of wood together? And not even to his own design, but to someone else's? He says that really he's a cabinet-maker, but he can't keep a family on that, so he has to do this. Compromise! I say I'd go out to work happily enough, even gratefully, but how would the children get to school? Roy doesn't drive. He has one of those peculiar disabilities which mean if you see a large object coming – like a truck – you drive into it, not away from it. A disability driving instructors fear, for there is no curing it. Or so Roy says. I wonder. I wonder about all kinds of things, since my father died, since I started this affair with Geoffrey. No, I didn't start it. Geoffrey did. We live in the country, after all, and the cock looks round the hens, and thinks, I'll have that one this morning, that pretty little feathered thing; and so he does.

We ought to move back to the city, where there's less pollen to fuel Roy's asthma, and I can get a job, and the children can catch buses. But I can't live without seeing Geoffrey. Not now. I would itch so much with desire I'd scratch myself to death and end up like my mother. Gone. When we part he says 'see you round,' but he never says how or where or when. He doesn't like me to be secure. I just know that somehow we see each other at least twice a week: I'm out looking for mushrooms or blackberries, or he just happens to be driving his Range Rover through Polydock when I'm shopping; and once I knocked on his door when I knew she was out and he was in, because I can see everything from my window, and he had me on the bed, his and her bed, her side, and then said, 'don't ever do that again', so I didn't. It's don't-ring-me-I'll-ring-you land we're living in. But he rings me. He does.

What do I do now, how do I get him, how do I make him leave her and take me? He can have me with or without the children. Roy can have those. My life can't go on with Roy for ever, humdrum and without passion. I shall never love anyone now but Geoffrey: the sheer power of my loving must make him love me: my hate for her will make her ill and make her old and die, and then he'll need someone to look after the children, and I'll be there. Roy doesn't need me: he's married to his architectural models.

Geoffrey took me to the tea-rooms at Pennyham today, for all the world to see.
'I'd love a cup of tea,' he said, on the hay in the big barn, withdrawing himself from me, leaving me all a-shudder as usual with unfulfilled desire, but all the better to remember him by and all the more eager next time. 'This is thirsty work,' he said, and we went to the Golden Goose and had tea and scones; and there was a dark-haired girl serving who went quite pale and shaky at the sight of him and me. You know how it is, you know: someone else's husband flirting with you, the wife's sitting opposite trying not to notice, you wait for the quick flicker of anxious eyes before deciding that's it, that's enough, and moving on. This was more than a quick flick and an anxious look; it was a white,

open-mouthed stare, and I had no intention of moving on, not for Sandra, not for her, not for anyone.
'Who's that?' I asked.
'That's Ellen,' he said, 'that's last year's model. Don't worry.'

I didn't worry. I took his hand to my mouth and held it there, for all the world to see. She fled to the kitchen. She was only a waitress; not worth a half of me. I didn't care who saw, and neither did he. All the world!

He ate his scone with big delicate fingers, big delicate fingers with which he paddled in me, and Sandra passed by outside and because we were sitting at the table by the window she saw us, and she came in and just stood by the table, in her headscarf, windcheater and clumsy leather boots. She reminded me of my mother. I have a photograph of her, standing just like that, on an autumn day, taken unawares. 'What's the matter with you?' he said to her. 'I can't be in here seeing Ellen, can I, because here I am having tea with Judith from across the way! You two really ought to get together some time over the school run. A hundred miles a week!'

She looked at me and I looked at her, and I smiled and she wept and ran from the room, and all the customers, the neighbours and the distant relatives, for that's what it's like in the country, turned and stared.

'Eat up,' he said. 'One thing in all the world I can't bear and that's a jealous woman.'

I'm winning, I thought, I'm winning. She will die from grief and his displeasure, and I shall be queen in her place, as is only right and fitting.

It was time to collect the children from school, and when he'd quietly finished his tea he allowed me to go. My thighs were agreeably bruised and sore. He didn't make love to her, not any more. He'd said so.

'Marriage is for the procreation of children,' he'd said. 'And that's been seen to, after all. What you marry and what you fancy, they're two different things.' He had a low, deep, soft voice. It caressed when it wanted to, bullied when it chose. What it said was what I believed.

I let her collect her children first from the school gate, and drive away. Then my Colleen and Kieron got in the back of my car. I don't let them in the front. It's safer in the back. I'm a nervous driver. My mother was killed in a car-crash, after all. She'd had a row with my father in the morning, and died in the afternoon. The whole house would shake with their rows. I was on her side, but hated her for not being happy all the same, and then I hated her for being dead, for making everything impossible: for example, that I could never make her happy. I promised the children ice-cream. I was alive and exultant; the sun was sinking. The autumn landscape was sodden and green and wonderful, multi-shadowed. There are lots of little hills round here, and sudden valleys and sudden views. Even when mad with love the beauty of it all impinges upon me.

I drove along the ridge-road, the A561, not crowding Sandra at all. I could afford to be kind. He had claimed me in public, and disclaimed her. The A561 was the main road between two small towns – not quite wide enough for the traffic it had to carry, always part closed for roadworks as they took out a curve here, or widened there, trying by half measures to make what was dangerous safe, and only half succeeding.

It was Carnival time: the time when floats from all over the West Country – which have taken their creators a year to devise, make and render mobile – gather in Bridgwater to begin their magical mystery tour of the West, and this road was one of the main routes along which these fantastical rolling monsters travelled. They would sometimes take up almost the entire width of the road, to the great handicap of the traffic and the great delight of Kieron and Colleen. As I rounded the sharp corner into the outskirts of Shillingford I found the road blocked. Before my eyes a petrol tanker was skewing and slipping one way across the road, a carnival float, an orange and green balsa wood and foam monster, fifty feet high, mounted on a long trailer, surrounded by pink polystyrene dwarves, and towed by a tractor, was skewing the other. The monster toppled on top of the tanker. The tractor tipped on its nose in someone's front garden; the tanker's cab tipped into the stone wall on the other side. The back of the tanker mounted the back of the trailer. The single car between me and this major traffic event jammed on its brakes. So did I. The car in front was Sandra's. I went into the back, but only slightly. Even so, my car being old and hers new, her crumple zone crumpled dramatically. My children squealed – I could see hers bobbing about in the back, presumably squealing too. I saw her eyes, pale and anxious with something other than wifely martyrdom, in the mirror. I saw men running away from the accident: the trailer driver somehow out of his cab, on to the wall, away. Fire! I thought, and I knew she thought it too. I restarted the engine, backed as fast as I could, which was very, very fast, and she followed. The children, catching fear, were suddenly dead silent. I gave her room to turn, then turned myself; a neat, rapid, three-point turn which any driving instructor would have admired, though in a place to turn him pale, on a blind corner.

But, listen, I looked after her and her children too. I was the opposite of murderous, when it came to it. We were both round the corner when the tanker went up and the green and orange balsa and foam giant too, in a black stench of flame and fire, which – as I found out later – by some great good fortune killed no one. Fathers were not yet home from work: mothers were on the school run, or walking. Shillingford has the misfortune to be a fraction under three miles from both Pennyham and Pollydock, which means the local authority won't pay for a school bus. (I'm sorry about these names, but if you live round here you have to put up with the truly unbelievable. If people who live in towns tend to believe the country has been invented for their benefit, it is hardly surprising.) Three houses were burned to the ground that day and new rules were laid down for carnival floats and the movement of same that very week.

We took the long, difficult way round to Polydock, and home, over the levels. We didn't have to speak. She just smiled briefly, as I let her pass and go first. She knew the way home: I didn't. I followed behind, but meekly, not harassing. My hands were trembling on the wheel. Fear shakes you back into sanity.

I can't tell you how beautiful the evening was, or the little wet leafy roads, between the tall, tall hedges. If a hedge is high and the road runs low between them, you know the road is old, has been there for ever, or at any rate since people started wanting to get from one place to another, and this was always the best and shortest way to do it. Even Kieron, seldom moved by natural glory, said, 'doesn't it all look nice,' and Colleen said, 'don't say *anything*. We'll have a crash,' and the last rays of sunlight glittered and caught in the gold leaves of the beech trees as they formed an arch above us, and Sandra's car went on ahead, showing the way.

As the sky darkened, the light from the blaze over in the east was pierced by orange and green streaks. It reminded me of Mrs Leaf's funny cakes, the ones I shouldn't laugh at, and of my father's paintings, going up in smoke – he'd used a lot of green and orange, and painted very, very thickly, which meant very expensively, and my mother had complained about that, which I'd thought was unfair of her. A man had to paint what a man had to paint. If I'd gone harder into the back of Sandra's car, who would have been killed, her or me? Probably both of us. In my mind it had always been her, and I'd always been safe.

I knew it was all nonsense. Of course Geoffrey slept with her. (Why shouldn't he: she was there, and he wasn't so very fussy as to who he entered, or where, or how.) He had no intention of leaving her, was just acting rooster in the farmyard, and it was my fault for letting him; not his fault for doing it, or her fault for being hurt by it, if fault lay anywhere, which I doubted. I'd be last year's model too, soon enough, when my own marriage was sufficiently mangled to make him feel properly effective, properly seigneur of the lands round about. We were living in what had been the bailiff's home. No doubt his father had had it off with the bailiff's wife, and his father's father with her mother, and then they'd all stood round and watched the bull mounting the cows, and felt truly part of nature.

A pink flare leapt in the sky. One of the dwarves, I supposed. Even this far away, with the car windows closed, you could smell burning. Sandra switched on her headlights, and I switched on mine.

So I loved him, and that was partly animal, the good part, and partly full of hate, the bad part; and all mixed up with him preferring Sandra to me, and my mother's death and my father's paintings and the bonfire I had made, and shouldn't have, and I had hardly been sane since then.

All I could do now, by going on, was hurt her more. It was true that if it wasn't me it would be someone else. There were a dozen women thereabouts, bored and on the school run, who'd wrap their thighs round his, as excitedly, as

desperately, as marvellously, as me. We all think we're
something special, I daresay; men certainly do! It had just
better not be me that did it. Let it be someone single, more
purely victim. I loved him to hurt her, and it was demeaning
to all of us.

She skidded on leaves and went into the ditch. I stopped.
We all got out, and surveyed the damage. She said nothing.
'I think it's a bit too hot for me to handle round here,' I
said. 'We'll be selling the house very soon.'
'Going back to the city?' She had a slightly nasal voice, and
I had a flash of the old arrogant contempt, but another
explosion, violet this time, brought me back to my senses.
She was just ordinary. So was I. So was he. So were my
parents – he and she, no different from many of our friends,
only writ large on the canvas of a child's mind, by reason
of her early death, and never properly reduced by time and
experience and understanding to ordinary size.
'I should think so,' I said. 'All this driving about, just to
get the children to school. It's different for you; you belong
here.'
'Don't sell the house without telling Geoffrey,' she said. 'I
think he wants it back. It used to belong to the farm.'

It occurred to me, briefly, that if he'd been trying to get me
out, this was the right way to go about it, but I don't really
credit him with quite so much duplicity. Of course it might
have been unconscious on his part. He came from noble
baron stock, after all.

We didn't mention Geoffrey, apart from in the role of
possible house-buyer. We didn't have to. She recognised
an abdication when she heard one, and accepted it gra-
ciously. She had always been the rightful queen.

We pushed and levered her car back on to the road. She
drove off, I followed. She went into her big house, I into my

own lesser one. Roy looked up from a model of a new Canadian university he'd been working on for some months. He had trouble placing so many fir trees.

'So there you all are,' he said. 'I was worried. Some sort of accident on the road. There was a newsflash on local radio.'

'Here we all are,' I said. 'Safe, sound, and back to normal.' I made tea.

'I've been a bit mad since my father died,' I said to him in bed that night.

'I know,' he said. 'Hell-bent on destruction.'

'I think we'd better move back to the city,' I said. 'As soon as possible.'

'Anything you say,' he said, and an unkind person might have thought he was unduly passive, but I knew that he only waited for me to say what was in his mind, when I eventually came round to it, thus saving time, argument and energy.

Who?

Howard had trouble remembering names. Faces were easy enough, especially if in a familiar setting, but putting a name to that face was often quite beyond him.

It seemed a minor enough fault in an otherwise pleasant and agreeable man – a good father and a good husband, doing well in his chosen sphere of business. A secretary and a card index helped him with the names of his customers, and if the names of his neighbours on their executive estate sometimes eluded him it was perhaps hardly surprising. 'We're all so alike, that's what it is,' said his wife, Alice, a little sadly. She felt herself to be unexceptional, and sometimes wished it were not so. 'Try to cook something new for dinner – like liver and avocado – and you find the whole estate's done the same thing, on the same day!'

Howard was thirty-eight, broad-shouldered, fair, not particularly tall, not exceptionally good-looking, but presentable enough. He was Area Sales Manager (North-West) for a firm which made agricultural machinery. Alice was four years younger, plump, short, with carroty red hair and a freckled, everyday kind of face, and legs she preferred to hide. They had three children – Samantha, Thomasina and Sylvester – shortened, of necessity, to Sam, Tom and Silv. Howard sometimes couldn't remember their names, either. He offered, as an excuse, the notion that the sex change which went with each abbreviation was enough to confuse anyone.

'Perhaps you should put their names on your card index,' said Alice, a little tartly. 'Or perhaps you should try and spend more time with them, and a little less in the office, or at the pub.'

Well, everyone complains. Little hurts and reticences pass between couples and get swallowed up in the great flood of togetherness. Alice and Howard were happy enough, and so were their children until, one day, when they had been twelve years married, Howard went to the doctor to complain of recurrent headaches, met the doctor's wife Elaine, and fell in love.

Elaine was bending over the T–Z section of the filing cabinet when Howard came up to the desk. He coughed; she turned, straightened, and as she came up looked him full in the eye. Neither smiled – their regard was intensely serious – and in those few moments the lives of both changed. It was as if, they told each other later, they recognised each other. That is to say, they knew in advance what was to come: how they were to move into the light, leaving others in the shadows.

When she had filled in the appointment he required he said, 'Can I see you after work? It's our wedding anniversary, so it can't be for long, but never mind.'
She replied, 'Of course. I'll tell my husband I've gone to see a friend.'

He knew she would accept; she knew he would ask. Neither felt obliged to tell lies to each other, only to the rest of the world. And what a delightful conspiracy that turned out to be – the mixture of agony and excitement, shame and thrill. Alice believed lies, and Elaine's husband Brian accepted excuses. Two lovers, pitted against the world, fighting for light, the escape from the dark. Love at first sight – full, powerful, sexual, forbidden love!
'We were destined,' said Elaine.
'Two halves of one whole,' said Howard, 'that somehow got split.'

They slept together the day after they first met.

'Will you come to bed with me?' Howard asked, quite straightforwardly.
'Of course,' she had replied.
They went to an hotel for the night. He said he was away on business: she said she was visiting a friend.
'This isn't lust,' he said, halfway through the night. 'It's love.'
'I know,' she said. She was taller than he was, with large dark eyes and a soft, tremulous mouth.

There seemed nothing they couldn't do, or shouldn't, and everything they wanted to do, with the light on and their eyes open.
'I've never known anything like this before,' he said.
'Neither have I,' she said.

And yet they were just two quite ordinary people, not particularly beautiful, or romantically inclined, or given to this kind of behaviour. Howard had been unfaithful once or twice, but discretely; Elaine, never. Nor did custom diminish their attraction for one another. The more they had, the more they wanted. The more they knew, the more there was to discover.

And how they talked! They could say anything to each other, without fear of being thought foolish. Every detail of their individual lives they could hand over to the other, in the knowledge of safe-keeping.

And every moment they were apart was terrible: restless, scratchy, miserable – they were addicts deprived of their drug.

As for Alice, Sam, Tom and Silv, and Brian, William and Frosty – they inhabited a dim world, where people mouthed and gaped and spoke words which could not be heard.

'Perhaps I'd better label the children,' said Alice, sadly. 'They're beginning to feel quite upset. And Howard, you're looking so pale! They work you too hard.'

'We can't go on like this,' said Howard to Elaine. 'It isn't fair to anyone.'

'We have to be together,' said Elaine to Howard. 'Surely they'll understand.' Elaine had confessed to Howard that she'd never really loved her sons, not as she felt a mother ought. Now she understood why. She had never really loved their father Brian. She'd liked him well enough, and found him not unattractive, and felt safe in his company, and mistaken these feelings for love. Were she to have children with Howard, how different her feelings would be! As it was, William and Frosty would be better off with Brian. Wouldn't they?

Her mother had gone off and left her when she was eight, and the neighbours had been very shocked – as they wouldn't be these days. It happened all the time – but that was about all. She, Elaine, had been happy enough to be left with her father; she was all right now, wasn't she? So would the boys be, and do Brian good to have a taste of what she'd been putting up with without any help from him all these years. No; no one would suffer – except her, as usual. She'd miss the boys, of course she would, far more than they'd miss her. But they'd come and visit.

'I can't go on living a lie,' said Howard to Elaine. 'It's not fair to Alice for me to go on living with her, when I'm in love with you. I love Alice: she's done nothing wrong: she's been a good wife and mother within her lights – but I'm in love with you.'

Within her lights! What a dim, feeble glimmer they gave off, compared to the incandescent flame that was Elaine.

She would close his eyes with her lips, and his whole inner world be ablaze with light and certainty.

He thought it was best to do it suddenly: simply not to come home one day, but leave a letter to be found later. It would save arguments, recriminations, bitterness.
'I don't think I'm being cowardly,' he said to Elaine. 'I just think it's the best way. Of course she's going to be upset, and I'm truly sorry. But, you know, she never asked me if I wanted children. She just assumed I did, and went ahead and had them.'
'Poor Howard! There seemed to be so little communication between you and your wife,' lamented Elaine, and already she used the past tense. That was the weekend before the notes were left and the new life started.

They didn't like to plan too much. Somehow it took away from the magic of everything. All the world loves a lover, and the gods help those who help themselves, and destiny was on their side – matters of mortgages and money and matrimonial homes would sort themselves out in time.

They left their notes, packed suitcases, and went off to a hotel in Blackpool, where they toasted their future in champagne.

'He'll have to get a relief receptionist and pay her a proper wage,' said Elaine, 'and that's going to upset him more than anything.'

'I think her mother will understand,' said Howard. 'She gave up everything for love, after all.'

Alice's mother, as a girl, had been to Dartington Hall (a fee-paying school for the children of the musical intelligentsia) but eloped from there, at the age of sixteen, with a long-distance truck driver. (Alice, rather disappointingly, after all that, had inherited her father's looks and temperament.) Alice's mother had once said to Howard, 'The reason you can't remember names is because you don't believe in anyone else's reality, only your own,' and Howard had felt there might be some truth in it, and had wanted to discuss it with Alice, but she'd been changing a nappy.

Alice's mother didn't understand. Nor did Alice's father, or Alice's children Sam, Tom and Silv. Nor did Alice. No one seemed to understand true love.

Alice went to their solicitor and had their joint bank account stopped, and rang up his boss at headquarters, and would even have got through to Howard himself had he not sweet-talked the switchboard girl. (She'd been one of the discrete infidelities: the only thing he ever kept from Elaine – who now owned his heart, his soul, his future.)

A private detective turned up at the Blackpool hotel and Howard and Elaine were asked to leave.
Howard marvelled.
'The institution of marriage is an amazing thing,' he said. 'Everyone cheats on it, but defy it openly, as we did, and see how the ranks close. Solicitors, bank managers, employers, hotel-keepers – all turn against the hapless renegades.'

But he thought all was well lost for love of Elaine.
'Look here,' said his boss, 'I hear you've been taking this woman round the farms, on business trips. And not just leaving her in the car but taking her round the fields, holding hands, that kind of thing.'
'We're in love,' said Howard. Somehow the simplicity of it all rang slightly false.
'I don't want anyone disloyal on my staff,' said the boss. 'And this is what this is. Rank, heartless, disloyalty to a good wife. I'm very fond of Alice.'

He'd come to dinner once, saying 'take no trouble, please.'
Alice had served rabbit, which he couldn't eat, being an
Australian, but he seemed to have forgiven her. At any rate
he fired Howard.

Howard responded by threatening to sue under the Unfair
Dismissal laws, but Elaine dissuaded him.
'We'd have our names in the paper,' she said. 'It wouldn't
be fair to the children.'

Elaine had telephoned Brian, just to see how the boys were,
but he'd put the phone down on her. She'd called round to
collect a few things but he'd shut the door in her face and
a neighbour told her, anyway, all her possessions were down
on the rubbish dump, being picked over by all and sundry.
Brian had put them there.
'So it really has to be a new life,' Elaine said.
'Of course,' said Howard.

They held hands all the way down to London.
'How wonderful,' said Howard. 'Journeys used to seem so
long; now they seem so short.'

They felt alive: felt their own selves both within the other
and within their own bodies. There were no children to
deflect emotion and delay response, or spoil the strange
stillness that sometimes hovered in the air between them,
as if the whole universe watched and waited, attending the
joining of two bodies. Momentous! Love at first sight. True
love!

They took a room in London and were surprised and rather
aggrieved by the rent demanded, and by the dinginess of
the street. Elaine feared lead poisoning. But she got a clerical
job in an estate agency next to the Underground station.
She was older than the other girls, and felt strange without

the protection of her wedding ring, and shocked by the language they used.

'They're so crude,' she complained to Howard. 'I feel quite sorry for them. They can't know what sex is like or love is all about, or they wouldn't talk about it the way they do.'

Howard applied for thirty-two jobs and got none of them. Well, there was a recession. Alice, contacted by letter, declined to sell the grandfather clock and send Howard the proceeds via a poste-restante address as he suggested.

'It's my clock,' he observed to Elaine. 'She is nothing but a heartless, mercenary bitch.'

'We have each other,' she said, her leg warm and soft across his, at night. 'And you'll get a job soon and we can live on my money until you do.'

Alice's uncle, of all people, managed to trace Howard and turned up to reproach him, and demand money, almost with menaces.

'People amaze me,' said Howard, having sent him away with a flea in his ear. 'Anyone would think we were back in the fifties! What is marriage, after all, but a scrap of paper? Surely these days it's recognised that a man has a right to fulfil his emotions – to follow his destiny through?'

Elaine, having few people to chat to, confided her story to the landlady. True love plus sacrifice – equals real romance! Surely?

'Five children between you!' was all the landlady said, disappointingly. Then she gave them notice. They humped their suitcases to another similar room. It didn't really make a great deal of difference which end of the street they looked out on, and in fact the bed in the new place was a little wider, and a little less squeaky.

'It's all right for Alice,' said Howard, signing on at the Job Centre. 'She can stay snug and secure in the matrimonial house and live off social security because she's got the kids. But a man has to labour for the rest of his life and pay out God knows what in stamps, and never see a penny return.'

Did God know what? Perhaps. Elaine telephoned Howard from work to find out how he'd got on at the Job Centre.
'Darling!' she said.
'Who's that?' he asked.
'Elaine, of course,' she replied.
'Who did you say?'
'Elaine.'
There was a silence. Then –
'Oh, sorry, darling. I was dreaming.'

Nevertheless it had been said, and was the beginning of the end. He knew that she knew, and she knew that he knew, and so forth, that although love flowed out of him, freely and passionately, it was the love itself that mattered, and not the object of the love. They were both, when it came to it, strangers to each other.

Oh Mary Don't You Cry Any More

'We live in Paradise,' said Shirley to her two girls, Gracey and Lisa. 'Paradise! There is so much to be grateful for.'

Gracey and Lisa went barefoot, not from poverty, or ignorance, or lack of shoe-leather, but because the climate was good and feet grow better unconfined by shoes.

'The original inhabitants did well enough without shoes,' remarked Shirley. 'If they didn't need them, why should you?'

The aborigines, the first Tasmanians! 'But they're dead, all dead horribly, and narrow and tall and black besides, and Lisa and I are alive, and plump and small and white, and the pebbles feel sharp between our toes,' Gracey sometimes almost said, but never did, for Shirley's sake.

Gracey and Lisa wore well-washed denim trews which showed their pretty bodies to advantage, Shirley said, and simple blouses and their hair grew long and thick.

'You don't have to spend much on girls,' said Shirley. 'Not if everyone pulls together. And it's wonderful what you can pick up second-hand down at the market, or by swapping with friends. It's years since we've been into a clothes shop.'

Lisa's eyes were perhaps a little narrow, her face a little pinched, as if the world squeezed in upon her rather hard. Well, she was two years younger than Gracey and had spent proportionally longer without a father. Gracey's eyes opened wider and wider as she grew, facing life unafraid, Shirley said, welcoming experience. Gracey's mouth grew softer and fuller as puberty neared, not tighter and narrower, as often happened to the girls on the mainland, where the ground baked and the hot dry air sucked softness out of the soul. This was Tasmania – Paradise, as Shirley said. No wonder Gracey was such a beauty.

'The girls and I have fun,' said Shirley, 'we really do! Who needs money? The beach is free and the sun and the air, and the people are so wonderfully kind. Life is what you make it!'

She would laugh, wryly, at the turn of fate which had led her into exile with her engineer husband.

'If a husband has to leave you with two young girls to support, then he'd better do it in Tasmania, rather than anywhere else in the world.'

No one was surprised when he left: Shirley was into yoga rather than working, playing the guitar rather than ironing shirts, and left him at home looking after the girls while she went to meetings and lectures and mind-expansion groups.

'Just because you've brought me here to the end of the earth,' she'd say, in those days, 'there is no need for my mind to sink back into it.'

She'd give him books to read but he did not understand why there was any necessity to read them. He didn't live in his head a minute longer than he had to. He loved squash, and bush-walking, and beer.

'I don't love him,' she'd weep to her friends. 'It was a terrible mistake. We are just not suited.'

Presently, she found someone she thought she was suited to, and flew to the mainland for a secret weekend, but that was a mistake too, and her husband found out, and felt it was the last straw, and she was too proud to persuade him that it wasn't, and he left.

Now he lived in Melbourne; he'd found someone else: he sent money back every fortnight, but he'd never been generous: the air-fares were terrible; he hardly ever saw the girls. He had a new baby son.

'We have each other,' said Shirley, 'Shirley and Gracey and Lïsa, strong against the world! Not that we have to be strong, the world is a friendly place. If you smile at it, it smiles at you! What I really mean is, united *with* the world!'

Shirley meant the girls to grow up positive and optimistic. If she'd made a mistake – well, two mistakes, first in marrying their father, secondly, in leaving him – her children weren't going to suffer for it.

How they laughed and sang about the house, all three of them! Shirley played the guitar. 'Where have all the young men gone?'

The sun shone in the summertime, over Paradise: in the evenings the wall of Mount Wellington hung deep blue over the town, in the mornings, if you were up on time, stretching sleepy eyes, it was greyish pink.

'It's a wall to protect us,' said Shirley, but Gracey wasn't so sure. Did the mountain protect, or threaten? Gracey had been up to the other side. It was scrubby and bare and like the moon. It was inhuman: it didn't like her or like anyone. One day it would shrug and shake all Hobart into the sea, and not think twice about it. There were ghosts in Hobart. Horrible things happened. A man climbed into a water tank to escape a bush-fire and was boiled alive. A sea captain ran his ship into the harbour bridge and a piece just fell out as if it was made of Lego and everyone who happened to be on it was killed. There was a beach where the first settlers had tied the aborigines to stakes and waited for the sea to rise and drown them.

'Paradise!' sang Shirley, to now efficient guitar chords. She'd scraped and saved and raised the money to pay for classes. Gracey went to dancing lessons once a week.

'So we don't have a freezer, or a car in the garage, but we have each other, girls, and good friends!'

The sun beat on the little clapboard house and the rain drummed on the tin roof, and gaps widened. The friends of Shirley's youth, the witnesses to her mistake, were married to husbands who were growing richer year by year. These days they brought champagne to picnic lunches on the beach: they got themselves trained and found part-time jobs. They looked uneasy when Shirley brought out her guitar.

'We were all hippies in our youth,' they said, 'but of course the world's moved on!'

What did they mean, 'moved on'? It went round, as it always had. Some were good, some were bad, and you knew which side you were on. By night lights sparkled and danced in the bright, watery air, as they had always done. Go due south, and there was Antarctica.

'We're not at the bottom of the world, girls,' said Shirley. 'We're at the top of it.' And she took the globe out of its stand and replaced it upside down, to prove her point, and they all laughed. Their little family, suspended in Hobart, Tasmania, Australia, the Southern Hemisphere, the World, the Galaxy, the Universe, Space.

'Christ,' said one of her friends, 'if only Shirley wasn't so fucking *brave*' and Gracey overheard. She listened at night and sometimes thought she heard her mother crying. Or was it just the wind keening around the house; dead men wailing for lost life? Tasmania is a windy place.

Father's money came more sporadically, didn't go so far. The State stepped in, and helped.

'You see, girls,' said Shirley, 'the universe is kind. People help each ·other. The thing to do is repay: don't ever let something be for nothing! Work hard, do your best.'

Lisa did her maths homework far into the night. Gracey worked and worked at her dancing; she could raise her left leg nearer to her nose than could anyone else in her class.

Shirley got drunk one night at a beach barbecue and drifted off into the sand dunes with Hamish Hunter.

'Girls, I don't want you to be puritanical about sex. Life is love, and touching, and closeness. Don't let anyone ever tell you it's wrong.'

Only Hamish Hunter was Stella Hunter's husband and Stella was Shirley's best and most supportive friend, and it was a small town, and if Stella forgave, which she did – well, everyone had been drinking: poor Shirley, she couldn't be expected to live like a nun the rest of her life, and there weren't many spare men drifting round, in a community where there were one hundred and forty women for every one hundred men – but it was certainly some time before everyone forgot, and somehow afterwards Shirley was on the outside, not the inside. She held her head high.

'Straighten your backs, girls! Walk tall! My beautiful girls – all I ever wanted in the world. Proud spirits, brave and free!'

Gracey sang prettily. Guests would observe it. Shirley always made a point of asking people round to Sunday brunch. She'd make vegetable soup, and beans and bacon.

'People don't want a fuss,' she'd say, 'just delicious home-made food and good conversation and real friendship. That's what life is all about.'

Gracey suspected people came because they thought they ought, not because they wanted to. There seemed to be some kind of rota. The Perkins and the Webbs came every fourth week: the Hamiltons every third – and usually the wives came without the husbands: the men so often had pressing engagements or business matters to attend to. Gracey did not mention her suspicions to Shirley: she sang as loud as she could, and as prettily, doing what she could to drown the keening wind.

'Good heavens,' they said. 'She's a born singer: a natural dancer! And how pretty! Gracey's going to end up on the stage: she'll be an international star, wait and see!'

Louder and louder, sang Gracey.

'I'm so proud of you, Gracey,' said Shirley. 'You're something so special.'

And if Lisa felt jealous, she didn't show it. Lisa struggled to learn the piano, to complement Shirley's guitar and copied out songs for Gracey to sing. They were mostly the folk-songs Shirley loved: 'The Sweet Nightingale', 'Now is the Month of Maying', 'Oh Mary Don't you Cry Any More'. They suited Gracey's clear young voice: her precise diction. They were pure and original, full of hope and love and life with an underlying hint of melancholy.

And now Gracey trembled on the edge of childhood and adolescence – vulnerable. Shirley looked at the local boys with fear. Who would be good enough for Gracey? Did she understand how precious she was, how rare and special and sensitive? How talented?

'But supposing she does what the other girls do?' Shirley agonised to Stella, who was now running the Mature Students (Part-Time) Study Centre. 'Supposing she falls in love with some local boy, at seventeen, marries at eighteen and is a mother by twenty?'

'It might be the best thing she can do,' said Stella. 'To have someone to look after her.' She spoke rather stiffly. Her own eldest daughter had done just all those things, and now Stella, who used to be so young, was a grandmother.

'I've brought them up to look after themselves,' said Shirley, 'to be self-reliant. To know there's always a way round things. That if you want something, you must go right out there and get it.'

Stella looked round the little home, with its thin rush mats on the floor and its cracked mugs on the shelf, and thought of Shirley and Hamish on the sand dunes, enfolded. 'It all depends,' said Stella, shortly, 'what it is you want.'
'The girls have never gone without,' said Shirley.
'Umm,' said Stella, and gave Shirley up. Well, she'd done her stint.

Autumn came. Gracey's shoe size sprung up from five to seven. She was going to be a big girl. Over in Melbourne, her father's wife gave birth to a daughter, and air-fares rose again. Never mind. The season cast a golden cloak over the island. The sea glittered and was quiet: the layered hills, purple embossed, hung still waiting over the bay. Soon the great winds, the Roaring Forties, would start. Not yet. In the meantime, the valleys and the hills rejoiced, and everyone lifted up their hearts.

'Paradise,' said Shirley. 'Paradise!' and Gracey's pretty voice filled the garden, floating out through open windows, and Lisa at last managed the accompaniment to 'The Sweet Nightingale'.

There was to be an end-of-term cabaret at the school. All the girls who could dance would be in it. An official from the mainland was coming to select three girls for the interstate competitions. Gracey's chance! Four changes of costume were required. Parents must provide them. The dresses and headwear were easy enough: Shirley could run them up on the machine, from scraps of fabric, but the cost of the shoes was prohibitive. Gracey would need silver tap, red satin pump, black strap heels and squash shoes. Four pairs! Impossible.

Shirley wept; so did Lisa. Gracey was brave.

'Look Mum, honestly it doesn't matter. I'll pretend to be ill. I'll stay home on the night. It's all right.'

Shirley prayed. God provided the answer.
'God helps those who help themselves,' He said.

'We work for the money, girls,' said Shirley. 'All of us. We have something to offer, after all. The world won't let us down.'

Hobart market must be the loveliest market in the world. On the cobbled waterfront, in the shade of great civilising English trees, stalls are laid out with space to spare. The light that glances off the sea dances back from cut-glass decanters, and sun-polished aubergines, and Star-Wars ear-rings, and mirrors on the 'Literacy for Nicaragua' stall: and a couple of students sing 'There is a House in New Orleans', and someone else plays 'Greensleeves' on a flute, and the days of hope are back again. Calm, prosperous people walk to and fro, meeting friends; children, elated by the heady air, dance and skip. The police keep a low profile. It is the world before it lost its innocence.

Here, on the last Saturday morning in April, Shirley, Gracey and Lisa took up their pitch, in the main thoroughfare. Shirley sat on the cobbles, and played the guitar. Lisa held on to the music sheets, and moved the open guitar case the better to receive the twenty- and fifty-cent pieces they expected. Gracey stood and sang.

> 'Oh Mary don't you cry any more,
> Oh Mary don't you cry any more . . .'

Her little voice piped shrilly. She was a child, not a woman, after all. Passers-by walked on without hearing. Gracey's voice, so charming, so miraculous in the family room, here in the open air lacked the power to command. Shirley had forgotten to bring the blanket: Gracey's feet were bare. The cobbles were not so clean and rain-washed as they had assumed: there was in fact a patch of oil where Gracey stood and piped her song.

They moved to the edge of the kerb. Those who did hear moved by, embarrassed or appalled. Gracey saw a school-friend – well, she'd known that would happen.

'You sound lovely, darling,' said Shirley. 'Isn't this fun! And look at all the money!'

Gracey looked. There were perhaps twelve coins in the guitar case. Three dollars at most.

> 'Oh Mary don't you cry any more,
> Oh Mary don't you cry any more . . .'

The first winter wind stirred up along the quay. It moved slowly, strangely: stripping one tree at a time of its leaves. Dead men's fingers, powerful and industrious.

'Oh Mary don't you cry any more . . .'

The wind had reached the tree in the shade of which Gracey stood. A shower of leaves beat down around her.

'Oh pretty, pretty! A shower of gold!' cried Shirley.

The wind blew harder. It blew the lid of the guitar case shut; it snatched the music sheets from Lisa's fingers; it blew the song right back into Gracey's mouth, into her lungs. She sang, but there was no sound, only the dreadful whoosh of the wind, the coming of Winter.

Up and down the market glass smashed and wood slammed, and used clothing flew up into the air and the trestle on which Middle Earth herbs were displayed collapsed, and the song was driven back into Gracey's mouth, and she was saved.
Gracey cried, at last, little-girl tears.

'Only the wind,' said Shirley, on the way home, 'only the wind, without the wind it would have been okay. We would have been all right.'

But Gracey knew it wasn't so.

Redundant!
or
The Wife's Revenge

Well now, friends, let's have a little light relief. Let me tell
you the story of what happened to Esther and Alan in the
twenty-fourth year of their marriage. It was an episode
distressing enough for those involved, although no doubt
diverting and instructive for their friends. And what are
friends for, but to provide the raw material for debate and
exhilaration? (You may remember Esther and Alan in the
earlier years of their marriage; when both went on a diet
and Esther left home, briefly, and you may be surprised to
find that instead of the son they had then, they now have a
daughter, by name Hermes. But that's the prerogative of
the writer – to change the rules as work proceeds. If you
can't accept it, close the book!)

Envisage now one of our new palace hospitals: a concrete
tower without, nicely carpeted within, with grave young
things in white coats and folders stepping in and out of slow
lifts, and the occasional dressing-gowned patient coughing
or limping or spluttering, having wandered out of the
patients' day rooms, and little alcoves here and there fitted
with tea-bars, staffed by jolly volunteers, where the visitors
can buy white sugared buns and a fix of caffeine. And where
the feel of seedy anxiety mixes with the lingering stench of
gangrene and floats in the purified air; and paint the walls
with whatever gloss colour the designer decrees, they will
still pale and roughen too soon with the notion of things
running down, running out – of desperate saving measures,
which will never quite work. Any cure can only be temporary, after all.

But that's the public wards, and we are meant to be here
for light relief. There's a private wing too, and that's where

Alan is. What did he work all those years *for*, if not for a little privilege? Things aren't so serious in the private wing. Money's a fine cushion for a worried head.

Mind you, Alan had the cushion snatched away, rather suddenly. Bang, thump! It happens to the unlikeliest people, these days. Redundant!

What's he doing here? He's having a face-lift. That is to say, he had one, a week ago, not to mention a cut and a stitch or so in the epicanthic fold above the eye. That takes years off. And ageing executives who want jobs had better take as many years off as they can. But Alan's not healing very well: the bruises don't fade, the tissues don't join. Why? Mr Khan the surgeon is worried.

Well, that's what Mr Khan says. We can hardly suppose the condition of Alan's epicanthic folds keep him awake at night. Other things do that. Pony the nurse for example; longing for Pony does on occasion keep him awake. Mr Khan is a cosmetic surgeon of enormous wealth and great skill. (People certainly get richer dealing with the discomforts of the privileged than they ever do dealing with the sufferings of the humble.) He is married to Mrs Professor Khan, a brain surgeon, of beauty, presence and renown, who terrifies him. Mrs Khan even has morality on her side, since she works for the National Health Service, in what her husband refers to as the Free Wards. He works there sometimes too, of course, for form's sake and because he gets a little tax relief, repairing burn cases and torn flesh. But Mrs Professor Khan will never, ever, agree to work in the private wing. She will never be rich, not really rich, but she will always be virtuous and she sleeps very well at night. Pony is neither virtuous nor rich nor beautiful nor brilliant, but she is young, very young. If she doesn't sleep well at night at the moment, it's because she keeps having to get up to spend a penny, having been made pregnant by Mr

Khan. At this very moment, as Mr Khan steps over the threshold from the public to the private wing, off lino and on to carpet, she is waiting to tell him the news.

Mr Khan is dusky and immeasurably charming: he comes from somewhere on the Indian sub-continent: he has dark, almond-shaped eyes, heavily fringed: he has sensuous fingers. He makes love in the spirit of the Kama Sutra: he hums love songs as he operates, as he shapes a little bone here, remoulds a little flesh there: remaking man, and woman too, in an image better than God himself managed. How can Pony resist him? She doesn't. Pony is small and pixie-faced and has blonde fly-away hair flying away beneath the white frilly cap they wear in the private wards. She's a nurse by the skin of her teeth: her father is an ex-Minister of Health. It gives her a boldness with specialists an ordinary nurse would never have.

Mr Khan sweeps down the corridor: he is king in his kingdom. Where he goes nurses look deferentially and patients look admiringly, and offer thanks. Many wear burnouses, even here in hospital; and women chadors, but their eyes glow in warm gratitude, above the black and virtuous folds.

'Mr Khan! Mr Khan!' Pony breathes, stepping out from behind a portable sterilising unit left untidily in the corridor by a porter who went on strike yesterday for increased pay, and will probably do the same tomorrow. All is not well in our hospitals, especially in the private wings. Not often do rich and poor come into quite so intimate contact: it is inflammatory!

Mr Khan stops briefly, and smiles kindly at her; so some early morning mercenary, fresh and spruce from his military bed, tuned and bright for killing, might pause to smile at some little Persian kitten. He moves on: she runs after him.

194

Other nurses have good strong quiet sensible shoes: Pony manages to break the rules and wears little heels; for medical reasons: her insteps demand them. Even so, she has to gaze up into Mr Khan's face. It is very agreeable, for both of them. Mrs Professor Khan is taller than her husband.

'Well, Pony?'

'Bobby,' whispers Pony. 'I'm pregnant.' And her little face radiates enchantment, wonder and gratification.

'Oh,' says Mr Khan, stopped in his tracks. Then he resumes walking.

'What are we going to do, Bobby?' asks Pony, falling into step beside him.

'We'll have to talk about it,' says Mr Khan, 'but not now, not here.'

'You're always so busy!' she mourns. 'But then you're so important. Just like Daddy!'

Ah, Daddy!

'It's true,' says Mr Khan, 'that many people depend upon me. In the meantime, I love you very much and your news makes me very happy.'

Pony beams.

'Bobby,' she says, 'I have to tell you that your wife was waiting for you in her office just now but she went home. I told her you were busy, and so you are! I was right. She's so busy too, isn't she? She waited only twelve and three quarter minutes.'

'I love my wife as well, Pony,' Mr Khan reminds her, 'but of course not in the same way as I love you. Over the next week or so we'll work something out. Now, to business! How is Mr Lear?'

(Mr Lear is, of course, Alan. Once he was Alan Sussman, but that was when he had a son, before he had a daughter, and in the days that he was vaguely Jewish, and consumed by an inner angst: these days he is tormented by practicalities, such as losing a kingdom and an income and, of course, in the manner of fathers everywhere, tormented in various ways by his daughter. Grown children go too soon, or go too late, or to the wrong place or, worst of all, don't go at all.

'I'm very worried about Mr Lear,' says Pony, composing her face into a grave nurse-like mask. (Well, she's not exactly losing sleep over Alan, any more than is Mr Khan. She regards him in the way nurses do regard patients – as essentially fictional characters.) 'He does seem so depressed. I mean, clinically depressed.'
'Oh dear,' says Mr Khan, 'anti-depressant depressed?'
'He was once diagnosed as depressed by his GP,' says Pony, 'and was given them. I asked him how they'd worked and he said they gave him nightmares and I said that was only imagination, and he said quite so. I don't somehow seem to get through to him, Bobby. Perhaps he has been badly hurt by women?' And her little lips tremble with sympathy, and Mr Khan pauses again, to admire her sweetness, and to instruct, which he loves doing, and which his wife, over the years, gives him fewer and fewer opportunities so to do. 'There is certainly some reason,' says Mr Khan, 'why the healing process is delayed: why the tissues refuse to knit: why such a simple operation as a face-lift, which should cause a mature man no trouble at all, has proved so traumatic in this particular case. My sweet Pony! To think that you are carrying my child! How fortunate women are: all a man can do is tinker with creation: a woman is creation itself!' And he continues his stride down the corridor, with Pony trotting after him.
'Bobby,' says Pony firmly – not for nothing is she her father's daughter – 'actually, men create babies too. I see this one as being as much yours as mine. I just do the carrying around! I don't even have to do that for us any more. We could take this baby out of me now, deep-freeze it for a little, and put it back in somebody else's womb altogether, and both of us watch it come out, hand in hand.' She is referring to advances in gynaecological technique recently

accomplished only a few yards down the corridor from
where they are standing.

'Not quite, Pony, not quite yet,' says Mr Khan. 'Though
no doubt in time such techniques will be perfected, and I
take your point.'

It is at this moment, while Mr Khan and Pony are locked
in their loving war, that a little party of three sweep by
them. Esther goes first, lean and freckly and passionate, for
all the world like Katharine Hepburn in Venice in *Summer
Madness*, a woman, though fifty, clearly in her confident
sexual prime. Behind her go a pair one could take for brother
and sister; Freddo with Irish good looks, broad-shouldered,
slim-hipped with bright blue eyes and thick black hair and
a sharp thin nose – wearing his best navy suit for the
occasion, and his working boots. Freddo is Esther's lover.
And Hermes is here too. Hermes, as you know, is Esther
and Alan's daughter. She is twenty-four, going on fourteen,
pretty as a picture, bright as a button and cross as two
sticks. Hermes feels badly done by.

Pony is out of sympathy with visitors. They mess up the
rooms and upset the patients. She stands between the Lear
entourage and her charge.

'Where are you going?' she asks. Mr Khan admires her
courage. Only his wife has as much.

'To see Mr Lear,' said Mrs Esther Lear, 'in Room 341. I
know that is his room. It was on Reception's computer.'

'He is not supposed to have visitors,' says Pony. Hermes
and Freddo prepare to turn back, but Esther will have none
of it.

'I am his wife, my dear,' says Esther. 'And husband and
wife are one flesh.'

Pony has that superstitious fear of the word 'wife' common,
thank God, to the mistresses of adulterers, and it is she who
stands aside. The Lear party pass on.

'It isn't right,' complains Pony to Mr Khan, who is standing in rapt fascination, staring after Esther Lear. 'I know he wants his face-lift kept secret from his wife. He told his family he was on a redeployment course for redundant executives in the North of Scotland. He wanted his new face to be a surprise for them. He told me so. He confides in me, you know. And he doesn't like his wife one little bit. They live apart.'

Mr Khan shakes his head reproachfully. 'Mr Lear should not have told lies. There is nothing to be ashamed of in cosmetic surgery. It is natural for employers, in these dismal times, to want their employees to look young and handsome and fresh, and to inspire confidence in others. A man often looks older than he feels: in such cases to have a face-lift is not conceit, merely sensible.'

Pony has heard him say such things many times.

'So that's the wife!' he says. 'Mrs Lear! She seems a higher type than the husband.'

Pony hasn't heard him say this before, and she doesn't much like it. She feels rather tired, and thinks perhaps she'll go home to her parents' house in the country, for the weekend, and weed their flowerbeds.

Esther, at the door of No. 341, turns on her followers and forbids them entry.

'Hermes, Freddo,' she says, 'you stay out of here.'

'You'll only have a row with him,' says Freddo in his succulent young voice, with the slight over and under tones of Irish (Southern) mist and charm.

'We are far more likely to have a row if there are witnesses,' says Esther, briefly. 'You should know that by now.'

'I'm coming in with you, my darling,' persists Freddo. 'The bastard will only upset you.'

There is no stemming the flow of his goodwill, his desire to look after and protect, his Lancelot complex, as Esther

describes it. So Esther diverts the flow. How skilled she is, after years of family life, in inter-personal relationships! 'Freddo dear, I need you to stay here and look after Hermes. She should never have come in the first place.' Hermes darts her mother a wounded and recalcitrant look. 'This is between her father and me.'
'Now you are accusing me of tagging along,' says Hermes, tears rising.
'See, Freddo,' says her mother, 'she's in no state to be left alone.' So Freddo stays, with his quasi stepdaughter. They sit beneath a palm in an upholstered alcove especially designed for surplus visitors, thus caught short by family passions. Hermes sits sulking, putting as much space as she can manage between herself and Freddo. Freddo stares at himself in a little gilt mirror and observes some slight slackness beneath his own chin, and experimentally lifts it. He now has a Chinese look.
'I spy Chinee with a lace lilt,' he says.
Hermes looks down her small, straight, perfect nose, and pretends not to belong to him.

Alan sits up in his hospital bed, his bandaged face turned listlessly towards the wall. Beside him books stay unread and orange juice undrunk. Esther sits herself beside her husband, her nearly ex-husband – the final decree will be in only a couple of weeks – and takes his hand in hers, and feels it grow tense.
'I didn't meant it to go so far,' she says, being these days someone who likes always to put the general before the particular. Women in domestic situations tend to do the opposite. 'I didn't mean it to come to this.'
'It hurts to talk.' He won't meet her eye.
'It always did, darling,' she observes, and leans over to adjust his head bandages. He shrinks, and wants her to know that he does. He doesn't trust her. She has come here for some sinister motive.
'The bandages have slipped! Let me help you. What do the

nurses *do* round here, except stand about and chat up the doctors? You can hardly see at all.'
'I don't want to see.'
'But, darling, it's Spring outside. Look out the window. Daffodils.'

Alan says that he doesn't like daffodils. They are too common and too yellow and Esther says no doubt he has seen too many Springs turn into too many Winters, which sounds rather more like the Esther he knew, or of late has come to know.
'At least,' he concedes, 'you didn't bring your lover. I suppose we must be grateful for that.'

Esther is glad he has raised the subject. She loves talking about Freddo to Alan.
'He's waiting outside,' she says. 'He wanted to come in to protect me from you, but I said since you were a sick man, I'd probably be safe, for once.'
'I don't want to hear about your lover.'
'You brought the subject up,' says Esther, 'and I think you *should* hear, because you might make a new relationship yourself one day and you won't want it to collapse like all your others. Freddo is always kind and considerate. He never finds fault with either my body or my mind. He accepts me: he admires me. He makes me happy. You must remember what it's like going round with the young and amorous and uncritical. You did enough of it, when safely married to me. But young girls do seem to prefer married men, don't they. They can put in practice without risking involvement. But there is something very sad and unwanted and defeated about a heterosexual man unmarried in his middle years. Don't you think?'
'Esther,' says Alan, 'I didn't ask you to come here. I didn't want you to come. Would you kindly go?'
It is somewhere in Esther's nature to accept rebuke.
'I'm sorry,' she says, in a small voice, quite like the old

days, when she had apologised for everything, including the
weather, and had weighed five stone more. 'I'll behave.'
And she looks at him with true sympathy, but not for long,
just long enough to ask:
'Does it hurt?'
'Yes,' says Alan.
'It's not supposed to,' she says. 'You're probably imagining
it. When I heard you were in hospital, and what for, I rang
up the BMC and made enquiries. They were very helpful.
They said you might experience discomfort, but they didn't
mention pain.'
'It hurts,' he says. 'There is pain.'
'They also told me,' she remarks, 'what it was likely to cost.'
'Did they?' He's vague, too vague.
'They assured me you'd look ten years younger. I said what
a pity it was there were some parts the surgeon's knife
couldn't improve.'
'Potency,' says Alan, declining to take offence, 'is a matter
of self-esteem.'
'Poor Alan,' says Esther.
'It has all been a great humiliation,' he says.
'I know what those feel like,' she says. 'You taught me.'
He lets that go. She tries again. 'Your daughter Hermes is
outside, keeping Freddo quiet. She'll come so far to show
her sympathy, but not quite all the way.'
'Perhaps she'll run off with Freddo,' says Alan, hopefully.
'How much of my redundancy money have you paid him?'
'It isn't your redundancy money, it's mine. The Court
awarded it to me, taking note of your despicable behaviour
during the last years of our marriage. Only a couple of
thousand, to start him up in business. He has a nice little
shop now: it keeps him busy and happy all day. So when
you sell the house over my head, as you so often say you
will, and kill yourself, as you so often say you will, there'll
be someone able to look after me.'
'When did you ever need looking after?'
'Oh, once, once,' she says, sadly. 'I am what you've made

me. Alan, I didn't come here to quarrel with you, I only came to ask how you got the money for this really very expensive and perfectly unnecessary cosmetic surgery, when Hermes' Cordon Bleu classes have to be paid for and the roof is leaking and your solicitor's fees must be enormous, because you keep insisting on going to court over trivial issues, which I always win, and there is no one in the world to care whether you look young or old. How did you pay?'

He is silent for a little and then he says, 'I took out a second mortgage on our house.'

It is her turn to be silent. And presently she says, with ominous calm, 'I don't believe you. You're trying to upset me. How can you take out a mortgage without my signature?'

'Mostly in these offices,' he says, 'they're on the husband's side. They'll stretch a point or so.'

She believes him. Believing him, she shrieks and flies at him, belabouring his bandaged head with quite powerful fists. He is already poised for escape having, after all, been married to her for many years and being able to predict her reactions – but gets his foot trapped beneath too-tightly tucked hospital blankets and can't slide out of the bed as easily as he has imagined. He shrieks for help and she shrieks abuse. Hermes and Freddo come running in. Hermes will not intervene physically but cries out to anyone who will listen, 'They're always doing this! I'm so ashamed! No wonder I'm so neurotic!' And Freddo tries gently to restrain his lady love, crying, 'Oh my darling gentle lady!' but she elbows him savagely aside. It is left to Pony to restrain Esther with a cunning neck-lock from the martial arts in which she is trained, and by the time Mr Khan has arrived, in response to his bleeper's urgent alarm tweet, some kind of order has been restored. Esther is brilliant-eyed but quiet in the corner of the room, with Freddo stroking her hair and regarding Alan with a curled lip, and Hermes is weeping quietly, and Pony is adjusting Alan's bandages.

'It's all right, Mr Khan,' says Pony, 'I don't think any of your wonderful work has been spoiled.' And she mutters, 'Visitors!' under her breath, but quite loud enough for Esther to hear.

'Mrs Lear,' says Mr Khan, in his mellifluous voice, 'will you come with me to my office? I think we should talk. It is true that in normal times physical violence can release tension in a helpful way, but these are not normal times for your husband. He needs your love and support. The cheek scars are safe enough, but I have raised the epicanthic folds, and they are particularly vulnerable.'
He pronounces his v's as w's; Pony loves it. Wulnerable! She sighs her admiration. Mr Khan preens.
'He should not, for instance,' Mr Khan goes on, 'laugh too much.'
'My father,' remarks Hermes, 'was never a great laugher. He should be safe enough.'

Mr Khan sends Hermes and Freddo down to the canteen to wait for their mother, and desires them to choose herbal tea rather than coffee. Coffee, he says, can break the fine capillary nerves in the cheek, and righting them can be quite a business. 'Some things,' he tells the silenced, desperate assembly, 'our patients can't help. Such as the passage of time, or the inequities of a natal fate. Things like coffee, alcohol, over-eating, over-indulging in sex – people wrinkle up the face quite drastically – they *can* help, but usually won't. You do not,' says Mr Khan sadly, 'meet the finest and best of mankind in this particular wing of the hospital.'

Freddo and Hermes, much reduced, go for herbal tea, resolved to abjure coffee, Esther accompanies Mr Khan to his office, and Pony sits on the end of Alan's bed, to calm him and soothe him in the interests of the proper knitting of tissue. The process was known to Sister Tutor as 'chattering on' and she was a great believer in it, and Pony was an adept pupil.

'Friends,' says Pony, curling her little slim legs, 'are all very well at visiting time, but if it's nearest and dearest out of proper hours, then there's nearly always trouble. I think hospitals should be kept for the patients, don't you? Sister Tutor always told us that hospitals are sanctuaries: and that the mind must heal before the body can, and what most patients come in for is peace and quiet. A broken leg, she'd say, is a plea for help: and what the nurse must do is find the source of the inner pain. Go easy on the pain-killers, she'd say: most patients need pain to assuage their guilt. When in their own estimation they've suffered enough, the pain just goes. Pain-killers merely confuse the patient and drag the healing process out. Sharp and short, she'd say, or easy and long, and in these days of cutbacks and queues for hospital beds, easy and long is plainly immoral. Sister Tutor is a wonderful woman. So wise!'

Alan isn't listening: he is tenderly moving his jaw, beneath its bandages, and is alarmed by the degree of movement the bones now seem to have.

'Do you think something's given?' he asks.

'No, no,' says Pony, soothingly. 'You just began to use your jaw properly. Shouting "you bitch, you bitch" the way you did, you really exercised your mouth. Sister Tutor was a great believer in catharsis. Now you've got what you really wanted to say out, you'll find speaking much easier! Isn't that wonderful? Good! I think we're really on the way to recovery!'

And she slips off the bed and does a little dance about it. Alan can scarcely believe his improvement merits so extreme a response.

'Everything's going so perfectly,' says Pony. 'And now I'm pregnant too!'

'Good heavens,' says Alan, gloomily.

'Why, don't you like children?' She's anxious.

'Not much,' he says. 'No one seems able to cook them properly.'

She looks at him blankly, not taking the joke, and he is ashamed of having made it: she is very bright and pretty and rescued him from his wife's fists. He responds properly, as she deserves.

'That's wonderful!' he corrects himself. 'I didn't know you were married.'

'You're so old-fashioned,' she says. 'But I soon will be! It's Mr Khan, you know.'

'I might have known it. Only yesterday he showed me photographs of his wife and children.'

'He feels he ought to, that's all. She looks all right in photographs, but she's terribly boring. She's a brain surgeon. He can't possibly love her, except in a conventional sense.'

'Is there another sense?'

'Oh yes!' breathes Pony. 'But how could someone of your generation understand?' And she speaks of the passion which melts her bones, and the feeling of the heavens uniting, and the sense of destiny, of the ultimate fortune, the great adventure! Herself and Mr Khan! He from so far away, spirited into this very hospital: and she having done her training here, almost by accident: and thus they'd met. Fate has led them together. How else to explain it?

'Ah yes,' says Alan, turning his face back to the wall. 'All that.'

In the meantime, Esther is talking to Mr Khan, in his large cool office. A photograph of Mrs Professor Khan and the two children, all on horses, stands on his tidy desk. 'It is no use living in the past, my dear,' he says.

'Don't you "my dear" me,' says Esther. 'And there is a great deal of use in living in the past. Anger keeps me going! To think how I lived! All those wasted years!'

'Do you want to tell me, my dear?' He gazes into her bright blue eyes with his own soft brown ones. He admires her. She reminds him of his wife – an intelligent and forceful woman, unbowed down by that necessity of being good which so afflicts English women: the sense that things must be put up with, whatever they are, and no complaints allowed.

'Tell me why the mention of a second mortgage should make you so very, very violent!'

'There was a time,' says Esther, 'and I lived through it, before the trouble started, when women were proud to be wives, and admired men, and ran homes, and loved to do it well, and the name housewife had dignity and substance and mothering was all the rage, and I mothered Hermes. And then Hermes was nineteen, and I wanted her to leave home, and didn't at the same time, because then what would my purpose in the world be? I had reached the time of my come-uppance as wife and mother, and I realised it, and Alan couldn't, and Hermes wouldn't.

'Picture the scene! Myself in my love home in the suburbs, with the roses in the front and the lawn at the back, big enough for a game of croquet and summer Sunday drinks, and serviced by myself: the wife, no matter what her talents or her aspirations were, existed in those days to service the family. And the family, without a doubt, was better off for it. Well, there's a dilemma!

'And then one summer evening came and I was waiting for Alan to come home. I was cooking the dinner. I am a very bad cook, but that was neither here nor there. To cook was my function. Alan liked formal meals, of the kind he took out at business men's restaurants at lunchtime. And he was always slightly aggrieved at the food I set before him, as if feeling the lack of a menu, a choice of dishes. I was in a muddle: the mixer had spattered unhomogenised mayonnaise all over the kitchen: a bolognaise sauce was catching

in the pressure cooker – you could tell by the smell of the steam – and Hermes was writing an essay on the kitchen table, and I said, which I shouldn't have:
"Can't you keep your books to just one area of the kitchen table, Hermes?" And I suggested she work in her room, where she had such a nice reading lamp, a Christmas present from her father. She reminded me that it had been I who had actually bought the lamp and put his name upon it, as usual, and I explained, as usual, that Christmas was the busiest time of her father's year, she mustn't be upset by his apparent neglect. "It's the time," I said, "that the main Presentations and Conferences take place."
"It's the time the office parties take place," Hermes corrected me, and went on to say that office parties were annual orgies and I went on to say she knew nothing about it, and she said she might not but Val did – Val often worked in offices – and I said, "Who is this Val? You keep talking about him," and Hermes said, "It's not a him, it's a her," and while I digested this and got ready for trouble ahead, and took out the flour to thicken the gravy, Hermes sidestepped and started in on me.
"You don't make it less greasy by adding flour," she said, "you just add carbohydrate to cholesterol."
"Your father loves gravy," I said.
"You're trying to murder my father," my daughter said.
"Why should I?" I asked. "Since he supports us and looks after us, and we are the meaning of his life?"
"You are a slave," said Hermes.
"I am a housewife," I said.
"Val says you are a slave," said Hermes, "and what you do is unpaid shit-work, and what you cook is murder. You want him to have a heart-attack and claim on the insurance," and I replied that all this was only a stage Hermes was going through, and she said, "What? Being a lesbian, a stage?" and since it was the first I'd heard of it, perhaps I didn't react properly, merely asked her not to mention it to her father before he'd even begun his soup – you know how

children will wait on the doorstep for the tired and weary worker, in order to spring bad news upon him – and explained to her how bad the times were, what with oil prices shooting up again and the recession and the rate of exchange – I can never remember whether a low pound is good or bad, can you? And so forth. And Hermes said:

"Mother, I don't believe you are a stupid woman. You went to college to get a degree. I think it is marriage that has made you stupid. You have lived your life through your husband. You have dedicated yourself to him, and given the scraps to me, and there is nothing left of you, nothing, except a parrot wittering phrases, and when I go, when I do go, you won't have him, because when I go, Father goes. I feel it. And Val says so."

"Hermes," I said, "surely it's time you left home."

"Oh yes, that's right," she cried out in her bitterness. "Turn me out in the last year of my finals! It's because I'm a lesbian! Val says lesbians must expect opposition, driven from pillar to post."

"Oh, do move your books, Hermes," I said, "and not a word to your father about being a lesbian until Mrs Thatcher has sorted out the economy a little."

'Of course I only said that to annoy her, and I shouldn't, but life can get very boring.

'Hermes screamed and threw a book, which caught the pressure cooker and spilt the stew and knocked the gravy all over the floor just as Alan came into the room, back from work.

"Do run along, Hermes," I said, and she did, and Alan raised his eyebrows at the mess and I said I was sorry things were so behind today, Hermes was being difficult, we could no longer blame it on adolescence but perhaps she was feeling the pressure of exams and Alan said where's the whisky and before I remembered I said in the fridge and got a lecture about whisky being served at room temperature, so I offered him gin and then said sorry again, because we'd run out of mixers, and he said what did I do all day, darling, and I said what I really wanted to do was to get out of this: start a new life: take out a second mortgage and get myself qualified, and he went into his set piece about my being a) too old to start anew and b) too loveably muddle-headed to cope outside the home.

"Darling," he said, "if you'd ever been out to work you wouldn't be talking like this. It is one long humiliation and curtailment of human rights."

"Darling," he went on, "you'd have to pay a housekeeper to do your work; they get paid more these days than office workers. We'd be running at a loss."

"Darling," I remember him saying, "had you thought about tax? I'd have to pay more if you went out to work. I would really resent that."

"Darling," he then said, "you're a traditional woman and that's the way I like it, even if you do put the whisky in the fridge."

'And I gave up and told him, unwisely, about Hermes and the fact that Val was female, whom we had assumed to be male.

"Well," said Alan, "these things can be nipped in the bud. One can take steps."

"But sometimes," I said, knowing Alan, "by taking steps to make matters better, one makes them worse."

"Darling," he said, "trust me to know what I'm doing," and I felt a sudden twinge of backache.

'I remember I used to get quite bad backache, in those days. I took it to the doctor, on occasion, who would always say, what did I expect, at my time of life, so I'd take it home again, with a prescription for Valium. I was going to be a doctor once,' says Esther to Mr Khan, 'but my father said it was a waste of the nation's resources, not to mention his, since I'd only get married and have children. He was quite right, as it turned out. That's what I did. Have you noticed,

Mr Khan, how many women there always are in doctors' surgeries, and how few men?'
'That may be,' says Mr Khan smugly, 'why it's women who outlive men.'

While Esther tells Mr Khan such sections of her life story as she feels to be relevant to her grievances, Freddo and Hermes drink herbal tea in the canteen. Hermes is cold and sulky but Freddo barely notices.
'I'd rather drink horse-piss,' says Freddo, sipping a fine yarrow concoction.
'I don't doubt it,' says Hermes.
'Some people do,' he assures her. 'It cures rheumatism.'
And he tells her she is old-fashioned, and she says she isn't interested in his opinion of her, and he says she'd better be, because he'll be her stepdaddy soon enough, at which Hermes begins to weep gently into her camomile tea.
'Why can't my parents' generation keep itself to itself?' she moans. 'Why does it have to come banging back into ours? Face-lifts for him, young lovers for her! At least my grandmother had the decency to grow old from a comparatively early age.'
'Och, my darling,' he says, and slips a consoling arm around her waist, 'sure in mythology it happens all the time. First the mother, then the daughter!'
But she's too lost in her own woes to feel the pressure of his hand or catch the tenor of his thoughts, and begins to repeat over and over:
'It's all my fault.'

'It was all Hermes' fault,' Alan is saying to Pony, at that very moment, and he tells her how he had first gone calling on Val, to nip in the bud any possible undesirable relationship his daughter might make. He felt in those days that he was not a sufficiently attentive father and that the least he could do was take definitive action from time to time. Esther, at Alan's command, has searched for and found Val's address amongst Hermes' papers. And so Alan had gone off to visit after work, grey-suited and brief-cased, and bolstered by a sense of being altogether on the right side of society. A gaggle of young persons on roller-skates nearly knocked him down: Val lived in a racy and expensive part of town. Her front door was chequered in silver and green. He found that strange and sinister. When Val opened the door to him he was taken aback. He had expected some tough-jawed young woman in denims, but found instead a shimmery young woman dressed in green silk with almond eyes set widely apart, and short, shiny fair hair: she was what he thought women should be and dismissed at once any notion that the friendship between her and Hermes was suspect. How could it be? He was irritated with Esther for having suggested it in the first place. How now was he to explain his presence? "Well?" Her voice was husky: it turned his heart over. "I'm Hermes' father." It was all he could think of to say. "How rare," she said, "for a man to define himself in relation to a woman. And how welcome! Do come in."

And she stepped to one side and he stepped past her, and caught a delicate whiff of her perfume, or soap, or shampoo, or something ridiculous, as he went by. Esther always used medicated soaps and shampoo.
'And then? And then?' asks Pony, for Alan's voice falters and is still.
'What do you think?' asks Alan, his nostrils dilating a little, caught in the sadness and wonder of amazing times, gone by.
'Of course, I know you're very attractive, but someone like that, your daughter's age – why would she want to?' asks Pony.
'You have not seen me at my best,' says Alan stiffly, speaking out from beneath his bandages, 'or you wouldn't ask. Why you and Mr Khan, come to that?'

Mr Khan reclines on a sofa in his office. He is telling Esther about Pony.

'I love the little thing,' says Mr Khan. 'I tell you this because I want you to know that I too am tempted, I too am human. I too am fed up with marriage. I am in no position to judge others. Of course, I love my wife as well as Pony.'

'Of course —'

'And I shan't leave her. How can I? She has never deserved it.'

But Esther isn't listening.

'I blame Hermes,' she says. 'I really do. If she hadn't been so silly, or if I hadn't mentioned her coming out to Alan — girls these days come out into lesbianism as they used to come out into High Society — none of it would ever have happened.'

'It should never have happened,' says Alan, regaining his composure, 'but it did.' And he tells Pony in rather more detail how it had all come about. How Val had lain back on embroidered cushions, while Alan paced and apologised. Shimmering and glimmering up at him: pale limbs against luscious fabrics.

"Of course it all sounds absurd now I'm here," he'd said. "How could you possibly be a bad influence on Hermes? If she were to grow up even remotely like you —"

"We're the same age, Alan."

"Yes, but you're so *original.*"

She'd seemed surprised.

"Perhaps you're accustomed to the company of very un-original people?"

"You find me suburban?" He'd considered himself, and sipped his whisky sour. "I daresay you're right. The modern equivalent of the Yeoman of England. Sutton Man! I'm a senior executive in a big company, as it happens. International. Of course the UK operation is a fairly minor division of the whole, but more funds are being diverted here from the States and I have a reasonable prospect of going on the Board."

"You don't have to give me your qualifications," she'd remarked. He was confused. Why was she lying back amongst cushions; what did she mean by it? Twenty years ago it would have been an open invitation for him to throw himself upon her, but who was to say what the signals were, these days? Perhaps she displayed the length of leg, the curve of the breast, the better to cry rape? Or perhaps it was just how she always welcomed guests: reclining on a low sofa, laughing and languorous. And how now was he to construe her last remark?

"I think you are the most beautiful, extraordinary girl I've ever seen in my life," he'd said, giving up.

And she'd considered this, and stopped laughing, and become intense.

"Am I supposed to be flattered, or honoured, or both?"

"I was merely telling you what I thought," said Alan, and then feeling that perhaps in her circles 'thought' was not an okay word, amended it to 'felt'.

"No," said Val, "you weren't. You were expecting me to be grateful for your good opinion of me: which is really only a prelude to saying you want to go to bed with me, now, and go home to your wife after a couple of hours and hope to God I'll forget the whole business. And if I telephone you at your office your secretary will say you're out, but you'll ring back after your meeting, which you won't: and you can rely on me not to ring you at home because on the whole girls like me – or the kind of girl you think I am – are frightened of wives, and feel guilty about sleeping with married men, which is, after all, like sleeping with father to annoy mother."

How could she read his mind? He'd wanted to leave. And even as he prepared to go, she'd stretched, cat-like, and said, "But certainly, if it's what you want, I'll go to bed with you. I just think you ought to be more honest."

That frightened him.

"I think I'd better go."

She did not make the expected move to detain him. She suggested he give her regards to his wife, whom she had heard so much about from Hermes.

"You are more like a piranha-fish than a woman," he'd complained. How could the mind be so sharp and wounding while the body so warm and yielding? "Thank God I am happily married!"

"Then you just go home to it," she'd said, as if to a naughty child. He'd shuffled and shivered. He'd said he'd ring her in the morning, when she was feeling better, and started again for the door, and changed his mind, and said:

"It's such a relief, you've no idea, finding a woman who can look after herself."

She'd looked up at him with darkening, receptive eyes, no longer laughing, or mocking, or hurting, and he'd said, surprising himself, for during his ins and outs with various secretaries and colleagues' wives over the years, he'd never said it, keeping at least some loyalty to Esther, "I love you." He amended it to, "I think I could love you," at once, but nevertheless it was said.

Alan falls silent again. Pony stares at him in alarm. There are tears in his eyes.

'You mustn't let your mind dwell on unpleasant things,' she says.

His hand goes to his neck, remembering Val's small white fingers, and how they unknotted his tie, unbuttoned his shirt. Her green silk whatever it was, was no hindrance to passion. There seemed, with Val, so little difference between dressed and undressed. Esther was always somehow embattled behind her clothes.

'It's not unpleasant,' he says. 'It's the difference between then and now that's painful, that's all.'

Now Mr Khan holds Esther's hand in his and tells her his troubles.

'My wife works,' he says. 'She is a brilliant brain surgeon. She saves a dozen lives a week. Some of course come out as vegetables, but death's the alternative, and her vegetation rate, as we call it, is lower than anyone's. She has right on her side: all I have is money, but rightness weighs heavier in the scales of life. Our home runs like clockwork. We have a housekeeper and a timetable pinned on the wall: we take turns fetching and delivering the children: dancing lessons, fencing, music: we fit everything in. Clockwork! Why then do I love Pony, who is nothing, not even a very good nurse? I will tell you. Because she worships me, she adores me, she doesn't understand me. But how can I leave my wife? It would destroy her.'

Esther looks down with some satisfaction at her lean, made-over, well-loved self, and says,

'It might be the making of her.'

But he'll have none of that.

'She is made already,' he says. 'That's what I can't stand. Our love-life is fantastic, fantastic. Pony lacks imagination, not to mention stamina. But it's Pony I want. I need her inefficiency. Look at me! My life is running out!'

'All our lives are running out,' says Esther sadly, 'but Alan used to be preoccupied with how much faster my life was running out than his. He thought it justified his horrid little affairs.'

'Affairs are not necessarily horrid,' protests Mr Khan. 'Sometimes they are beautiful, beautiful! I see Pony's little dancing legs beneath her crisp white nurse's skirt, and my heart turns over! I, Mr Khan, at whose frown the whole department of cosmetic surgery trembles! That this little creature, this little nurse, should wrap me around her little fingers — is not there wonder, and hope and amazement in this?'

'I became hopelessly entangled in her web,' says Alan to Pony. 'She was Eve and she held out the apple of knowledge to me, and I ate of it, and was cast out for ever.'

They lay together, Alan and Val, in her satin bed. It was afternoon, the best time for stolen trysts. All passion spent, Alan lay on his elbow and gazed down at her perfect face, the sweep of her long lashes, the curl of hair beneath the ear. Her skin was dewy.

"You have everything before you," he said to her, "it gives you a special quality. Youth, future, intelligence, hope: all shine through you!"

Her large eyes shot open.

"Alan," she observed, "you are a terrible lover."

He was taken aback. He thought he had done well enough. Was this what the new woman said to men, at such times?

"I beg your pardon?"

"You have no idea at all," she said, "how to go about it."

"No one else has ever complained." He was haughty.

"I daresay not," she said. "But then perhaps you only encounter people with no standards."

Alan rose and dressed himself, vowing never to return.

"It seems the least you can do for your wife," said Val, "when you do find time for her, is to afford her some small sexual satisfaction. I am more and more on your wife's side. I am really thinking of giving up men altogether. At least women know what to do, and when, and how."

"Good God," said Alan, looking for his tie, "sex between men and women is an expression of love. It is purely instinctive. One does, after all, what comes naturally."

"No," said Val, "one does not. Sex is an acquired skill. Some have a natural talent for it, of course, the way some people are born able to draw beautifully, but application and training is still required. And you've simply never bothered."

Alan had taken quite considerable offence.

"I'm going now, Val," he said, "and I'm not coming back. You've gone too far. A man turns to a woman for comfort, reassurance, and a sense of completeness."

"Surely," said Val, "a man would turn to his mother for

that. A lover offers something different."
"I don't like the way you use the word lover. Men are lovers,
women are loved."

Val sat up, bare breasts poised above the oyster silk.
She seemed surprised.
"I am your lover. You are mine. We are equal."
At that he turned back to her, and sank back upon the bed:
his resolution had failed. He could not do without her.
She seemed neither gratified, nor disappointed, whether
he stayed or whether he went. It occurred to him that she
had no expectations and, having none, found the world
immeasurably interesting. He thought he wanted to be like
her, to divest himself of the boring habits of established
thought: the little spats of righteousness and self-justification
from which he suffered. He wanted to be born again, body
and soul.
"Aren't you going?" she asked.
"No. I find it too interesting. I want to change. I want to
join your new world."
"Ah," she said. "Well, if you're going to stay, if we're to
continue this relationship, you're going to have to learn to
do better."
"But you'll teach me?"
"I haven't time," she said. She was taking exams in Design
at the RCA. She rose and drank some spring water from a
bottle and dug her sharp teeth into a red apple, naked as
she was.
"I think you'd better buy a manual."
And he lay on her bed, Sutton Man in a good grey suit and
pale blue tie, and wondered what had hit him.

'Hermes tried to tell me about Alan and Val,' Esther is
saying to Mr Khan, 'but I didn't want to listen. I was
frightened. I knew everything was changing. I remember
one evening in particular, Hermes was going berserk because I was darning socks and I was trying to explain to

her how important it is that a man's feet should be comfortable, and how I knew it was old-fashioned, but I liked doing it – it's really quite a skill – and how it seemed wrong to me, simply to throw things away and start again, and how if she loved a man she'd know what I meant.

'And Hermes said, "And where is my father now? This man you love?" and I said he was working late at the office, which I knew was a cliché, but like all clichés was no doubt true, and even if he did stop by at the pub now and then – and he did sometimes come home smelling of whisky – I could hardly grudge the poor man a drink. "I think he rather smells of musk," my daughter said.

"Musk?"

"Val wears musk," said Hermes. "It's disgusting."

"I thought Val could do nothing wrong!" I said.

"Val can do a lot wrong," said Hermes darkly.

"Dear me!" I answered brightly. "And you used to be so fond of her. What happened? Did she steal one of your boyfriends? Well, I'm afraid girls do! It's a mistake ever to put too much trust in a girlfriend!"

Hermes shrieked that she couldn't live in this madhouse a moment longer, and I said then don't, darling, don't, and she became pale and grave and begged me not to turn her out before her Results – Results had been looming large in our lives lately – and I said she could always go and stay with Val, couldn't she, all of the time and not just some of the time. Hermes still stayed over with Val a couple of nights a week.

"Val keeps turning me out of her bedroom because she's entertaining her middle-aged executive lover."

"Oh dear," I said, "I do think girls should stick to their own age-group. There's always trouble if you mix the generations."

And she said, wonderfully darkly, "Quite so! He's old enough to be her father, not to mention mine," and I nodded and went on darning socks – I only really ever darn socks to aggravate Hermes – and she said, "Mother, I am trying to tell you something," and I looked her in the eye and said, "That's very thoughtful of you, darling, but your father has been particularly loving of late and I don't think there is anything in the world I want to know. Now be quiet."'

Alan lies in bed and recovers from the sudden uprush of remembered desire; it is Pony's turn to offer confidences, as Sister Tutor always said she should.

'All I have to offer him is love,' says Pony, dewy-eyed, 'and the baby, of course. Isn't it strange, how I keep forgetting about the baby! The first time I set eyes on Mrs Professor Khan was when I'd just started working in the department. We were having a case conference, Bobby and I, and she walked in and sent me to fetch coffee, as if I were the maid. I thought then, I'll get my own back on you, and when Bobby made the first pass, I didn't slap him down or anything, and before I knew where we were, we were in bed and in love. So it's all her fault. She brought it on herself, and now she can be a divorced brain surgeon and as for me, I shall be married to a specialist. I am, after all, daughter of an ex-Minister of Health!'

But Alan isn't listening.
'I blame Hermes,' he repeats. 'If only she'd kept her silly, malicious little mouth shut, Esther would never have known, and the whole thing would have blown over.'

And downstairs in the canteen, Hermes pours her heart out to Freddo, since he's there.
'Of course, my father never *liked* me,' complains Hermes. 'He wanted me to be a son, if anything. It was always him and her together, Alan and Esther, keeping me out. They were lovers, really, in spite of Val and all the ones that went before, and that's what Val didn't like, that's why she had to get between them. Being with my father was her way of

getting close to my mother. She never had a family of her own: she envied mine, I think, more fool her! I've always felt orphaned. The children of lovers are orphans, they say. Isn't that sad!'

Freddo remarks that Alan and Esther didn't look too like lovers to him, the pair of them screeching and carrying on, and Hermes observes that that's the only model of love she has, and why she never means to get married, and he strokes her cheek in an understanding way, and she actually feels comparatively understood.

'But of course,' says Esther to Mr Khan, 'not being jealous didn't last for long: not for more than an hour or two. I had my rights as a wife, although Alan had been explaining to me for long enough how minimal these were. And so, as Hermes had gone weeping and complaining to bed, I too went tapping at Val's green and silver chequered door and saw for the first time the exotic creature who was Hermes' best friend.
"I'm Alan's wife," I said, and she raises her eyes to heaven and said, "Why do women always define themselves in relation to men?" But she let me through and I went into this vulgar brothel-like room, all crimson wallpaper and cushions, and there was Alan sitting on a low sofa, looking completely out of place with his pink tie askew but thank God clothed, and I went into the kind of shock one does go into when the evidence of one's eyes and the conclusions of one's reason simply don't co-ordinate.
Alan was as casual and relaxed as could be.
"Esther," he said, "how did you know I was here? Val's been doing some typing for me."
"I used to type for you," I said, "until recently."
"Yes," said Alan, "but you made so many mistakes it really wasted more time than it saved. Which is why I'm using Val, and didn't tell you, because I didn't want you to be hurt."

"I see," I said, and then, playing for psychic time, "I only came to see if Hermes was here, actually. Her results are through."

"What are they?"

"A lower second," I told him. "Still – better than a third."

"Christ," said Alan, "that's dreadful. You should have made her study, Esther. But no, you had to just let her run wild from a child. She simply never got the hang of academic work." Need I mention that Alan only ever got as far as business college, and flunked that?

"Now," he said, "I suppose I'm going to have to see her through some expensive secretarial college. She might have made some kind of effort. But no, you've brought her up to regard me as money-bags, Esther, which is hardly surprising, since that's how you see me."

Now through this quite irrational but familiar tirade, Val had been gliding up and down on her jewelled bare feet – I think it was some kind of eastern sandal she was wearing – staring first at me, and then at my husband, who was clearly her paramour. He may have got his tie back on but his feet were bare – and the skin crumbly and papery and veiny too. I don't know why she, who could have had anyone, chose Alan, though Hermes did tell me later that she was neurotically obsessed with married men: she just couldn't resist splitting marriages, and that once it was done, she lost interest, but I think it was simpler than that. I think she just welcomed experience, and anyone who knocked upon her door, she would let in, and in, and in – it was admirable in its way.

"If I ever have children," Val observed, "I'll do it on my own."

And I said to her, "You've been sleeping with my husband."

"Not sleeping," said Val. "There's not been too much sleeping. There are simpler words, but your husband doesn't use them. Men are such romantics!"

I thought she should offer some apology, or show some shame, and said so, but Val said no, why should there be, so far as she could see the less time I had to spend with such a person as Alan the better. Was he always so rude and insulting? It occurred to me, with a shock, that that's what Alan was. Not right, and honest, as I had assumed, merely rude and insulting.

"Why do you put up with it?" my rival now asked. "No, don't answer that. It would go on for pages! In brief, what choice does a wife have? Only now you've caught him in flagrante delicto –"

"Val!" Alan was alarmed. "All you've been doing is my typing. I must apologise for my wife's insane insinuations. This is all most embarrassing. Nothing has happened here tonight!"

"Well, actually I agree with you," said Val. "A lot of plungings and shakings and terriers catching rats, but when it comes down to it, nothing. My soul is quite untouched. He's a terrible lover, Esther. May I call you Esther?"

"You may call me Mrs Lear," I replied, I hope with dignity, and admitted that I didn't know what sort of lover he was since I'd married him so young, and was a virgin at the time, and had no standard of comparison at all. And Val cried out, "One man in a whole lifetime! How perfectly dreadful!" and Alan hustled me out of her house, unable, I later concluded, to stand two women talking together and himself no longer the central part of the action.'

Down in the canteen Freddo suffers a spasm of rage with Alan, Esther's tormentor, and allows himself to hope that something will go wrong with the face-lift. How could any man treat a good woman so, Freddo expostulates, and Hermes asks him about his wife, left at home in Ireland, and he says 'That's different. I was just her meal-ticket. Ireland, anyway! All they want over there is a man to give them a baby, and a wedding so the priest doesn't send them to hell for it, and then they're through with men for ever. Sure, and isn't all that the way God intended?'

'Then why don't you go back where you came from?' asks Hermes, triumphantly.

'Or why don't you come back over there with me?' he asks, not noticing the intended insult.

'Of course,' Esther says now to Mr Khan, 'the first thing Alan saw when we got home, after I had interrupted his evening with Val, was the socks I had been darning for Hermes' benefit. He picked them up and looked from them to me, and back again, and it is true the socks were cream and had been darned with rather yellowy wool, and I said something like, "Look, I've been darning your socks." And he said, "But Esther, I can't possibly wear these! They're bodged, cobbled, lumpy and uncomfortable. You haven't even matched the colours properly!"

'I sat and considered the day I'd had, and the day he'd had. Eventually, I said, "I suppose Val darns beautifully." I hadn't mentioned Val since he'd dragged me out of her flat, and he hadn't brought the subject up, and he replied, "Of course Val doesn't darn beautifully. She wouldn't dream of doing anything so menial. She is independent and proud."
"But I heard her say you were a bad lover; she insults you," I observed.
"We understand each other," Alan said. "We deal in truths, not lies. Those were not insults, those were compliments. But how could you understand? You're thirty years out of date! Val embroiders, actually. She does all her own cushions. She is remarkably talented. There's almost nothing Val can't turn her hand to. She befriended poor Hermes out of kindness: I can't think what they have in common. Poor little Hermes! What a mess she is."
"I suppose," I said, as brightly as I could manage, "Val's better in bed than I am, too."
"She certainly turns me on, Esther," he said. "To use a modern expression."
"So what do you mean to do about it all?" I asked.

"Do?" he enquired. "Why, nothing! What should I do?"
"You're not going to give her up? You know, how husbands
are supposed to when the wife finds out?"

'But he wasn't. Why should he? That was an old-fashioned
notion. He wouldn't desert me. He wouldn't sleep with me
either. He'd spend weekends with Val and weekdays with
me.
"I am only truly alive in Val's company," he said. "I am
sorry if it hurts you, but we must speak the truth. Val has
taught me that."
"Yes," I observed. "For someone so young she has taught
you a lot." At which he said she was an old soul. He took
it I didn't want a divorce. He said most women of my age
thought half a husband was better than none, and I said I
supposed that was true, and he said now that was settled
we could be friends, even if we couldn't be lovers, and asked
me to fetch him a scotch. He didn't mind if it was cold; in
fact Val had taught him to appreciate iced scotch, and I
said – oh, Mr Khan, do you know what I said? – I said "get
it yourself." And that was the first step to freedom. "Get it
yourself." One small step for a woman, Mr Khan. But a
great step forward for women.'

Well, well! Press on: look forward, not back! You must hear
these people out. What do we have friends for, but to lend
an ear to their preoccupations and complaints? In time they
will do it for us, when the white nights come, when the
detail of what he said or what she did or what I felt keep
sleep away, and a dreadful sense of injustice consumes our
hearts with fire – not fair, not fair, what did I ever do to
deserve this! – and the panicky feeling that something must
be done, something, but what? weakens the bones. Then we
will need our friends, as they once needed us. So hear friends
out: answer the phone when they ring and do it in person
– don't leave it to the machine. They may seem mad to love
such a one, or such another, but of such stuff are we all

made. It isn't really madness, you see; rather it is the concentrated sanity of hope.

So, now, what's Hermes saying in the canteen over a third cup of yarrow tea? (Yarrow loosens the tongue and soothes the nerves. Freddo's now on borage, that pretty blue flower which the Greeks used, to assuage the grief of those bereaved. And remember that Freddo's lady love is closeted with Mr Khan, a suave and foreign charmer, and Freddo doesn't care for that, although increasingly impressed by Hermes, who – now her silly sulks have gone – can be seen to be pretty, and merry, and charming, with very silky, very white, very young skin. While her mother's, to be honest, is not what it was.)

'It was all so dreadful,' Hermes is saying, 'but I couldn't make Val see that it was. Even my tears didn't move her. She maintained that she was sleeping with my father for my mother's sake, in particular, and women's in general, and with me because it was every woman's right to be homosexual, and so far as she was concerned, nothing need change.'

Freddo looks at her, appalled.
'You didn't actually –'
'Yes, we did, actually. Why not?'
He can't answer. He breathes heavily.

'Val said that people have to be confronted with the consequences of their actions,' observes Hermes. 'She said my father was at fault for trying to cheat my mother, and my mother was at fault in always seeking the easy way out, and that those who live by wife and children deserve to die by them, and I was at fault in still living under their roof, and so knowing past my time what was going on. She didn't seem to think she was at fault at all. And I said yes, she was, it was her fault I'd only got a lower second! She couldn't answer that.'

'You mean you and her actually –'
'Oh shut up, Freddo. And she said why didn't I just come to bed and forget about it: she said we had three lives, waking, sleeping and sex, and each is a refuge and rest from the other two. And I said I wouldn't. I thought she was disgusting, and she said have it my own way, and at that moment there was a ring on the bell, and she asked me to answer it, but I wouldn't, because I knew it would only be one of her lovers, and it was. It was my father. Do stop looking at me like that, Freddo, I'm sure you had homosexual relations with other boys when you were in your Catholic seminary.'
'Only ever against my will,' says Freddo.
'And Daddy burst in and said, "darling" in a disgusting, throaty voice, and Val said, "I thought you'd gone home." She didn't sound welcoming in the least, but Daddy took no notice. He's wonderfully thick-skinned. He told her he was moving in with her. He couldn't live without her. She was his education, his life, his future, his everything. "Oh dear," said Val. She was trying to stop him coming into the bedroom, where I was, but he didn't notice. He had a suitcase with him; he wanted to unpack. He told her he was expecting promotion, and then he'd leave home and the two of them would live together in a split-level bungalow, just built, he'd found on the outskirts of town. He knew the builder: he'd get it at a good price. It wasn't too far from where the family lived so he could keep an eye on them. And I said, "Oh, thank you, Daddy," and watched him jump a mile. I liked that. But he pulled himself together very quickly and said how about me running home to look after my mother? It's time I did something to earn my keep, he said, and I said I had as much right to be in Val's pad as he did. That shook him but he went on about Mum needing me, on account of how she was in the dark, really

in the dark, because they'd had a row, him and Mum, and Mum had tried to murder him, throwing an electric heater at him while he was in the shower, but all she'd managed to do was fuse all the electricity in the house, so he'd packed a suitcase in the dark and come straight round to Val's – he'd made up his mind. He'd chosen Val and a new life. How could anyone be expected to live with a murderous, violent woman like my mother? People had to take the consequences of their actions, he said – he'd got that from Val – so I got dressed and went home to look after poor Mum.'

'Dressed?' asked Freddo.

'Put on my coat,' she amends. She is beginning to want Freddo's good opinion. Yarrow makes its drinkers soft and nice. 'And as I left I heard them arguing. Val was saying but she liked to live alone, and Alan was saying but she'd said she loved him, and Val said but that was in the heat of the moment, and he said all our moments are heated, my darling, wait till you see the new house: picture windows and a magic eye garage. He and Val could jet-set all over the world: he'd go to the conferences by day while she lay by the pool, and in the evenings they'd see the town – and all Val did was look at my father as if he was mad, which I really think he was. Poor Daddy! Then Val asked Daddy what he meant to do about Mum, and he said she would be entitled to half the marital home, and she'd always wanted to work and be independent: now was her chance.

'And that was when Val, to her credit, told him to go away. "I think," she said, "that in my scheme of things, in my plan for Utopia, I underrated people's capacity for just sheer simple appalling depravity."

'And Daddy went to a hotel for the night, and I went home, but couldn't get into the house because the front door was locked.'

'I was inside by then,' says Freddo, 'with your sweet lady

mother, and sure and all we didn't want any intruders.
Nobody bursting in, you understand.'
'It was my home, too,' says Hermes, reproachfully.
'And sure wasn't it a special occasion! To find true love in
the space of a few minutes! Sent out by the Head Office to
right a power failure at No. 19! I knocked at the door, and
called out, so as not to alarm those within, "This is the
Electricity Board, Sir Lancelot himself, come to bring light
into the lives of the helpless!" and who should come to the
door but your dear lady mother, all swollen up with tears.
A damsel in distress! It's often like that when the power
fails. Someone's thrown something. We found a torch, we
found a ladder, we found the fuse, and she told me I meant
Sir Galahad, and not Sir Lancelot; Sir Lancelot merely ran
off with King Arthur's wife, and I shone a torch down from
the top of the ladder on to her upturned face, and she smiled
up at me through her tears, and sure my heart went out to
her, and I knew I must dedicate my life to this poor woman's
happiness and up we went to the big soft bed.'
'My father's bed!'
'Sure, and hadn't he failed in his duty to it?'

Alan sighs, and Pony adjusts his bandages.
'It won't be long now,' she says. 'Your bandages will come
off: you'll be back in the world again.'
'The world!' he complains. 'The world conspires against
me. Step out of line and wham! bam! it gets you. No sooner
did I have to face the fact that Val had been playing with
my affections, than I was summoned to the Director's office
and there, instead of receiving the promotion I expected,
was handed a redundancy notice. Certain branches of the
business were being closed down: they no longer needed
me. The recession, my dear, is like age: it closes in gently –
one can't believe it! That it should apply to oneself –
impossible! There was quite a substantial redundancy pay-
ment but that was not the point. Being suddenly pointless,
useless, was the point: waking up in the morning and having

nothing but the mood one woke up in! I didn't tell Esther what had happened. I let her think my aura of quiet despair was because I had given up Val on her account. And therefore that she, Esther, was to blame. But she didn't take it as she usually did – trying to assuage the guilt I laid upon her with nervous coughings of apology, and little placatory offerings – a new shirt here, a pair of socks there, acquired by virtue of economies she had made in the housekeeping. No, not at all! I kept looking up and finding her smiling to herself, and when I moved back into her bed it was as if she'd scarcely noticed my absence. It didn't occur to me she had a lover. I pretended to go off to work every day, but really went to the public library instead, and in the company of a dozen or so others similarly engaged, studied and responded to the advertisement columns of the news-papers. As the recession bit harder, the vacancies grew fewer, and still I had not found a job. Grief over the loss of Val – and that went deep – and the sense that I had made a fool of myself, and in front of my own daughter too – had aged me. My hair was noticeably grey. I went to many interviews – but no one offered me a job. I was depressed, miserable, and angry, and I drank too much, and it showed.

'One day I decided to tell Esther all, and face her mirth and wrath – she, whom to the employed man had seemed an object to disregard and all but despise, to the unemployed seemed formidable. And I went home mid-morning.'
'That's never wise!' says Pony.

'To be sure,' says Freddo to Hermes, 'your mother is a frightening woman when she's roused. I was happily in the dear soul's bed one morning, as was my wont —'
'How you have the nerve,' exclaims Hermes, 'to criticise *me*—'
'My darling,' says Freddo, 'what I do is natural, what you do isn't, and sure and isn't there AIDS to prove it? God's punishment on the sinful!'

She opens her mouth to protest, but he'll have none of it,
'– as was my wont,' he repeats, 'when there's the sound of
a key in the lock, and she jumps out of bed mother naked
and goes to the top of the stairs.
"Esther, Esther," hubby says, "where are you?"
"In bed," she says. "Why aren't you at work?"
"Didn't you get up at all this morning?" he asks, looking at
her naked shame.
"Sure and I did," she says, "but I got back into bed," and
I hear her calling me, "Freddo!" and hubby says, "Who's
that?" and I go and stand beside her in my birthday suit,
and she says,
"His name is Freddo, and he is the man I love. I am only
half alive in your company, I am all alive in his. I'm sure
you don't mind. If you do, I'll move in with him during the
week and spend the weekends with you."
And doesn't the poor devil look as if he's going to burst into
tears, and I tell her to stop it, and it comes to me that she
only wants me to get back at him, and I say so, but she says
no, she wants me *and* to get back at him.

'And then she asks poor hubby to go and fetch her some
whisky, and, speaking personally, she says, she doesn't like
it on the rocks, and then he does begin to cry, and I go and
get dressed, and when I get back she's standing on the top
stair, and he's on his knees, blubbering and trying to kiss
her feet.'
'Don't, don't!' cries Hermes, appalled.
'Sure and it shows he's a man of proper feeling. Many's
the time I've kissed your sainted mother's toes. Hubby
straightens up, seeing me, and says, "I won't have that man
in the house," but all she does is laugh and says, "what I
say, goes" and tells him she's landed a job writing cookery
captions in a magazine and can live as she chooses now.'
'And perfectly dreadful it was,' says Hermes. 'To have a
mother working! She never cooked food and she never
washed clothes and if Dad said where are the cornflakes

she'd say in the corner shop, and if I said where's my white blouse, she'd say under the bed, where you left it, and if he said "let's start all over again, my dear" she'd say, "I haven't time to talk now. I have a meeting at nine. Make sure you take the cat to the vet and hire a carpet-cleaner for the stairs, and cook something for supper that won't spoil, because I'm working late at the office tonight. I'm working and you're not."'

'That's just like her real sweet darling self,' says Freddo. 'A woman of spirit!'

'She drove my father out,' says Hermes, 'whether she meant to or not. One day she found she'd set one too many empty plates before him; he walked out and hired a bedsitting room and started divorce proceedings, and she defended them. And what the solicitors didn't take of the redundancy money, you did. My mother is a monster. My father made her so. No wonder I'm a mess. But I'll never leave home. I'll get everything I can from the pair of them, for ever and ever and ever!'

'You're your mother's daughter and I love you for it,' says Freddo and leans across the table and kisses her on the lips. 'It was you I was after, all the time. And sure, now I've a little business set up of my own, couldn't we get together? Only where will we live?'

Alan falls asleep in his bed. Pony creeps out of the room. Mr Khan says to Esther, 'You are a very, very attractive woman, my dear,' and his slender, talented hand creeps towards her ageing but more than sensuous knee, and Esther rises quickly and says she must just look in to see how her husband is, glad for once to claim him as such, and at this moment Mrs Professor Khan steps over the divide where the lino turns to carpet and the free wards stop and the paying wards begin, in search of her husband. And of course she encounters Pony, who is about the same business.

Of course they encounter each other. You will know from your own experience, that when caught up in one of these wildly interacting groups – and most of us are from time to time; particles of dust flung into the air and jiggled about in some overwhelming magnetic sexual field, when tears flow and hysteria mounts – that there is just no getting away, until it has worked itself out. Flee to the Sahara and who will you see on the first camel but your lover's husband's secret boyfriend! Surprise, surprise! The Force is with you. The Force is strong. The Force is all the fun and horror in the world: it is an overflow of energy from the making of babies.

So that is why I say that naturally Pony encounters Mrs Professor Khan.

'Good morning, Mrs Khan,' she says demurely, hating and despising this woman who shares her lover's bed, by right. Of course we, unlike Pony, admire her. She is what all women should be. Competent, assured, working nobly in the community, realising her potential, fulfilling her aspirations, organising her children, seeing her husband as decoration – she is so superior to him she can scarcely admire him. And he admires her, but he does not love her. How can he? He loves Pony. He loves what he can look after. Dear God, what *is* to become of us all?

'Professor Khan,' the older woman corrects her.

'I'm afraid Mr Khan is rather busy,' says Pony, boldly, laying down rights of ownership. Mrs Professor Khan pauses, examining her with curiosity, as a very large cat will a very small bird.

'So am I, my dear,' says Mrs Professor Khan, kindly. 'Very busy.'

'He's with the wife of one of the face-lift patients,' Pony says. 'She's rather upset. You know how important Mr Khan thinks the family gestalt is, when it comes to healing.'

'I am sure he will comfort her,' says Mr Khan's wife, 'as one human being will another. He is very good at that. Sometimes I feel he takes it to extremes. But then, he has all the time in the world.'

And she smiles sweetly, and Pony realises her loved one is under attack.

'There is,' Pony blurts out, 'such a thing as *love!*' and her eyes brim with sudden tears.

'Only for weak minds, little girl,' purrs Mrs Professor Khan. 'Do *you* fancy yourself in love with him? I suspect you do. Try not to get hurt. My husband falls in love twice a year, once at Christmas and once at Easter. You must be last Christmas's event, and Easter's coming up – and you not over it yet. Oh dear! But at least you don't have a brain tumour! We must try and keep things in proportion.'

And she sweeps on and Pony wails her distress and indignation, just as Esther passes by.

'Oh dear,' says Esther, recognising the nurse who earlier restrained her with a neck-hold from the martial arts, 'what can be the matter?'

'What am I going to do?' the younger woman sobs. 'I'm pregnant!'

'But that's wonderful!' says Esther. 'The one justification for love. It produces babies. You should be very proud and happy.'

'But she'll never let him marry me.'

'Oh, marriage!' says Esther. 'That's different. That is difficult. Never mind. Social welfare will always keep you, and give you a one-bedroom flat, and I'm sure the father will do what he can to help you – though then of course your benefit will be cut, so you might be better off saying you don't know who the father is – and you will have the baby for ever, living evidence of the power of passion. What more do you want?'

'But I got pregnant on purpose,' says Pony, 'so he'd marry me.'

Esther stares at her, quite stopped in her tracks. 'Well,' says Esther, 'nothing changes,' and she goes on in to wake her husband from his fitful, barely achieved slumber.

Mrs Professor Khan faces her husband. He is smaller than she.

'I have been wanting to speak to you for two days,' she says. 'You were asleep when I came in last night, and gone before I woke up,' he says. 'Such is the fate of many busy and accomplished couples, of course.'

'I think you should know,' his wife says, 'that I have been asked to join a peripatetic life-support team, centred in Moscow, to attend various Heads of State in the East. It is a two-year appointment. I mean to take it.'

'But what about me?' he asks.

'There is already a cosmetic surgeon on the team. I'm sorry.'

'What about the children?'

'They have their father,' she responds calmly. 'And they already regard you as the primary parent.'

Indignation boils over. He jumps to his feet, blood suffusing his smooth, sensuous, olive skin, to the great danger of his capillary nerves.

'You mean to leave me behind,' he cries, 'as *nanny*!'

Down in the canteen the waitress coughs. Freddo and Hermes are so closely entwined as to be a threat to common decency. They suit each other. Both are of an age, both are strongly sexed, and both highly opportunistic. Thank God they have found each other. They ignore the waitress's cough. Now the manager will have to be sent for.

'I won't have you seeing this Val,' he says, 'that's all.'

'She's locked up house and gone to the Harvard Business School,' says Hermes.

'Leaving her pad empty?'

'Yes.'

'Then we can squat!' he cries, in triumph.

'All I ever wanted from my parents,' observes Hermes, acquiescing to his plan, 'is that they should be happy. It's all any of us want. Not good, not rich, not perfect – just happy. And they failed me.'

Thus, accepting her fate, she attains her maturity, albeit in Freddo's company.

But of course what to the children appears to be abject misery, appears to the parents to be merely richly textured life – the intricate and fascinating games that couples play in the struggle for fairness and permanence within the home.

See now how Esther holds Alan's hand, pulling him and her from the brink of separation – and the Final Decree only days away!

'I'm sorry,' she says, now. Listen to her!

'So am I,' he says. Good God!

'You know I got pregnant on purpose,' she says, 'so you'd marry me. It wasn't an accident.'

'I had no idea,' he says. 'Poor little Hermes!'

'I haven't much pity for Hermes,' says Esther. 'We gave her life, that should be enough for her. We put up with her for years.'

'Then if only she'd go,' says Alan, 'we could actually start our married life.'

'Are you proposing,' she says, 'that we should get back together?'

'I am,' he says. 'Now that I look ten years younger I'll get a job soon enough. Employment's all in the mind, you know.'

'Tell that,' she says, 'to the three and a half million!'

But she kisses him through the bandages.

'You must get these ridiculous wrappings removed,' says Esther, 'and come home at once to me.'

Mrs Professor Khan is taking a little time to placate her husband.

'We can't put our personal happiness before the affairs of the world, Bobby. Our leaders must be sound in wind and limb and brain, if the people of the globe are to sleep soundly in bed at night.'

'You'll be unfaithful to me,' he laments.

'Not for the sake of pleasure,' she assures him, 'or from any particular inclination. Only to steady my hand.'

He suffers, or appears to.

'You know how it is,' she says, 'before a big operation. For the likes of us sex can only be therapeutic. Don't pretend otherwise, to me. We are neither of us stupid people.'

'I can't bear it,' he says, defeated.

'What?' she enquires. 'My being unfaithful, or my not being stupid?'

He does not reply, and since she does not like time to be wasted, for lives truly hang upon her minutes, she leaves. Pony is lurking outside the door. Mr Khan calls her in.

'And what are we going to do about Freddo?' asks Alan of Esther. 'You can't just ditch him.'

'I can,' she says.

'Women are heartless.'

'He was only ever entertainment at best, revenge at worst.'

'You mean,' says Alan, 'you think he's cooling off and you want to get in first.'

'Probably,' she admits.

And at that moment Hermes and Freddo come in, having been ejected from the canteen, hand in hand, and flushed with the discovery of the real, the true, the inevitable, the inimitable LOVE. And their elders and betters look at them, and quell such envy, jealousy, rage and resentment as rise in both their breasts, because the sun is no longer in mid-heaven, but beginning to sink, and they have each other, and tranquillity, and the golden glow of the evening, or else they have nothing.

'Hi,' says Esther, calmly, 'you two.'

And after Freddo and Hermes have left, the sooner to consummate their passion, Pony bounces in, all smiles.

'Mr Khan's coming to take off your bandages,' she says.

'Your tests are through and all is well. And what's more he's going to give all this up and retire early and divorce his wife, and marry me, and look after his children himself; and all for love of me. So put that in your pipe and smoke it!'

'Happy endings,' says Alan.

'Happy beginnings,' says Pony, 'and just as well. I almost thought I'd have to have a termination, but since I run the "Nurses Against Abortion" here in the hospital, wasn't I half in a fix!'

And presently Mr Khan enters, with extra trolleys and nurses, and ceremoniously unmasks Alan, and returns him his face. He is a little irritable with Pony, who keeps dropping the scissors and losing the swabs, but she seems to like his irritation.

'What an inefficient little thing you are!' Mr Khan says, and she simpers and giggles and the other nurses envy her. Betrothed to a specialist!

'Behold,' says Mr Khan, as Alan's face emerges, 'the new man! Match for the new woman!'

Alan examines himself in the mirror. He sees with a new clarity. He sees the truth.

'I look older,' he says, 'if anything.'

But that, of course, is the great penalty. The more we know, the older we get. The body quite withers away, in the harsh light of wisdom.